ROSTOCK

CONNECTION

ALSO BY MAX HERTZBERG

The East Berlin Series
Stealing The Future (2015)
Thoughts Are Free (2016)
Spectre At The Feast (2017)

Reim Series
Stasi Vice (2018)
Operation Oskar (2019)
Berlin Centre (Bruno Affair 1) (2019)
Baltic Approach (Bruno Affair 2) (2020)
Rostock Connection (Bruno Affair 3) (2021)

Other Fiction
Cold Island (2018)

Non-fiction
with Seeds For Change
How To Set Up A Workers' Co-op (2012)
A Consensus Handbook (2013)

After the experience of the East German political upheaval in 1989/90, Max Hertzberg became a Stasi files researcher. Since then he has been a book seller and a social change trainer before writing his debut novel, *Stealing The Future* (2015).
Visit the author's website for background information on the GDR, and guides to walking tours around the East Berlin in which many of his books are set.

www.maxhertzberg.co.uk

ROSTOCK CONNECTION

MAX HERTZBERG

Book 3 of the Bruno Affair trilogy

OV Press

P 1 2 3 4 5 6 7 8 9 10

Published in 2021 by Max Hertzberg
www.maxhertzberg.co.uk

Copyright ©Max Hertzberg 2021.

Max Hertzberg has asserted his right under the Copyright, Designs
and Patents Act 1988 to be identified as the author of this work.

Cover photograph copyright ©Jörg Blobelt, licensed under the
Creative Commons Attribution 4.0 International Licence.

Map derived from work copyright © TUBS licensed under the
Creative Commons Attribution 3.0 Licence.

Text licensed under the Creative Commons Attribution-Non-
Commercial-No-Derivatives 4.0 International License. View a copy
of this license at: www.creativecommons.org/licenses/by-nc-nd/4.0/

c/o Wolf Press, 22 Hartley Crescent, LS6 2LL

A CIP record for this title is available from the British Library
ISBN: 9781913125110 (paperback), 9781913125134 (large print paperback),
9781913125127 (epub)

Set in 10½ on 12pt Libertinus Serif

All characters in this publication, except for those named public figures who
are used in fictional situations, are fictitious and any resemblance to real
persons, living or dead, is entirely unintended and coincidental.

JUNE 1984

A list of main characters and a glossary of GDR and German terms are available at the end of this book.

1

BERLIN LICHTENBERG

June 1984 was the month I won the lottery. Being offered a fortnight at one of the Firm's guest houses on the island of Rügen sounded nice enough, but after the field operation last winter I wasn't keen on another trip to the Baltic coast. So I swapped holiday places with a colleague: my place on the beach for a quiet room in the forest near Berlin.

The colleague was all smiles when we sealed the transaction with a handshake, thinking he'd got the better half of the deal, but I wrote his name in my notebook, knowing I'd ask him to pay back the favour one day. Then it would be my turn to smile.

So I was content enough when I began clearing my desk on Friday evening before my leave began, already looking forward to a fortnight with no reports to write or assess, no operational situations to analyse and no superiors to appease. Just one more file to complete, then a wee glass to celebrate, I told myself, not supposing for a moment that Lieutenant Colonel Schur of Counter Intelligence was about to drift along the corridor and into my office.

But drift he did. When he pushed my door open without knocking, I stood up—back stiff, eyes straight ahead—uneasy in the knowledge that visitations by superiors, particularly when unexpected, always bring complications with them.

"Comrade Reim," said Lieutenant Colonel Schur by way of greeting, gesturing with an unlit cigar to let me know I should sit down. I waited for him to find his seat, then lowered myself into my chair, spine rigid, hands clasped on the desktop in front of me.

"I've been looking at the report on Secondary Operational Procedure Merkur," he said, making me wonder why the interest, a full four months after the case had been closed. "You wrote the report, didn't you, Comrade Reim? Not so straight-forward, that operation, so well done for getting to the bottom of it all."

It was a compliment, but no response was required, and anyway, the lieutenant colonel was still talking:

"But of course, if Major Kühn and I hadn't covered for you, things would have ended quite differently. You would have been in some difficulty, wouldn't you?"

Marvellous how the brass rewrite history to cast themselves as the heroes of any operation. In my recollection, the KGB used me and then pulled rank to make sure my superiors couldn't complain. It must have stung when they realised they'd never know how the case turned out.

I opened the drawer and pulled out a clean ashtray for Schur, anything to break the steady gaze he was pointing in my direction. He lit his cigar and puffed it into life, then took it from between his fleshy lips to admire the little glow he'd managed to produce. I used the moment to wonder how much of the real story this officer knew. I don't mean what I'd written in the dolled-up final report, but the real facts of the case.

He stood abruptly, leaving me scrambling to get out of my chair, and with a nod and a wave of his cigar, he left my office. I remained on my feet for a few moments, waiting to see whether he would come back and tell me why he'd popped in, but hearing his heavy footsteps recede down the corridor, I crossed to the door and shut it.

Back at my desk, I reached into my drawer for a glass. I took a drink and asked myself whether the head of a different section had just come all this way to persuade me I owed him a favour?

I looked at my watch: five to seven. That was me for the day, in fact it was me for the rest of the month. All I still had to do was pile the files into the safe, put the bottle in my bag in case anyone came snooping in my absence and put the seal on the safe and office door. After that, I'd be free until the first Monday in July.

I was pressing the *Petschaft* into the disc of wax on the door of my safe when I heard the phone. I thought about leaving it to ring, but a glance at my wristwatch showed the minute hand just shy of the top of the dial—my twelve-hour day wasn't yet over.

"Meeting with Major Kühn, tomorrow morning at seven," said my immediate superior, Captain Dupski.

"My leave starts in less than two minutes." Normally I wouldn't argue, but two weeks furlough was short enough without my boss organising meetings for me on my first day off.

I was talking to a dead phone. Dupski had hung up, and I knew that come the morning, I'd be right back here at Berlin Centre.

2
BERLIN LICHTENBERG

The first day of my leave saw me standing in the corridor outside my boss's office. I could hear the buzz of voices through the closed door, but little else. Early Saturday morning is a quiet time on the brass's corridor, even if other parts of the Lichtenberg complex were as busy as ever.

The door didn't open for another ten minutes, and when finally I was commanded to enter, it was no surprise to find Lieutenant Colonel Schur, the one who had drifted into my office the previous day, seated next to Major Kühn, the head of my own section. I marched in and came to a stop at an appropriate distance from both Kühn's desk and Schur's thin knees.

Schur had one of his cigars going, and despite the open window, the room was tinged with pungent smoke, although neither of the officers seemed to notice the thick atmosphere.

"At ease, Comrade Second Lieutenant," said Kühn, glancing over the expanse of his desk at the ranking officer occupying the visitor's chair.

"After you, Comrade Major," said Schur, waving his cigar generously.

"We may have a task for you, Comrade Reim, something to fit your ..."

"Individual skill set," offered Schur, using his cigar to point at me. The tip was dull, perhaps it had gone out.

"Absolutely." Kühn gave Schur another glance, then turned back to me. "Comrade Schur's department has a minor difficulty, and the comrade lieutenant colonel suggested you'd be the right man to get to the bottom of things."

Schur nodded along, looking rather pleased with Kühn's tactful formulation. He leaned forward, deposited his extinct cigar in the ashtray and took over the briefing, such as it was.

"The comrade minister, General Mielke, has expressed concern that my department may have fallen behind in the acquisition of operationally relevant material. He made the point that the comrades over in Foreign Intelligence, HV A, have been more productive in certain endeavours." He leaned forward again, but instead of picking up his cigar, he addressed my boss. "You're sure Reim is the right man?"

Kühn wasn't expecting this attempt to shift any future responsibility for choosing me, but he quickly recovered. "You said it yourself, comrade. You felt the Merkur case was satisfactorily resolved, and would not have been but for the political-operational and professional efforts of Comrade Second Lieutenant Reim."

"If you say so." Schur leaned back in his chair and peered at me through thick lenses. "I have been given sight of a selection of the material that HV A is using to impress the comrade minister. The material makes for uncomfortable reading—it appears to have been channelled through an unofficial source in the imperialist intelligence agencies."

I sharpened my ears in interest. In his delicate way, Schur was saying a contact in a Western security agency was passing information to HV A. And if reading the material had made the lieutenant colonel feel uncomfortable then the ultimate source was probably one of our own.

"We require an urgent operational analysis of the material in order to gain an overview of the operational-political context," the lieutenant colonel was finding his pace now, spouting the usual jargon that we use at the Ministry to distract ourselves from what we're really doing. Schur's department, Counter Intelligence, had failed, and their rivals over in Foreign Intelligence had run to General Mielke to tell tales. No wonder Schur was under fire from the big boss.

It can sometimes be hard to stand there like a little soldier doll and at that point I could feel the corners of my mouth tightening into a smug grin. I liked hearing when other departments were the focus of the Comrade Minister's ire, it meant his attention was elsewhere, that my section was evading his capricious scrutiny.

"Comrade Major Kühn has kindly offered your services, he tells me you have a formal background in operational analysis —just the man I'm looking for. You are therefore seconded to my department with immediate effect."

The nascent sneer slackened on my face and I turned to my boss. "Permission to speak, Comrade Major?"

"Go ahead, Comrade," said Schur before Major Kühn could respond.

"Comrade Lieutenant Colonel, Comrade Captain, I am currently on leave-" But I didn't get any further, I noticed how Kühn's eyes had darkened.

"Change out of uniform and report to the comrade lieutenant colonel's secretary."

Taking that as my signal, I left the two senior officers to gossip.

3
BERLIN LICHTENBERG

"Second Lieutenant Reim reporting," I told the secretary.

Without acknowledging my presence, she lifted the phone and spoke into the receiver. Just a sentence or two, then she returned her attention to an electric typewriter.

Since she hadn't told me otherwise, I stood around, waiting to see what would happen next. I was tempted to light a coffin nail, but I'd left the pack on my desk and I had to make do with propping up the wall and examining my fingernails.

I didn't have to wait long, the phone rang and the secretary picked up, writing herself a note as she listened. She hung up and looked at me for the first time, her fingers pinning the note to the edge of her desk. I leaned over to read what she'd written.

U-Bahn Tierpark, wait opposite car-park

"Hold this in your left hand," she told me, picking up a folded copy of that day's Neues Deutschland newspaper.

I took the paper, and left Berlin Centre to walk down the hill to the underground station.

I didn't have to wait outside the zoo—as soon as I emerged from the U-Bahn station, newspaper in my left hand, a Trabant sputtered out of the car park, rumbled over the tram tracks and pulled up a few metres down the road. Once I reached the car, I leaned down to see the driver—he wasn't in uniform, but I could tell the type from the way he was perched in the driver's seat, staring straight ahead: *Uffzi*.

The NCO remained eyes front as I opened the door to climb

in next to him, and we sat in silence as he took us south, over the Spree and towards the motorway. I knew there was no point asking where we were going—if his orders had included letting me know the destination, he would have done so as soon as I clambered into the vehicle.

Nevertheless, I was still able to read road signs, and I watched with interest as we turned first onto the Berlin Ring, then onto the Autobahn to Frankfurt.

We took the exit for Storkow, heading south then turning right onto a narrow cobbled lane. The dusty forest grew close to the road, overhanging branches had been splintered and broken by high vehicles. A granite post marking the verge leaned drunkenly into the bushes.

A sharp curve to the left hid the village until the last moment, the faded yellow sign announcing the name of the place was illegible with grime. In a second or two we were through the settlement, turning onto a concrete track that fringed the edge of the forest.

The Trabant halted at a red and white painted boom, and I peered through the dust-speckled window at the BT9 tower that commanded the approach track.

A soldier in army grey fatigues sporting the yellow piping of the signals regiment on his shoulder boards came out of the guardhouse, stooping to take the documents handed over by my driver—grey booklets in a plastic wallet, these were military IDs rather than the green hardboard of MfS clapperboards. The sentry flicked through the pages, bent down again to compare our faces with the mugshots, then handed the papers back.

A wave at the guard hut to raise the boom, then a salute as we entered the base.

We drove slowly between two fences—the slabs that made up the track were freshly laid, but already roughened and buckled from heavy use. The air was charged with the scents of hot sand and pine resin, and the branches from the forest reached over the fence to meet above us.

An open gate, 300 metres after the first, allowed us to exit the enclosed zwinger, and we drove through to the main site of the camp. Pre-fabricated buildings of assorted sizes and purposes were in various states of completion, the three-storey accommodation blocks to the left looked ready to move into, and my driver halted the car outside the first of these.

"Room 27, Comrade Second Lieutenant," he said, holding out one of the grey military passes. "You're expected."

I clambered out of the Trabant, leaving the Party newspaper behind, and mounted the steps to the door of the block.

A couple of workmen were wiring up fluorescent light fittings in the stairwell, and I edged carefully past the ladders on the stairs. More sparkies were at work in the corridor off to the side, but the second-floor corridor seemed remarkably finished—all wiring in place, lights working, doors and frames tacky with fresh paint. Even the plastic nameplate holders for the room number and occupant details were waiting to be filled.

Pausing outside office number 27, I examined my new military identification booklet. Flipping it open, I checked the details: name of Schultzke, Bernd, a few months younger than me, but lucky enough to have my features staring out of his photograph. The various entries for kit issued and qualifications gained had been filled in by different hands, dated back as far as five years ago. If I hadn't known it was fake, I would have believed I was a signals lieutenant.

I knocked on the door and, gambling that I wouldn't find a particularly senior officer in a half-constructed camp, went straight in.

I was only half right. A captain in NVA uniform with the same yellow piping on his shoulder boards as the sentry at the gate looked up as I entered.

I stopped just inside the door and put the fingers of my

right hand to my temple, my feet together, left thumb along trouser seam and eyes forward.

"What do you want?" It was said with force, but the voice was a little high to carry much authority.

"*Unterleutnant* Reim, reporting for duty, Comrade Captain."

"Shut the door, get yourself over here." He gestured at a chair on my side of the desk so I got myself over there and sat down.

He had a square face divided by a broken nose and hollow cheeks. His eyes, when finally he looked at me were grey, overhung with heavy eyelids and thin black brows.

"First of all, you're not here. Comrade Reim is not, was never, nor will ever be here. Understood?"

4
FOREST EAST OF BERLIN

I didn't need to understand why the captain had told me I wasn't standing in front of him, and I didn't object either. Superiors have a habit of handing out demonstrably false statements, but there's never a reason to query them.

"In future, if anyone ever asks, you were on leave. You had a lovely time, doing what you'd normally do while on holiday," he continued. "While you're here, you're not to leave the base without escort, you're not to have any contact with the civilian builders on site, and if you speak to any member of the armed organs you're not to communicate matters concerning the work you'll be doing."

This was basic stuff—apart from the bit about not being allowed off-camp, that was unusual. The idea of spending my leave in the middle of a building site didn't fill me with joy.

"This will be your office. Here's the key to the door and the keys to the safe. *Petschaft* for use when sealing the safe and room door. Sign here." The captain put two keys, an aluminium seal and a form on the desk. He had a Thuringian accent, not strong, but still enough to make him sound out of place in the Brandenburg forest. He continued his lecture as I signed on the dotted line.

"A set of the Wolfram material is in the safe—your task is to evaluate overall authenticity and establish possible provenance of the material. Provide me with a list of records you wish to cross-reference and any personnel queries you intend to make. Questions?"

Everything he'd said had been rapped out as if I was taking

dictation rather than instructions, but as he moved from behind the desk his tone softened. He held his hand out and I stood up.

"Hauptmann Ewald, HA II," he said, meeting my eyes. "Officers' casino is in the next building, RD will sort out your accommodation and uniform."

After he left I stood by the window for a while, smoking. There wasn't much of a view—another building, same model as this one, stood a few metres away, behind that the forest loomed. I opened the window for long enough to allow the smell of pine and the hammering of heavy machinery to roll through the gap, then picked up the keys from the desk, took a look at the sealed safe—a heavy-duty version of what I had in my office back at Berlin Centre—and decided that whatever was in it could wait until I'd reported to rear services and found myself a second breakfast.

I took a wander around the building site before going for breakfast—garages for heavy vehicles were being erected at the far end of the site, a fuelling station had already been completed, and work was continuing on a boiler house. Round the back of the accommodation blocks, I found bulky signalling equipment resting on pallets, waiting to be hoisted into what looked like it would become a Class-E bunker. Beyond that, a tall mast, wires and antennae as yet unfitted, had been erected on a low mound.

Rear Services weren't easy to find, in the end I tracked them down to the basement of the staff building, next door to the one I was based in. The *Uffzi* in charge examined my pass and turned to a set of binders that lined a shelf behind him. Pulling one down, he sorted through the pages until he found what he was looking for, then compared the details on my *Wehrdienstausweis* to those on the page. Unclipping the rings, he took several sheets out, ran his forefinger down a list on the second page and went to find the various supplies.

Summer field uniform, summer service uniform, winter field and service, underwear, basic toiletries, and finally, shoulder boards for a second lieutenant with the same yellow piping as all the other uniforms I'd seen in this place.

There was another check of the paperwork, several signatures and stamps before I was free to find my breakfast.

5
FOREST EAST OF BERLIN

Back in my assigned office, wearing my new uniform, I broke the seal on the safe and took out the files, untying string and laying them over the desk while my brain got to work with deciding how to go about the task I'd been set: reconstruct the extent of awareness the imperialist agencies had gained with a view to establishing the psychological, behavioural and political errors that had led to this penetration.

Or, to put it in everyday language: what did the West Germans know, and whose fault was it?

The documents I had in front of me—mostly evaluation reports rather than original material—covered a wide range of subjects, dates and sources. There was no common theme—reports on criminal activities from the late 1970s were mixed up with more recent information on the nuclear power station at Greifswald and up-to-the-minute information on sensitive political-tactical operations carried out by various departments in my own ministry.

The first job was to log the material, but unsure how to classify the information, I started by writing up a card for each report: title, theme, dates and places along with a note of any specific references to individuals or state organs.

It was solid work that would keep me at my desk for a while—in fact, the only people I spoke to during the first few days were the women in the canteen who served me food and sold me cigarettes and *Hauptmann* Ewald, who came in towards the end of each afternoon to check on progress.

★

By the third day, despite judicious dosage, my hip flask was empty, so at lunchtime I took a turn around the site. I found a brigade of builders in the furthest corner, unwrapping their sandwiches in the shade of a half-built vehicle workshop overlooking an overgrown helipad. Flasks of coffee and bottles of beer cluttered up a sheet of plywood that rested on a steel barrel in the centre of the group.

"How do?" I said, settling myself in the shade next to the workers and handing around a deck. Conversation had ceased as soon as I'd appeared, and I noted the suspicious looks as each of the men took one of my cigarettes. The pack did the full circle and the last man held it out for me. I took a nail then put the rest on the board. The silence continued while we smoked, only broken by the rustle of the unwrapping of greaseproof paper as some of the men began to eat their *Stullen*.

"I need a favour," I said when I judged the time was as right as it ever could be.

The man next to me wiped his brow with his sleeve and glanced at the shoulder boards on my fatigues.

"What's that then?"

"I need a couple of grenades."

The men understood, they'd all done their military service and knew the jargon.

"You want alcohol? Get your own like the rest of us have to —there's a *Konsum* in Alt Stahnsdorf." He threw another glance at my shoulder boards.

"Alt Stahnsdorf?"

"The next village. Turn right at the gate."

I shook my head. "Confined to barracks," I confided, giving the circle a half-smile.

A few of the builders had turned away, suddenly finding interest in the treeline and the stark shadows cast by the glaring sun.

"I'll pay you for your trouble," I told the man next to me,

pulling out a couple of twenty Mark notes. A *Nordhäuser* would set him back just over 17 Marks a bottle—if he brought me a couple of grenades, he'd get to keep more than a fiver.

Like the others, his eyes couldn't resist flicking to my shoulders. If I'd been able to get hold of a soldier's plain shoulder boards then this conversation would have been easier. But whoever I persuaded to do the run for me wouldn't be taking much of a risk—if word got out there'd be a few stern words from the gaffer, at worst a transfer to a different building site.

"I'll do it," said a beanpole sitting opposite me. He was young, his hair shaved almost to the skull, had probably just finished his own military service and remembered all too well how it is to be stuck on base with no access to fusel. He put his wrap of sandwiches on the board and reached across the divide, holding his yellow plastic builder's helmet out for me to deposit the cash.

"I'll see you tomorrow," I told him and left them to what was left of their break.

6
ALT STAHNSDORF

Having acquired a glass at breakfast, I spent the morning trying not to watch the sunlight reflect on its curved surfaces.

But when I wasn't staring at an empty glass, I made good progress through the files—having catalogued each report, I was now categorising my index cards by potential source: public domain, industry, *Volkspolizei* and MfS.

The largest pile was made up of material that had conceivably been gathered from the public domain—newspaper and media reports.

But my interest was focused on the other three stacks, these were the ones I planned to spend more time looking at.

I left the office at midday and strolled around the building site, sweating in my summer-issue field uniform. The builders were exactly where I'd left them the previous day, eating bread and sausage and drinking beer in the shade. The stringy young worker saw me coming and put down his penknife and cucumber and reached into his satchel for a couple of bottles of *Goldbrand.* I took the glass-jacketed projectiles and let them get back to their conversation.

Back in the office, I poured myself a swallow, knocking it back without letting any of it touch my tongue—the greedy kid had gone for the cheapest option, doubling his own share of the forty Marks I'd handed over.

I put the bottle and glass away, popped a *Pfeffi* mint in case Ewald was planning an early visit and continued cataloguing.

★

Captain Ewald did indeed arrive a little sooner than usual. He sat on the hard chair opposite me while I reported on progress, staring at the pile marked *Origin: MfS?* So far, he'd listened to my daily reports and not interfered in my work. But today he wore an impatient look.

"What are these?" he asked, pointing to the smallest pile.

"Information possibly sourced from the *Volkspolizei.*"

"And what does the material cover?"

"Art theft from the Grassi Museum in Leipzig, 1975; theft from graves and mausoleums, 1982, also in Leipzig; destruction of property of the people, Gera, 1980-"

"Any common elements?"

"Serious crimes, too serious to have been publicly reported. I'd guess the cases all required detailed investigation, which suggests the involvement of K1 in each case." K1— Department 1 of the *Kripo*, dealing in serious and organised crime, along with any political cases the comrades in the Ministry don't feel like handling. According to general rumour, K1 was supposedly a branch of the MfS, but really it was part of the police, same as all the other *Kripo* departments.

Ewald took the cards from that pile, spreading the first few along the edge of my desk. He frowned at my handwriting for a while before gathering them together and handing them to me.

"What about this pile—*Industry*?"

"Not so many reports in that category, and a clear concentration around the large *Kombinate,*" the state-owned industrial combines, "SKET Magdeburg, Ports Rostock, KKW Greifswald-"

"All of which have an MfS office directly on site."

Ewald sat back in his chair and lit a cigarette. I shunted the ashtray in his direction, but he didn't notice, he was too busy examining the freshly painted ceiling. His eyes rested on a crack that was already spidering its way from the corner above the window.

"When a K1 case is closed, the files don't go to the police archives, they're transferred to the local MfS offices for safekeeping," he continued to trace his thoughts, although he didn't follow them to the logical conclusion—at least not out loud. He didn't need to, I understood the implications: with the exception of the public domain material, each of these cards pointed to information that could be traced back to the MfS. Every case discussed in those reports had been leaked by someone with access to the Firm's archives.

"Focus on anything extracted from ministry offices." He put his hand on the third pile, the one marked *Origin: MfS*. "I want to know which department this traitor belongs to."

7
ALT STAHNSDORF

I spent the next two days with analysis: reading and re-reading the reports, noting any information that could help identify the sources. But the papers in front of me had been written in such a way as to deliberately obscure the provenance: no names, not even cover names were mentioned, and there were very few clues as to the classification levels or the perspective of the source.

Grasping at straws, I decided the sheer mass of material in front of me suggested I wasn't trying to find just one source, but several. Possibly even dozens. And going by the timescale of the events and the operations that had been reported on, these reports had been gathered over a period of more than ten years.

In short, I'd be glad to find anything more substantial than a vague pointer or two.

I gave Ewald the news when he turned up that afternoon.

"There has to be more material—something that isn't just a situation report or a general summary?" I said.

"That's all we have." Ewald shook his head. We'd become comfortable in each other's presence—I no longer stood to attention when he entered the room, and he always brought a flask of coffee with him when he dropped by. "If you can't find what you're looking for then go back to the beginning. If that doesn't do the job then work your way through the other categories."

★

I spent the evening with a glass or three of *Goldbrand*, thinking about the files. One particular report had caught my attention, and I didn't understand. A few years ago, the West German chancellor came on an official visit. He wanted to see a piece of art in Güstrow cathedral. So a plan was hatched to take him to the small town where he could see Barlach's sculpture, but also get to see how the happy citizens of the GDR live. Overnight, the town was practically emptied and the remaining residents were forbidden from leaving their houses and flats or going near their windows. MfS and police personnel were shipped in to play the role of the missing locals by filling the Christmas market and streets of Güstrow.

It was all hush-hush, but when you have over thirty thousand members of the MfS and police involved, stories are bound to spread.

Putting my glass down, I crossed to my desk, looking through the piles of cardboard and paper until I found the report I wanted.

Reading through, I realised what I'd missed until now. I'd been so desperate to tag the material with anything that could help identify the departments or individuals involved that I'd overlooked one basic identifying feature: geography.

The next morning, I began to re-order my index cards—this time by area. Just a couple of hours later I had fifteen piles on my desk, one for each district of the GDR.

I placed the cards for District Rostock at the far edge of my desk, Suhl, Gera, Karl-Marx-Stadt and Dresden were lined up next to where I was standing. Already after a few dozen cards I could see that I was onto something: the far north was filling up nicely, while the southern districts had very few cards.

By the time Captain Ewald brought my coffee that day, I had news for him:

"The traitor is acting alone, and he comes from the north."

8
ALT STAHNSDORF

"Classified material is mainly sourced from Districts Rostock, Schwerin and Neubrandenburg. Almost all the information from points south is either public domain or could be based on the kind of thing that colleagues talk about amongst themselves-"

"You mean gossip," Ewald interrupted. He sat on the edge of his seat, leaning forward to see the various cards laid out on my desk.

"An example: Federal Chancellor Helmut Schmidt's official visit in December 1981. There were just two stops on his tour: first, the government guest house on the Werbellinsee in District Frankfurt; after that, a trip to Güstrow in District Schwerin. Details on the talks on Werbellinsee are sketchy, no information about the accommodation, on Schmidt's escort, the subjects discussed by our Comrade General Secretary and the Federal Chancellor—not even a schedule of vehicles used to bring the party from Schönefeld airport. I think it's possible the report was based on newspaper and radio reports from here and in the West.

"But Güstrow—in a different district—the report on what happened in Güstrow is extraordinary: operational details of the plan to replace the town's population with colleagues; practically every comment made by Schmidt when he visited the Christmas market and the cathedral is included. There's even an account of that tête-à-tête Schmidt had with the bishop in the cathedral, how he attempted to exclude Comrade General Secretary Honecker by speaking in northern *Platt* dialect-"

"There were something like 50,000 colleagues from the Ministry and the *Volkspolizei* on duty that day," Ewald interjected. "Details will have been leaked after the fact. But security was tighter at the summit by the lake, fewer and more reliable personnel. Therefore: no idle talk. Your example proves nothing."

"No, Comrade Captain. But this report drew my attention to the correlation between geography and verifiable detail."

I showed him a few more examples—some of the reports covered information that would surely have been graded VVS —the most restricted security classification of all—operations I myself had never heard even the vaguest whisper about: the IMES depot south of Rostock where military hardware is stashed, earmarked for illegal export; or the fact that the BKK, the Commercial Co-ordination Division specialising in procuring hard currency, had recently stepped up their questionable activities at Rostock International Port.

"And you've found nothing at this classification level from central and southern Districts?" Ewald asked.

"A couple of items from Berlin, otherwise all pretty soft."

"We'll need to cross-reference classified information with the distribution lists of the original documents." Ewald stood up, preparing to leave. The next step in the investigation would be high above my security clearance—someone, somewhere had already overshot the rules when they let me see this material, and I knew I was about to be relieved of my task.

"Prioritise sorting the material from the northern districts. Once that's done, pack up the reports and any notes you've made then report to me."

As I watched Ewald leave my office, I could feel a smile climb onto my face. I'd lost a week of my leave to this job, but once I'd completed this final task my holiday by the lake could finally begin.

9
ALT STAHNSDORF

"I'm taking these to Berlin." Ewald slid the papers and my notes into his briefcase and stood up. "Keep yourself available, I'll be back in a few days."

I stiffened to attention as he left the room, silently cursing his retreating back. On reflection, perhaps the cancellation of what was left of my leave wasn't the biggest surprise, but I still allowed myself a moment of disappointment.

I looked around Ewald's office, but he'd left nothing behind —the place was quite literally empty: his desk was nothing more than a table, the doors of the steel safe hung open, shamelessly exhibiting its nakedness.

The next day was Sunday, building work was on hold for the day and the only movement came from the shifting haze of fine sand that swirled and meandered through the superheated air.

I took a turn around the base, starting in the south-east corner, just out of sight of the guard post. Beyond the main building site, a track took me between high pines to a clearing with a parade of empty barracks. I took a look inside the first couple—both were vacant of furniture and other signs of life.

This isolated corner of the camp would do me. I went back to my accommodation block, returning with the second bottle of *Goldbrand* and a camp bed. If I couldn't enjoy my holiday sunning myself on the edge of a lake, I'd have to do it here on the edge of a half-built military camp.

★

I went to see the builders the next morning to negotiate delivery of a couple of crates of beer. For an extra fee, they agreed to store the crates in a shed with their equipment, giving me the key so I could get myself a bottle whenever I needed.

Days passed. Waiting for word from Berlin, I lounged on the camp bed, drinking warm beer and watching the sky. A bird of prey swung by a few times a day, red body and forked tail, eyes piercing the hazy air, checking whether I was cooked through yet. One afternoon, a stork heaved itself over my clearing, wings dragging through the air. But other than that, just the light sand, the tall pines, the heavy sun and my beer. And with every bottle I tossed into the undergrowth on the other side of the fence, my resentment grew.

I understood the need for the secrecy that had brought me to this place—Lieutenant Colonel Schur's pride was on the line here, perhaps even his position—but I'd played my part and as far as I was concerned my secondment was over. I ought to be in my holiday accommodation right now, going for a swim, watching dragonflies patrol the reeds, sipping fridge-cold beer from a glass and eating decent food.

But they couldn't keep me here for much longer—if I wasn't back at my office in Berlin Centre on Monday morning, there'd be some difficult questions to answer. So, at most, I had another week of hanging around.

In this game, you learn to take what small comforts you can find.

I shifted my camp bed out of the shade of overhanging trees, taking care to stay out of the way of the forest ants. Cracking open another bottle, I settled and pulled my cap over my eyes, ready for another doze.

My peace was disturbed by a soldier standing by my side, wheezing like a superannuated panzer engine on amphibious manoeuvres. I nudged the peak of my cap out of the way and squinted at the vague silhouette standing against the sun. It had a hand raised to its head, waiting for me to return the salute. I tapped a couple of lazy fingers against my forehead.

"Comrade Second Lieutenant," he panted, still trying to catch his breath. My eyes were adjusting to the bright sun, I could see the sweat trickling down his face. Poor kid must have run all around the base looking for me. "You're to report to Comrade Captain Ewald's office immediately."

Cursing, I dismissed the kid and chucked my nearly-full bottle of beer over the fence to join the others in the forest, then made my way back to the half-completed administration block.

I stopped at my own office first, downed a couple of *Pfeffis* and changed into a clean shirt. Another *Pfeffi* for luck, then along the corridor to present myself to the captain.

10
ALT STAHNSDORF

"Comrade Lieutenant Colonel Schur is in agreement with your assessment," announced Captain Ewald as I closed the office door. "Thoughts on next steps?"

What is it they say? *Never volunteer for anything.* But maybe I'd been drinking too much, maybe I just felt flattered that such a high ranking officer had expressed unqualified agreement with my evaluation. Whatever the reason, I was rash enough to volunteer an opinion.

"Working on the assumption that the informant is based in the north, then we should begin the operational search in those districts. Since the greatest concentration of both classified and highly classified material is linked to Rostock and the surrounding area, I suggest we begin with signals surveillance around the city-"

"Out of the question," Ewald broke in. "The fewer units involved ... Begin with an assessment of the political-operational situation in Rostock. After that, we can consider further operational procedures."

This was always going to be a lengthy operation and radio surveillance would never have been enough on its own anyway—signals intelligence might help to confirm my theory, possibly provide a lead or two, but after that we'd still end up with old-fashioned, snail-paced detective work to identify the informant and his handler.

But I was prepared to bet my illicit stash of alcohol that the last thing my superiors wanted to hear was that they'd have to wait to get their answers, and if they weren't prepared to ask for help from other departments, then they should be prepared to wait even longer.

"Have any of the files these reports are based on been identified?" I asked, trying to buy some time to think. "If we can examine the original distribution lists-"

Ewald was shaking his head, just as expected. "As I said—no other units to be involved."

"So if we can't search for the original files and we can't ask HA III for signals surveillance, then all we can do is focus on the chain of contact between the informant and his handlers," I said. "The imperialist asset will stay in the shadows, but he'll regularly use a courier, someone to take the information out of the country. Once we identify that courier, he'll lead us to our traitor." Ewald was nodding away as if that had been his idea all along and I was just catching up.

"Focus on border crossings in or near District Rostock?" he suggested.

"One rail and one road crossing on State Border West, another one if we include the Hamburg motorway crossing at Zarrentin which is just inside the next district." Before my post at ZAIG, I'd worked at HA VI, responsible for border crossings and tourists. I knew all the crossing points, but considering that Ewald had probably never been north of Berlin, I went through the list for him. "Then the two ferry ports to Scandinavia and four freight ports. And we shouldn't forget the limited road crossing to the Polish People's Republic."

"Ten entry points?" Ewald marvelled. "Fine, collate entry and exit records from those ten. We need to identify suitable candidates for operational surveillance, with a view to further processing in an operational procedure."

Life would be easier all round if we could just speak German with each other. What was wrong with saying something like: *we could cross-reference records from border crossings to see if anyone sticks out, then take a closer look at them?* But the Firm's work isn't about clear communication, it's about hiding from ourselves what exactly we're doing to other people.

"How long do you need?" Ewald steepled his fingers and puffed out his sunken cheeks.

I didn't reply, because any answer I gave would be a lie. As so often with these things, it all depended on luck. The more paperwork we had, the more files and information we gathered, the longer everything took. Whatever we were looking for was buried in the archives, but I might need to check a few thousand records before I found it. And if I was unlucky, I wouldn't even recognise it in the first trawl and would have to start again from the beginning.

"Fine. Start work on an opening report."

I took the boxes back to my own office, allowed myself a single shot of *Goldbrand* before sitting down in front of the modern Erika typewriter.

```
Operational Procedure WOLFRAM
Opening Report


- - - - - - - - - - - - -


1) Findings of political-
operational and criminological
analysis of material
```

I stopped and lit a cigarette. I could write the next few pages on autopilot, knew which paragraphs in the criminal code to cite and which ministerial standing orders to quote from. The usual thing to do was to include anything and everything that could conceivably become relevant. So to make sure I had all the bases covered, I thought for a moment before jotting down paragraphs 97 and 98 of the Criminal Law

Code, espionage; paragraph 99, treasonous communications and the only marginally different paragraph 100, which covered walk-ups, even if the foreign agencies decided not to bite.

Having completed the title page, and noted which laws might have been broken, I took another belt of alcohol and checked my watch. I could burn through this report in a couple of hours, maybe ninety minutes, but it wouldn't be in my interests to let Ewald know I could be that efficient. So I checked the office door was shut, pushed my chair back a bit to give my legs enough room under the table and prepared myself for a refreshing snooze.

When I woke up, the sun was still high, drumming heat through the window, but a glance at my watch told me it had gone six. Later than I'd planned, but I had no problem with making Ewald wait until the morning for the report because right now, I decided, getting *Jägerschnitzel* with Letscho and noodles at the canteen should be my biggest priority.

11
BERLIN LICHTENBERG

A note was waiting on my desk when I arrived at Berlin Centre on Monday morning: *Report to Capt. Ewald, HA II.*

It was just a couple of days after I'd handed in the report. There'd been some discussion about suitable operational measures—the captain had been keen to restrict the number of operatives involved and I'd been obliged to scale down my recommendations. An hour to rewrite and retype a couple of pages and Ewald accepted the report at midday.

I'd handed in my NVA uniform and an *Uffzi* took me back to Berlin, where I was just in time to get some bread and beer before the *Konsum* closed.

And on Sunday it had rained. The last day of my leave, the *only* day of my leave, and I spent most of it in the corner of my local bar, glowering at the clouds on the other side of the window and ignoring the civilian drinkers' inane banter.

"Come in, Comrade Second Lieutenant." Ewald was in a good mood, his broken nose twisted into a vague smile.

I came to a halt in front of his desk, but before I could assume the position, he gestured me into the visitor's chair. I set myself down and waited to hear the captain's good news.

"Comrade Lieutenant Colonel Schur approved your initial plan for Wolfram." I noted the stress he placed in the word *your*, making sure I was aware I'd carry the responsibility if my plan were to fail. "You may begin the operational procedure." He paused.

"You begin work immediately." Just in case I hadn't caught

the message the first time.

Since Ewald and I got on so well together and since we were both facing each other at eye level, I didn't bother requesting permission to speak, but just asked him straight out: "Has my department agreed to extend my secondment?"

His grey eyes examined me for a few moments, as if surprised that I didn't share his excitement, then he pushed the report I'd written over the desk towards me.

"You're to continue your current duties at ZAIG—Comrade Captain Kühn has agreed to lighten your load for the next few weeks—meanwhile, you will also work on Wolfram under enhanced conspirational rules."

In other words, the work would be unofficial and the overtime unpaid. It wasn't just my annual leave that I'd lost, they were going to take every evening and weekend I had until I succeeded in identifying the hostile-negative asset in our ranks.

"And the comrade lieutenant colonel is expecting a speedy and satisfactory conclusion to the operational procedure?" I ventured as Ewald narrowed his eyes. "You see, I can still remember my way around the files in my old department, HA VI, but if we had an operative more familiar with the material then we could reduce the time-"

"You have someone in mind?" Ewald interrupted.

"An old colleague from HA VI. Reliable, competent. Working with him, I could-"

"Name and rank?"

"Stoyan, Matthias, *Unterleutnant.* Based at HA VI main offices in Treptow."

"Begin work on OV Wolfram. I'll get back to you about Comrade Stoyan."

Did I feel guilty about volunteering my old colleague Matse? Not at all, I'd already sacrificed my whole leave for Operation Wolfram—it was time somebody else shared some of the burden too.

12
BERLIN LICHTENBERG

"You are only to access the archives here at Berlin Centre, never at HA VI—we don't need your colleagues in Treptow wondering what you're doing in the basement every evening," I told Matse Stoyan. He hadn't been pleased to be roped into the operation, and once he worked out that he wouldn't be seeing much of his wife and kids over the next few months he would be even less pleased. But he realised he didn't have any say in the matter and had enough sense to pipe down.

Schur or Ewald or whoever made the decisions over at HA II had taken less than a day to agree to the request to bring Matse on board—they were even keener than I to wrap this whole thing up. I tried to pass on that sense of urgency to my old colleague: "You want to spend time with your family? The sooner we find the target, the sooner life gets back to normal."

We'd been assigned a windowless closet in one of the basements at Berlin Centre, right next to where the copies of HA VI archives were held. Under normal circumstances, it would have been impossible to borrow files for even a few minutes without the archivist knowing, but in the summer of 1984, the central archives were temporarily displaced because some bright spark at the top of the Ministry had decided we needed yet another bunker, and the best place to build it would be under the archives. So files and archivists were currently displaced to whichever of Berlin Centre's cellars could be emptied at short notice.

Which meant the archivists now spent most of their time

running up and down stairs and across the yards between buildings, trying to keep track of their precious paperwork. By the end of each day, they were exhausted enough to abandon the cellars, and by 2000 hours there was usually just a skeleton crew to keep watch through the hours of darkness.

So with a little discretion and the right pieces of paper with the relevant permissions in our pockets, we were able to help ourselves each evening and weekend. And providing we put the files back in the right place, there was neither witness nor record to exactly what we'd been looking at.

I started thumbing through the statistical entry and exit cards from both the passenger ferry and the cargo port in Rostock, compiling lists of names as I went. The details of anyone entering the GDR more than four times over a two-year period were passed to Matse, who went off to cross-reference entries.

His first checks were with the police registration files—for the moment we were ignoring anyone who had registered their temporary residence as being outside the immediate area around Rostock—we'd get back to them if we had to, but right now, we were hoping for a hit on the tourists and business travellers who stayed in or near Rostock.

It wasn't exciting work, but there was a rhythm to it, and we regularly worked through the night, catching up on sleep at our desks during the day.

At the end of the second week we had collected several hundred names going back five years. I decided that was enough of a milestone to call for a temporary halt.

"Hold your glass out," I told Matse, who was still pining for his family. I filled him with a shot of vodka, then did the same for myself.

"Could it be the courier we're looking for never actually enters the GDR? That our target uses something like a radio to communicate?" asked Matse in a flat voice. I decided it was a rhetorical question and ignored him, but Matse didn't give up easily: "What about the other teams? How are they getting on?"

"All being taken care of, Matse. Don't worry yourself." He was fishing, wanting to know more about the operation I'd dragged him into.

His curiosity wasn't idle, the pair of us were giving up practically all our free time, hours of sifting files every night, and it would have been comforting to know other teams were working just as hard. If we missed our courier in the files, other teams might find traces of him in a radio microburst or a microdot glued on a personal letter. Experts would be examining the thirteenth full stop on page seven, checking whether it was a minute disc of film and not a drop of ink.

Except I didn't have the reassurances Matse was looking for. Not wanting to dishearten him with the news that we were all alone on this one, I did the next best thing: "Call it a night, shall we?" I suggested. "Go home, take the weekend off, remind yourself what your kids look like."

13
BERLIN FRIEDRICHSHAIN

When Matse and I took the stairs down to the dark basement room after work on Monday, I couldn't help but notice his lack of enthusiasm. He slouched in my chair and leafed through the pages of names I'd gathered as I poured the first two glasses of the evening.

"It'll take us until the end of the year to check all of these," he grumbled.

I didn't disagree, which was perhaps why his despair was proving so contagious. I stood beside him and picked up the top few sheets. "Let's hope we find him before the end of the year."

But Matse wasn't listening, he was looking at one of the sheets from the longlist. "Why didn't I notice that before?" he pulled the page towards him and tapped one of the names. "Heller, Herbert. He's a West German, but comes on the Gedser ferry—why would a West German get the ferry from Denmark?" he asked. "It would make more sense if he came over the western border by road or rail."

"Perhaps he lives in Denmark?"

"So we assume he lives in Denmark. But he's going to Poland—why not take the direct ferry from Copenhagen to Poland? Why come via Warnemünde and have the hassle of getting a transit visa for the GDR?"

I leaned over to read the notes. "Looks like he's been doing it for at least five years—transit visas Warnemünde to Poland until martial law, then a break, and now things have quietened down a bit over there, he's back on the transit visa again." It didn't seem that interesting to me, and I was impatient for Matse to vacate my seat so I could continue work. But Matse hadn't finished with Heller.

"Comes in on the midday sailing, leaves again the next day. That doesn't leave much time to get to Poland and back."

Unenthusiastic as I was about Matse's discovery, I still took a moment to think about what he was saying. "The ferry comes in at noon, he has twenty-four hours to get there and back," I thought aloud. "That's long enough to get to any of the cities in the west of Poland: Szczecin, Gorzów or Zielona Góra, he could travel to any of them. Spends the night there, catches an early train to Berlin and changes for the Neptun-Express to Copenhagen via the Warnemünde ferry." It was doable, but perhaps Matse was right—it didn't make sense to go to the trouble of sorting out two sets of visas then travel all that way for a single overnight stay. Not unless he also had business here in the GDR.

"I'll get his cards from the archive," announced Matse as he finally left my chair.

My colleague returned within five minutes, clutching a handful of statistical cards. He laid them out on the desk in pairs: Entry and Exit for each leg of each journey to Poland.

"Pomellen," I read over his shoulder. "That's the crossing point on the Berlin-Szczecin motorway. West German plates, too—so where does he get himself a West German registered vehicle from? He enters Warnemünde on the boat train, then magically finds a car for the rest of his trip to Poland?"

"That's not the biggest question," said Matse, pointing out one of the pairs of cards. The space for the exit stamps had been filled in by hand rather than with the usual varicoloured rubber stamp of the Pass and Control Unit at the border.

Matse went to the archive again to fetch the full records for the Border Crossing Point Pomellen, leaving me to look at the cards. The dates were frequent, but not quite regular—a trip every three or four weeks—a clear enough pattern. With renewed interest and a fresh eye, I started going through my longlist, looking for any other transit journeys returning within the week.

I was on the seventh page with no further hits when Matse returned, carrying a couple of box files. I cleared a space for him, and he laid out photostats of visa application forms, visa authorisation notifications and visas, vehicle registration papers and Heller's passport.

"Heller, Herbert, born Magdeburg 1941, currently resident in Flensburg, West Germany," I read aloud. "I'll ask for an official search of the Who's Who register tomorrow—we won't be able to slip a look at it without anyone noticing."

"Reim?" Matse was comparing the visa papers with the statistical entry and exit cards. His face was pale. "Look here." His fingers moved from the Warnemünde entry card to the matching transit visa. It had an entry stamp for Warnemünde, but no exit stamp from the Polish border. Matse's fingers sought out the card for the return journey: no entry stamp for the crossing at Pomellen, just the one stamp for exit at Warnemünde port.

"That's impossible," I whispered. Matse nodded. When a traveller enters the GDR on a transit visa, the time is noted and the duration of the transit is checked at the exit point to discourage dawdling. If a transit visa holder doesn't turn up at the exit point, we go looking for him.

So how had Heller entered the GDR on a visa for transit to Poland, but never actually made it to the Polish border? Not just once, but regularly? Alarm bells should have gone off at Pomellen and a search party sent out.

"When was the most recent entry?" I asked, looking at the visa application form with the mugshot.

"Entry Warnemünde on June 21st, left the GDR at Warnemünde the next day. Just over three weeks ago."

Herbert Heller was due another visit to the GDR.

14
BERLIN LICHTENBERG

Matse was trembling with excitement when he turned up at our cubby hole in the cellar the next evening. "Our friend Heller has a visa to enter at Warnemünde on Saturday," he announced as soon as he was through the door.

One of the reasons I'd chosen Matse was because his day job at HA VI was to keep an eye on visa authorisations. He was in position to spot Heller's visa application a week or two before they were brought to the archive, and that had bought us a bit of advance notice.

"Congratulations, you've won a trip to Rostock." I clapped him on the shoulder.

"Rostock?" he wasn't chuffed about that. Fair enough, I wasn't too keen on going to the coast either, albeit for different reasons.

While Matse didn't want to leave his family behind, I had worked up a serious dislike of the north during an operation last winter. But by sending Matse first, I hoped to avoid having to spend too much time up there.

"But why me?" he asked.

Good question. And, funnily enough, when I'd presented my plan to Captain Ewald, he'd asked the very same question: why send Matthias Stoyan rather than go yourself?

"We don't want to cause any unnecessary concern, do we?" I answered. "Passport Control Unit in Warnemünde wouldn't be happy if I turned up with no official reason. But you're in the same department as them, it'll be easier to explain what you're doing there. Tell them there's a review of procedures, you're carrying out an analysis of the standard operating sequences, something boring. They're used to that kind of manure."

"But they must know about the missing stamps on Heller's cards," Matse countered. "Don't you think they'll wonder when I turn up the very day Heller is due?"

"Which is why you're going up there first thing tomorrow, and why you'll stay for at least a fortnight. Just don't act too interested in the ferry passengers. All you have to do is keep an eye open for Heller when he enters the country and I'll take it from there."

He still didn't look very happy about his orders, so I made a final effort to cheer him up. "It's a cushy posting—an hour's work at midday and an hour's work in the wee hours when the night ferry comes in. You get the rest of the time off—go for a swim in the sea, hire a *Strandkorb* and sit around on the nudist beach all day—it'll be like going on holiday."

Put it like that and I was having second thoughts about not going myself. But Matse merely shrugged.

I patted him on the shoulder again. "I'll be there at the end of the week, and we'll be ready for our West German friend when he arrives on Saturday."

15
ROSTOCK LICHTENHAGEN

Matse Stoyan was waiting for me when I arrived in Rostock on Friday evening. He watched me open the glass door of the bar, bag in one hand, motorcycle helmet in the other.

"Why are we meeting here?" he asked, looking around the soulless room on the ground floor of one of Rostock's concrete suburbs.

I sat myself next to him and looked out of the window at the block opposite. The bar was as dull and devoid of life as the last time I'd sat here, but outside on the street, the young trees were in leaf, kids were making themselves heard, some cycling around, making a nuisance of themselves, others chalking up a *Hopse* ladder on the pavement.

I turned away from the window as the barman set up a beer on the table in front of me. Matse already had his, so we tapped our glasses and looked deep into each other's eyes.

"Why here?" he asked again.

"Need to avoid Warnemünde, too many of our colleagues snooping around," I answered. "What have you got for me?"

Matse took another sip of beer before answering. He leaned forward, and in a conspirational whisper that was wasted on the empty bar, told me about the work of the Passport and Control Unit: "The international train comes into Rostock Central Station and the through carriages for the ferry are unhooked. The passengers have already shown their papers when they boarded in Berlin, but PKE and customs go through the whole procedure again while en route to the port in Warnemünde. At Warnemünde station, the PKE unit is stationed along the platform while the *Transportpolizei* guard the trackside. When they've gone through all the passengers, the shunter is brought up to push the carriages into the belly of the ferry."

"So all checks are done on the train between Rostock and Warnemünde?" I asked.

"It's the same in the other direction. The carriages are pulled out of the ship by a shunter, and while the mainline locomotive is hooking up, PKE and customs board the train and do their stuff. If they haven't finished by the time they get to Rostock Central Station, they stay on board and get the next train back."

"So, practically speaking, our subject can't leave the train before Rostock?" I was thinking aloud, trying to visualise Heller's options once he'd entered the GDR.

"The international express trains only stop in Rostock, Waren and Oranienburg before they get to Berlin," Matse supplied helpfully.

"Let's assume he's going to Poland, despite the lack of stamps on his cards," I said, flipping open my road atlas, looking for the page that showed the main routes. I put my finger on Waren. "Good place to pick up a car, less chance of running into one of our colleagues, and a step closer to the Polish border."

"Oranienburg is good, too," Matse objected. "It's not any closer to the Polish border, but it's motorway all the way. Much quicker."

"But if he's in a West German vehicle, why take the risk of driving around the Berlin ring motorway? The *Volkspolizei* could pull him over, they keep an eye out for Westerners who have missed the turn-off for West Berlin."

"He could pick up the car in any of those places," Matse insisted.

I checked the road atlas again—it was about 100 kilometres from Rostock to Waren. "How long does the train take to

Waren?"

Matse pulled a timetable out of his pocket and flattened it on the table. "Just under an hour."

Since Ewald wouldn't let me involve other operatives, and I needed Matse to stick to his cover in order to avoid raising suspicion among his colleagues at the port, I was the only one available to follow Heller.

I would have liked to take the motorbike, it would give me more flexibility once the subject picked up his car, but there was no way I could match the speed of the train between Rostock and Waren, not on those roads, not even with the MZ.

So all I could do was wait at Rostock Central Station to check whether Heller alighted, and if he didn't then I'd join him on the train.

I signalled to the barman for another couple of beers.

"What happened over there?" asked Matse once we'd started on the fresh beers.

I turned away from the window, confused by his question.

"You keep looking outside, you've been staring at that block across the way ever since you got here," he explained.

"Nothing happened over there." But I couldn't stop my eyes from flicking up to the windows on the fourth floor.

"You know someone who lives there?" Matse guessed. He was looking at the building although there was nothing interesting about it. Just six storeys of concrete slab-build, same as hundreds of thousands of others across the Republic. "A woman?"

"History." I stopped looking out of the window and made a point of staring into my beer instead.

I thought Matse would catch my hint and shut his trap. But he didn't.

"You chose this place as a rendezvous, and you've done nothing but moon out of the window since you got here."

"Like I said: history. Now leave it." But then I surprised

myself, and instead of following my own advice, I allowed another few words to fall out of my mouth: "A contact person. You know how it is, every so often someone makes an impression ..."

"A woman?" Matse repeated his question, and I'll admit, I wondered for a moment why he'd immediately decided my behaviour could be explained away by the presence of a female.

Perhaps he was right to think that way, after all, his guess was accurate: it had been a woman who'd occupied that flat across the way. Anna Weber. And when we first met, I'd seen her as the usual challenge—an attractive lass I could try to seduce. But then I found myself working alongside her and my respect for her abilities grew, even though she was an agent for the other side. Unbidden, images passed through my mind: a charcoal portrait; Weber at the wheel of a tiny Fiat Polski; the Russian railway station at Wünsdorf.

History.

Even though things hadn't gone so well for her, I didn't lie awake every night thinking about her. Yet here I was, staring through the window like a lovestruck teenager.

"Drink up," I told Matse. "It's time to go."

16
ROSTOCK

The next day saw me in the shade of the platform canopy at Rostock Central Station as the carriages from the boat train were shunted up to the rest of the express. A *Reichsbahn* worker in dark blue overalls jumped down to the trackbed to attach the screw coupling as the conductor released the door locks.

Passengers boarded the train, but the doors on the two carriages from Warnemünde remained closed. I stayed where I was until the dispatcher looked up and down the platform, whistle held between her lips, green and red lollipop at the ready. As the whistle blew, I climbed the steps of the nearest carriage and waited just inside the door as it shut. The train pulled out, and I peered through the window for a final sweep of the platform, but save for the dispatcher, it was empty.

Once we'd left the station, I moved to the rear of the train, but my way was barred—the gangway connection to the final two carriages, the ones that had come from Denmark, hadn't been hooked up.

Unable to check the carriages, I had little choice but to sit on a pull-down seat next to the train door, ready to surveil the disembarking passengers when we pulled into the next stop.

After an hour in the stuffy vestibule, the brakes squealed and moaned as we slowed to a stop at Waren. I swung the door open and climbed down to the low platform, swivelling my head to watch the other travellers stumble down the steps.

The crowds swirled, resolving gradually into two streams:

one flowing out of the station, others eddying around the doors. Nobody remotely matched the description of a Westerner called Heller.

As the last few passengers hauled themselves up and into the carriages, I joined them, this time pulling open a door on the first of the two carriages that had come off the ferry.

I moved along the corridor as the doors clacked shut behind me, the train gathering motion as I peered into first one compartment, then the next. Finding no Heller, I passed through the rumpling connection to the next and final carriage of the train. The curtains of the second compartment were drawn, and without hesitation, I slid the door open to better examine the occupants: an old couple with grandchildren and more luggage than they could possibly carry.

"Wrong compartment," I said to their startled faces and carried on down the corridor.

The next compartment: five suits, all older than Heller, talking in what might have been Danish—or Norwegian or Swedish for all I knew. After that, an empty compartment, then two families. A prim old biddy keeping a tight grip on the handbag that rested on her lap. A young couple.

No Heller.

In desperation I doubled back, once again checking each compartment in the two carriages, earning hostile, curious and bemused looks as I went.

Heller was not on board.

I went back to the empty compartment and made myself comfortable while I waited for the next stop. Pulling the window down, I wiped sweat off the back of my neck. Heller hadn't left the train at Rostock or Waren, so where was he?

17
ROSTOCK

It took me several hours to get back to Rostock, late enough for shadows to be creeping into the square in front of the station. I ignored the yellow telephone box by the main entrance and walked a few blocks.

Finding a telephone hood on the side of a building, I called Matse at his lodgings to let him know I was back in town.

Hanging up, I checked the map of Rostock—it wasn't far to the Old Cemetery, so I decided to walk. I passed between the ivy-covered gates just twenty minutes later and took the central path, carpeted by weeds and flanked by mature lime trees, before turning off about halfway down to find the right section.

Matse was already waiting, I found him behind a barrel-roofed mausoleum, watching how the low sun glinted through the leaves of the neglected trees. He turned as he heard me step through the ivy that smothered the pathway.

"You followed him? Where did he pick up the car?" I was surprised how his eyes shone with excitement.

"He wasn't on the train. Did you see him come off the boat?" I asked.

"I was on the train but I didn't think anything of it when the PKE squad I was shadowing didn't come across him—just assumed the other squad would." Matse's voice slackened, his eyes losing their lustre.

"What about foot passengers? Or could he have got into a car or truck on the ferry?"

"That would be flagged up—the Pass and Control Unit

would give him grief for not using the method of transport stated on his visa."

"He's not going to get any grief—we as good as know that someone in PKE is covering for him!" If he had the connections to smooth over the missing entry and exit stamps on his cards, then he wasn't going to get smacked on the wrist for entering the country in a road vehicle instead of by train.

Matse shuffled his feet, the dead leaves under the ivy scraped and crackled.

"Can you get eyes on the entry stats for today's ferry? Check whether he actually arrived?" I asked.

My colleague shook his head. "The paperwork will already be with the District Administration. We'll just have to catch him tomorrow on his way back to Denmark."

"Assuming he even came through Warnemünde today ..."

But even if we caught up with Heller the next day, we couldn't follow him any further than the port without authority from Berlin. But it was the weekend—our request would end up in the sandbox until Monday, by which time Heller would be well over the horizon.

18
WARNEMÜNDE

Neither of us were enthusiastic about trying to pick up Heller's trail on his return journey—the best we could hope for would be to watch him leave the country again.

Nevertheless, duty called. If nothing else, we could at least report that he was safely out of the country. So at midday on Sunday I took a stroll along the lines of Danish and Swedish lorries parked up alongside the main approach to the ferry port. Most of the trucks had curtains drawn over the windscreens, drivers were catching up on sleep, but a few cabs were empty, the occupants at the *Intershop*, buying up stocks of cheap cigarettes and alcohol.

I wasn't comfortable about hanging around so near the port —I knew my colleagues from Rostock would be about, keeping an eye on those citizens who showed a little too much interest in the goings-on at the border. Sure, a flash of my clapperboard would get me out of any trouble, but only at the expense of letting the local units know that Berlin was poking its nose in.

I heard the boat train rumble and squeal along the tracks on the other side of the station buildings, and as if that were their cue, drivers returned with their *Intershop* bags and the lorries quivered into life. A white-mouse traffic cop appeared at the gate to the port and, trying to remain inconspicuous, I sauntered over to the railway station to take up position beside the yellow telephone kiosk, nicely out of sight of the cop.

The white mouse directed the cars into the port first—

mostly Western vehicles, plenty of large Volvos and Saabs—and I watched them go by, trying to make out the features of drivers and passengers through windows that reflected the bright noon sun straight back at me.

There was a hold-up at the gate, the cars queued back, hot air pulsing from bodywork and exhaust pipes, then the line lurched into motion again, jerking forward a car's length at a time as paperwork was examined at the entrance to the port.

The phone behind me rang, and I pulled open the door of the booth and lifted the receiver.

"I'm listening," I said into the mouthpiece.

"Subject was dropped off by a local taxi. Light blue Volga, leaving the port area now," said Matse down the line.

I hung up and hurried down the road to my MZ, sparked it up, ready for the Volga to appear. This was the main road to Rostock, so unless the taxi headed into the centre of Warnemünde, he would be coming my way.

And there it was: a blue Volga wallowed past on soft suspension and I fell in behind, allowing distance to develop between us once we'd left the coastal town behind. Other cars obligingly filled the space I'd made, but I never let the black and yellow taxi sign on the roof out of my sight.

Once we entered the outer edges of Rostock old town, I closed the distance on my quarry, following as he turned into a minor road, but I judged the angle wrong, my front wheel slid off a slick cobble and skidded out a little. Adjusting my balance, I righted the bike as the taxi pulled into a parking space.

Slowing and mounting the curb, I let the bike's momentum take me along the footway and around the corner.

With the bike on its stand, I stood at the end of the road, peering around the side of the building to where the Volga stood. A large man in a sailor's cap had levered himself off the slatted boards of a wooden drinks kiosk and was stepping over to the Volga at the curbside.

The driver, a short man, not in the best of shape, was waiting by the open car door. He handed the big man an envelope, shook hands, then set off towards the main road, in my direction.

I ducked back around the corner and stood by my motorbike, unsure whether to swing a leg over it and drive off before the short man reached me.

But I didn't. I waited. Because the man walking towards me was called Horst Lütten and I knew him. He'd assisted in an operation back in February—I say assisted, but he'd really been playing both sides of the street. I owed him for the bullet hole in my left biceps, not to mention for the loss of two valuable contact persons.

I should have left the scene. I had the information I'd come for—I'd made Lütten, and I had a good description of the taxi driver he'd presumably bribed for the use of the cab. But anger held me in place, preventing me from taking what I knew was the operationally expedient course of action.

When Lütten finally rounded the corner, I was waiting for him.

19
ROSTOCK

I pressed myself against the side of the house until Lütten appeared, then stepped behind him as he cleared the corner. I pulled his right arm up his back and turned him round quickly, slamming him face-first into the wall. Hard.

I held him there, one hand on his wrist, halfway up his back, the other pressing his head against the rough rendering.

"You're going to regret this," he gasped once he'd found enough breath. "There will be consequences."

"Shut your snout, Lütten," I hissed into his ear.

He went stiff. Maybe he recognised my voice, or maybe he just realised he was dealing with a pro.

Pulling his wrist a little further up his back, I let up the pressure on his skull and shifted a little to the side, just out of range of his free arm. Lütten obliged by moving his head round far enough to see me, and I stuck my thumb into his fleshy neck, hooking it under his jawbone. His eyes swivelled, trying to work out whether I was alone, but there wasn't much he could see without moving his head further, and he couldn't do that unless he wanted my thumb to dig even deeper into his mandibular nerve.

"Reim? What?"

"Funny you should ask that—I was just wondering the same thing."

"Always interfering ...." He gasped as I moved my thumb, just a little bit. Sweat pearled on his brow. "It's my manor, you've no business here!"

"I decide whether I've got business here, and right now,

you're my business. Tell me about the man you just dropped off at the port."

"Take your questions to the head of XV!" he panted.

Shit, that made it sound like Lütten's taxi service was not only official, but actually sanctioned by top-level brass here in Rostock.

"Greetings to Prager," I whispered in his ear before letting go of his wrist and jaw. I stepped away before he could make any moves.

I watched Lütten in my mirror as I moved back into the traffic on my bike, and he in turn watched me, alternately rubbing his elbow and his jawline. Why had I asked Lütten to pass my regards on to his sidekick, Prager? Why not just ask him to say hello to the man pulling his strings: Sachse?

Maybe because part of me still hoped *Oberleutnant* Sachse wasn't involved in this affair.

I can be naïve like that, sometimes.

20
ROSTOCK

The bar wasn't a good choice. It was near the Old Cemetery where I'd met Matse the night before, which is why I'd picked it out on the map, but the place was full of students, and I didn't exactly blend in with customers sporting ragged hair and beards, short skirts and long smiles.

The second mistake was that we hadn't arranged a backup. The bar was too close to where Lütten and I had just had our little chat, but this was the arranged rendezvous and with no way to contact Matse in time, I could only wait for him here.

So I sat at a table far away from the windows and kept an eye on the door. At least I'd managed to get the MZ out of sight—a local had taken ten Marks to store it in his garage. If Lütten was on the lookout for my bike, he'd have to look that bit harder.

Matse arrived late, but not late enough to give me an excuse to take my ill-humour out on him. Instead, I sat in silence, rubbing the tension out of my jaw while he ordered his beer.

"Who was in the taxi?" he asked once he'd worked out I wasn't about to start the conversation.

"A known operative. I need to go back to Berlin, report this. But you stay here as planned—we don't need PKE working out that you're interested in the subject."

"So did we do it? We were successful?" he asked, his eyes bright with pride. He was taking all of this too personally—it was obvious he'd just experienced his first field operation.

"We'll see."

★

I left Rostock immediately—I had no intention of hanging around long enough to find out what revenge Lütten was planning for the humiliation he'd been handed right in the centre of his own territory.

Heading down the motorway, tucked inside helmet and leathers, I had time to think. Why had seeing Lütten made me so choleric? Granted, I was angry with myself for my unprofessional response to his presence, but something about Lütten's sudden appearance had provoked me, and I needed to work out what was happening inside my head before our paths crossed again.

But in the real world—the one outside me, where other people make things happen—I had a problem. Lütten now knew—and by extension, everyone else who was involved would now know—that Berlin Centre was interested in the West German, Heller, and his dodgy transit visas.

I don't often lose sight of operational objectives, but this time I had, and I'd probably loused up the whole operation.

Just as my wheels took me down the motorway, my brain followed its own paths, tracing its own links. The last few months had been quiet for me—an easy desk job with regular hours, mindlessly shuffling paper around my desk and launching files into the maw at the dark, bureaucratic heart of the Ministry. I rarely saw the value of what I did—so far as I could tell, my work hadn't been instrumental in advancing socialism or defending international peace. But I slept at night, and I'd only recently learned how important that is.

I held some deep grudges. Sure, I'd buried them in paperwork and routine, but coming across Lütten had shown me they weren't so much buried, merely embalmed. And now those grudges were being exhumed and dusted off, they reminded me of my duty to keep some promises I'd made to dead people.

There it was, slow, but already tangible. Beginning at the bottom of my stomach and spreading out. Resentment at the waste of good operatives. Frustration at the loss of opportunities. Injured pride. All boiling and reducing into the kind of anger that couldn't be left behind with a twist of the throttle.

And this anger and fear and pain was down to one man: *Oberleutnant* Sachse of Foreign Intelligence.

The signs had been there from the start, his fingerprints were all over the files I'd analysed. I should have recognised the pattern weeks ago: Foreign Intelligence, HV A, was giving Counter Intelligence, HA II, a hard time, and whatever clues I'd found had all pointed to Rostock.

Rostock. Scene of my last field operation, on the hunt for evidence of a Western agent embedded in HV A. The hunt for paperwork that proved a first lieutenant named Gerhard Sachse was the agent.

At the time I thought I'd tapped the mother lode, that if I dug deep enough I'd have a chance to even up the score with Sachse, who had caused the death of an old friend and a new colleague. But I didn't ever get the pleasure of presenting the evidence to my superiors. In the end I hadn't been remotely close to forcing them to sign Sachse's death warrant because what little evidence I managed to pull together had been confiscated by a KGB major, who had his own interests to protect.

I welcomed the anger, the resentment and hate, because if Lütten, that unfit officer from Rostock, was getting his hands dirty then his boss, Sachse, was sure to be close by.

And that, I thought, meant I'd have another chance to take First Lieutenant Sachse down.

21
MOTORWAY, SOUTH OF ROSTOCK

I came off the motorway at the next junction, and took the main road to the nearest settlement, stopping by an open telephone booth attached to the wall of the village pub. Before I could start hunting Sachse, there was someone I needed to talk to.

I checked the list on the wall for the code from here to Berlin, then dialled a number that, although I didn't use it often, I knew by heart.

"Burratino requesting contact. Urgent."

"How urgent?" the voice at the other end of the line spoke good German, but with a slight Slavic accent.

I looked at my watch—I could be back at Berlin Centre by five o'clock. Ewald would be waiting, wanting a preliminary verbal report as soon as he saw me. But I decided I could push him back a little.

"2100 hours at the latest. Sooner would be better," I said.

"Your location?"

"Forty or fifty kilometres south of Rostock, heading to Berlin on the motorway."

"Phone this number again in ninety minutes."

The line was dead before I could answer.

Ninety minutes was time enough to wonder what instructions I'd receive when I phoned my Russian friends again. I doubted I'd get to meet the one person I needed to speak to, Major Pozdniakov of the KGB, but I knew I had to get word to him that the current operational procedure was about to bring me, once again, into conflict with Sachse.

It's not that I liked taking orders from the KGB—the brass in my own Ministry were difficult enough to deal with—but Major Pozdniakov held a protective hand over Sachse, and not even a fool would antagonise the KGB.

I phoned again once I reached Neuruppin, and was told to get myself back to Berlin and wait in the Mitropa buffet at the Pionierpark station in Wuhlheide park.

So a couple of hours later I was sitting at an outside table, surrounded by young mothers and children excited by the slow progress of a diminutive diesel locomotive along the park railroad, driven by a spotty youth in an oversized *Reichsbahn* uniform. The kids jostled each other to line up along the track and wave at the train of tiny carriages as the pubescent youth proudly pulled the whistle. The diesel chugged unsteadily around the corner, swaying out of sight and the kids returned to their mothers to recharge on pop and soft-ice.

Not only did I feel out of place in this family setting, but I was conspicuous, so I was relieved more than amused when I saw the middle-aged woman clutching a diminutive cone of soft ice cream, blithely pushing aside toddlers and parents in an effort to reach me. She sat down without bothering with a greeting, then looked around, paying particular attention to the occupants of the nearest tables. She needn't have worried —the shrieks and shouts from the kids' throats were loud enough that the *Muttis* around us had no chance of eavesdropping on our conversation.

"I am sent," she informed me.

I nodded. I couldn't think of a better response to her statement, and until she'd identified herself, I didn't have much to say anyway.

"I am *Motylek*," she informed me solemnly, using the codeword: Russian for butterfly. It was good enough for me.

"And I am Burratino. Thank you for coming."

She nodded gravely, which made her cheeks puff up and her double chins bulge sideways as they squashed against her chest.

"Tell the comrade major I'm engaged in an operational procedure which could potentially interfere with First Lieutenant Sachse's activities."

I don't know whether she recognised the name, she didn't react. Melted ice cream dribbled as far as her fingers, but she didn't react to that either.

"I've just returned from Rostock, tracing a Westerner who was being assisted by one of Sachse's colleagues. I thought it wise to ensure the comrade major was informed."

"Name of colleague?"

"Lütten Horst. Department XV at District Administration Rostock."

The woman stood, she still hadn't touched the cone enveloped in her large hands. A line of kids filed past, each holding the one in front, shouting choo-choo as they went. She waited until they had passed, then watched a waiter bring a tray of bottles and glasses to the neighbouring table.

The waiter departed, neatly dodging those children who weren't entrained in the Chattanooga conga. Finally, *Motylek* must have judged conditions to be acceptable, and leaned over, depositing pools of stickiness on the wooden table. "Thank you for information, we will contact." She turned to go, but I caught her free hand.

"Wait a moment. Should I report Lütten's involvement? My superior is expecting me at Berlin Centre."

"You did not see Lütten," she pronounced before stalking off, depositing her *Softeis* in the bin as she went.

★

I reported to Ewald as soon as I reached Berlin Centre, giving him a straight account of what had happened the previous day but marginally adjusting my report of that afternoon's events:

"I had no option but to cease operational pursuit of the taxi when a group of young pioneers entered the roadway."

"You lost sight of the taxi?" Captain Ewald was incredulous. "A bunch of kids ran into the road and you lost sight of the taxi?"

"It was a large group, Comrade Captain. Undisciplined and without adult escort, they failed to observe traffic regulations relating to the safe crossing of roads by pedestrians. After the incident, I spent several hours driving around Rostock in search of the taxi." I thought that was a nice touch, it explained the delay in my arrival at Berlin Centre.

"Your major told me you were good—but you're not living up to expectations." He looked over my shoulder at the door, was he telling me to leave? "Written report first thing tomorrow morning."

"Comrade Captain?" I waited until he was looking at me. "I informed Comrade Second Lieutenant Stoyan that I had successfully identified the driver of the taxi. I considered it important to maintain morale, it's his first political-operational assignment."

Ewald nodded and I turned for the door.

"Comrade Reim? Be better prepared next time."

22
BERLIN LICHTENBERG

After handing in my report the next morning, I shuffled the usual files and watched the hands of the clock sweep around to late afternoon. Once I could decently leave, I took the stairs down to the broom cupboard in the cellar and began the task of sifting the data that Matse Stoyan and I had collected over the previous weeks, looking for any other lead, any other suspicious movements in or out of the ferry port at Warnemünde.

There had been no word yet from the top, but I was sure Lieutenant Colonel Schur and Captain Ewald would send me back to Rostock next time Heller was due to come through. Privately though, I was pretty certain we'd never see Heller again, not after my confrontation with Lütten—at least not using that handle, and probably not coming through that port. But if he did come, we'd have advance notice, courtesy of Matse's day job over at HA VI.

Matse himself returned on Thursday evening. He burst into the small room, his face as dark as the exhaust fumes from a Russian truck.

"Matse, you're-"

"The last two weeks in Rostock? I got back today to find my department had booked it as leave!"

I got up and pushed Matse into the chair I'd just vacated, held out the half-empty glass I'd just been drinking from and watched him gulp down the vodka.

"Why the surprise?" I said. "Of course all of this is on your own time—if we'd been up there on an official operation it would have been logged, there'd be paperwork—and you know how paperwork has a habit of falling into the wrong hands."

"Wrong hands?" He stared at me, eyebrows still bunched together, mouth still wide open. I filled his glass and guided his hand in the right direction. He took another couple of swigs.

"This is how it is on political-operational duty—we sneak around, nobody is allowed to know what we're up to; we keep things off the books as much as possible. You're on the inside now, Matse, have to show some commitment. Take the political-operational life as it comes."

He nodded. His jaw was still a little slack, but this time he managed to drink the fusel all by himself.

"See that pile by your elbow?" I asked him. His eyes travelled to the few entry cards and a sheet of notes on the table, his free hand already reaching out to them.

"Those are our new possibles—I've found a number of Danes who come over regularly, they all register at addresses where one or more of our younger female citizens live. I need you to check them out, might just be a case of young international love, might be worth taking a closer look."

"But why? You said you recognised the man in the taxi."

"Just putting the dot on the i, doing our homework in case there are any questions upstairs."

Matse finished off the glass and put it back on the table, reached into his jacket pocket, and pulled out a sheet of his own notes.

"I brought something, too," he said. "Our friend Heller is due back on the day sailing on the seventh of August."

I read the details Matse had copied from the transit visa application. As he'd said, Heller was due to arrive in Warnemünde a week on Tuesday.

I sat down opposite Matse and poured myself a drink.

Perhaps Lütten hadn't told anyone about our exchange. Could he really be so embarrassed about allowing himself to be followed that he hadn't reported the incident?

Or, had he reported it, and he and his *Fischkopp* colleagues were planning a welcome party for me on the seventh of August?

23
BERLIN LICHTENBERG

I took Matse's notes upstairs and along the echoing corridors of HA II. The secretaries' office was sealed for the night, but I could make out a thin strip of light coming from under Ewald's door.

"This better be good, Comrade *Unterleutnant*," he said as I stepped into his office.

"Subject Heller has a transit visa for the seventh of August, returning one day later," I announced.

"Suggested operational measures?" Ewald closed the file he'd been working on and laid down his pen, all the better to concentrate on me.

"Having considered the covert nature of our operation, and having observed for myself the permanent overt and covert observation of the port by Border Troops and various departments of our own ministry, I suggest we restrict close operational activities to areas outside Rostock, namely on the territory of the Polish People's Republic. We can begin covert observation of the subject once he has crossed the border into Poland." I gave Ewald enough time to pull a face. Relations with the SB, the Polish secret police, had been strained since martial law was declared in 1981, and even now, a year after it had been lifted again, the Party and the Ministry were still suspicious of our neighbours beyond the River Oder.

Ewald pulled a scrap of paper towards him and jotted a note, then nodded to let me know I should continue.

"As a second measure, I recommend placement of at least two conspirational observers on board the ferry on the day the subject is due to return to Denmark. These operatives should establish the subject's residency in Denmark and observe the subject's further operational contacts."

Ewald jotted another note before laying the pen down. He clasped his hands on his desk, his heavy eyelids made it impossible to see where his focus lay.

"You don't like asking for the easy things, do you Comrade Reim?"

I didn't answer.

"Tell me this isn't the only angle you're looking at?"

"Comrade Captain, we are currently processing several other possibilities—young men from Denmark who appear to have established relations with young female citizens of our country. Furthermore, we are extending our analysis to data from other Border Crossing Points."

"In other words, you don't have any other leads? Fine, keep looking, and in the meantime, revise the operational plan to include your suggestions about Poland and Denmark. Bring it to me tomorrow morning and I'll sound out the chief, see if we can interest him in your ideas."

The chief took a week to make up his mind about my plan to follow Heller into Poland and Denmark. I wasn't surprised when he decided Poland was a no-go—relations with the People's Republic were too volatile to risk operating on their territory without involving the SB, but we couldn't do that without putting the operation on a more official footing.

I knew I was unlikely to get the go-ahead for working in Poland, which was the very reason I had requested it— crossing that option off the list may have rendered Schur more amenable to my second, less controversial, suggestion. And that's the way it worked out: Schur didn't object to the idea of operating in the capitalist country of Denmark, so my plan to post observers on both the ferry and the territory of Denmark was accepted.

While Matse and I worked ourselves blind on the growing stacks of paperwork in our basement room, Ewald selected the operatives to follow the subject onto the ferry and then wherever in Denmark he happened to go after docking in Gedser.

Tuesday the seventh of August dawned, but without observers in Rostock, and with the usual channels closed to us, we couldn't confirm the subject had entered the GDR. So Matse and I sat in our cubby hole and continued compiling and working through lists of foreigners who regularly passed through Rostock. The Danish men had, as far as we could tell from the visa and entry paperwork, turned out to be just as expected—foreigners using their relative wealth to attract young East German women. Not something I approved of, but not my problem either.

We crossed the Danes off the list and began analysing traffic through the other border crossing points in the district.

24
BERNAU

The next day, I rang the bell for number 7 in a concrete block of flats built just inside the old town walls of Bernau. Ewald buzzed me in and was waiting for me on the landing.

We entered the one-room flat, and a brief glance told me this place was borrowed by rather than belonging to the Firm. It was the little details that gave it away: the dust-free net curtains and clean but worn furniture, the up-to-date newspapers and TV guides in the magazine holder next to a couch that pulled out to become a bed, the dust catchers on the bookshelves and on top of the telly—the typical indicators that this was a home rather than a place to cache operatives.

Other than the discreet but handy distance from the capital —Bernau sits at the end of the S-Bahn line—the flat's main asset was clearly the grey and beige two-tone telephone on the coffee table in front of the threadbare couch.

I took one of the *Diplomat* cigarettes Ewald offered and we smoked in silence for a while, both watching the telephone, wondering how we'd bridge the hours ahead.

"There won't be any contact before they reach Denmark," Ewald offered. It was just his nerves talking—there was no need to tell me the two observers on the ship wouldn't have a chance to make contact until, at the earliest, landfall at Gedser.

Despite his obvious agitation, I didn't pick up on any of the stiffness Ewald had shown back at Berlin Centre. The man seemed to have two personalities—formal at base, more tolerant in the field. I decided to test the theory by taking a bottle of *Rotkäppchen* out of my bag and showing it to him before I took it over to the fridge.

"Something for later, if things go well," I said as I assessed the contents of the fridge. Lots of beer, an opened can of Eberswalder sausages, a triangular carton of milk with the top corner sliced off.

Ewald's grey eyes had tracked the sparkling wine on its journey from bag to kitchen niche, but he didn't tell me to put it away. As a test, it was lacking—I still didn't know how much tolerance he would have of alcohol consumption on duty, but at least I could console myself with a glass or two of sparkling wine once we had some results over the telephone.

As hot as it was in the small flat, it was hotter outside, so we kept the windows and curtains shut and put up with the still, dry air. At some point one of us turned the television on, and since we couldn't bring files from work with us, we passed the time by staring at the muted screen and flicking through newspapers.

"Have you seen the ship?" Ewald asked at one point, looking at his wristwatch. The operatives were late checking in, several hours late, but there was no point in worrying—there was nothing we could do even if things were running crooked.

"The ferry to Denmark? Big white thing. Elegant when she comes into port—all the tourists stop and stare. Maybe not the Westerners, but everyone else does."

"Dreams." Ewald muttered.

I didn't reply. We weren't in the business of dreaming.

"You should know, there's a question mark over your West confirmation status," he said, apropos of nothing. "Could be a problem if we need to send you to Denmark."

"Question mark?" I kept my tone even, casual, as if this were the kind of thing mentioned in the course of any conversation with a superior officer.

"The status hasn't been withdrawn as such, but a memo

was added to your file. I checked because we were thinking of sending you to Denmark if it became necessary—you've got the experience, and you know the case." He was still staring at the television, a repeat of some Hungarian animated film—presumably produced to teach kids the value of Socialist behaviour.

"What do you mean, a memo? When was it attached?" I allowed irritation to creep into my voice, but tried not to show just how alert I'd suddenly become.

He turned away from the television, his heavy eyelids making it look like he wasn't really paying attention. "Dated September last year. Anything happen at that time?"

I felt the pull of the beer I'd seen in the fridge. I wanted to fetch a couple of bottles, open them up, pour them out. Pass one to Ewald and tap glasses before I got a cigarette going. That would buy a minute, perhaps two, to get my thoughts in order. My throat was dry, already anticipating the first hit of cold, sparkling, bitter pilsner.

"September?" I repeated. How much did Ewald already know? But actually, it didn't matter, even if he'd read my full file, I shouldn't discuss anything with him. Not without clearance from much higher up the ladder. "There was a misunderstanding, I was under the impression it had been cleared up."

September. The month both my wife and my boss went missing—in our world, missing meant either dead or over there: beyond the border, in the West. Naturally, I'd been questioned about both disappearances, and naturally I had denied any and all knowledge.

"Something about your wife." Ewald got up to change channels on the television. It was an old-fashioned set with a knob like a radio to twist back and forth in search of the next frequency. I wondered whether he genuinely wanted to know what was on the other channel, or was being generous, giving me time to arrange my face.

"She was last seen in September. People don't go missing in our Republic," he said, echoing my thoughts. "Anyway, without a wife to remain here as collateral, your West confirmation is under review."

It sounded so reasonable, coming from his mouth: no wife to remain behind as hostage equals no trips to the West, even allowing for the fact that we'd been separated for over a year before she went missing, and had therefore been pretty poor collateral for quite a while.

"But I've been on several operations in the Operational Area since September—despite your memo." Ewald was still nudging the dial, trying to tune the television, and didn't see me wince as I mentally counted my various trips over the Wall. I came up with just one officially sanctioned operation in the West—the rest had been forays that had been off the record and therefore best never mentioned again.

"You had a shadow when you went to Cologne," he replied, sitting back down on the sofa. He didn't show any sign of noticing my inadvertent mention of trips in the plural.

"The HA II operation to Cologne and Bonn? You know about that?"

"I was the tail. I was with you right up until the point I handed you over to the covert observation post in Bonn."

Without thinking about what I was doing—my brain didn't get as far as asking for permission—I walked to the fridge, took out a beer and opened it with a fork handle. I would have preferred something with more percentage points under the cap, but at that moment it was a choice between a bottle of our unknown host's *Bärenquell* beer and a glass of the *Rotkäppchen* sparkling wine.

Far from being the golden-haired, blue-eyed defender of Socialism that I'd hoped my department thought I was, I'd been under suspicion since before I'd even transferred to Berlin Centre.

I took another mouthful of beer, Ewald showed no concern

about the dereliction of duty I was holding in my hand, he was flicking through the television guide I'd just put down. I stood, watching him, trying to work out what to say. This was my opportunity to try to quantify the department's reservations, try to quantify the risk. But before I'd managed to frame my questions, the telephone rang.

Ewald leaned over and picked up the receiver.

25
BERNAU

"*Komplexannahmestelle*," Ewald said into the telephone. He listened for a moment before replying. "We can pass your vacuum cleaner onto a mechanic—do you have the model number?"

Another pause while Ewald waited for the person on the other end of the line to speak. They must have said the right thing, because Ewald cited a code back to them then tucked the receiver between ear and shoulder to free up his hands to make notes on the log form.

I went to stand next to him, reading as he wrote down the time of first contact, then a series of Danish place names. I unfolded a map and located them easily enough: Gedser Port, Nykøbing, Rødby Port, all major stops along a railway line.

"Proceed and report back in the usual way," were Ewald's final words as he hung up.

"The subject took the train to Rødby port, is now waiting to board the ferry to West Germany," he added the name Puttgarden to the list on the sheet of paper in front of him. "Our operatives wanted permission to cross to West Germany, I told them to go ahead—so now I'd better get get back to Berlin and clear it with upstairs. You remain here, I'll relieve you at 0730 hours." He cleared his throat and as he stood between couch and door, he looked uncertain for a moment or two. Perhaps he regretted telling me about the memo on my file. Perhaps he regretted having given the two agents clearance to follow Heller across yet another international border.

"Wait!" I called as Ewald gathered his wits and turned for the door. "If you were with me on the way to Cologne then you know what that operation was about?"

"The death of Source Bruno." He nodded, then unlatched the flat door and left.

26
BERNAU

I finished my beer and turned the television up. There was nothing to do except wait—providing they could find a relatively secure line, the operatives would call once they had any news. I'd have to be patient with the other matter, too—there was little I could do about the fact that someone, somewhere in the Ministry was considering whether they should classify me as reliable or more of a liability. I'd just have to wait and see.

I opened another beer and returned to the couch.

The call came in the early hours and my voice was hoarse with sleep when I lifted the receiver.

"*Komplexannahmestelle.*"

"Do you take vacuum cleaners for repair?"

"We aren't able to repair them here, but we can pass them on to a mechanic. Have you got the model number?" I checked my watch and made a note of the time on the sheet of paper: 0447.

"The model we have is DO-7114."

"One moment." I looked blankly at the time I'd just written down, my brain still sluggish, then checked the slip of paper, the second number on it was a 3. I crossed it off.

DO for *Donnerstag*, Thursday, then add 3 to each of the numbers and ignore the carry. The code was correct.

"We have parts for the ...." I checked my watch, it was now 0448—check the series of random numbers at the top of the page and add the next one along to the middle two digits:

44+7. "The model 51, they should be compatible. Go ahead." I crossed the number 7 off the list.

With the checks completed and both parties satisfied they were speaking to the right people, the operative gave me the message. "We're in Cologne, arrived with subject seventeen minutes ago. Subject currently in the station buffet. Next scheduled trains are for Dortmund, Salzburg via Stuttgart and Munich, Vienna via Frankfurt and Nuremberg."

"Proceed," I told them. I noted down what had been said before going to the window for a cigarette. The night was slightly cooler and a good deal fresher than the air in the flat, so I left the window open when I went back to the sofa bed.

Ewald arrived the next morning just as the water came to the boil. I spooned ground coffee into a second cup without asking as he read through the phone log.

He took the cup without comment and paced the room. I sat on the sofa, ignoring him as best I could, sipping my scalding coffee.

"Anything else to report?" he asked as he came to a stop in front of me.

"Nothing to report," I replied without looking up. Everything he needed to know was on the piece of paper he still held in his hand.

Ewald continued his journey around the room. I hadn't slept well on the lumpy bed—being woken up at a quarter to five hadn't helped—and I was finding it difficult not to snap at him.

I swallowed more coffee and closed my eyes, but even then I could hear him goose-stepping around like an eighteen-year-old recruit on his first guard duty.

"What time should I come back?" I asked as I took my half-finished coffee back to the kitchen corner and rinsed the cup out.

Ewald paused and turned his wrist to look at his watch.

"Shift change at 1730?" he suggested.

That was good enough for me, I picked up my bag to leave. I had the flat door half-open when the phone rang, so I shut it again and went to watch over Ewald's shoulder. He had already written down the time, was checking the codes, crossing the next numbers off the list as he did so.

"Repeat message," he said. He hadn't written anything further on the notepaper yet, barely held the pencil in loose fingers. Then: "Proceed." He hung up.

Finally, he started writing up the notes: arr. 0732 Mainz main station. Subject picked up by black Mercedes 280 SE, registered in Wiesbaden. He wrote a series of letters and numbers, then began to decode them with the same series of random numbers we used to confirm the authenticity of the caller.

"Want me to check those plates?" I asked as he wrote out the rest of the registration number of the limousine.

"No, I'll run it through our records when I get back."

Wiesbaden registration, black limo. You didn't have to be Chekist of the year to work out who owned that car—I was prepared to bet that bottle of *Rotkäppchen* in the fridge that the car belonged to the BKA, the West German Federal Crime Agency. The same BKA that I suspected my so-called colleague, *Oberleutnant* Sachse, to be working for.

It was time to go, I needed to have a chat with a certain KGB major I knew.

27
BERLIN PANKOW

I left the S-Bahn a few stops early and went looking for a bar or café I could phone from. Housewives and veterans queued outside bakeries and food shops, pressing themselves into the narrow bands of shade at the foot of the high Berlin tenements.

A tram rattled past, windows slanted open and almost empty of passengers. I crossed the road in its wake.

Here was an ice cream parlour, the doors standing open but populated only by a shopworker mopping floors, pushing chairs and tables around as she went.

"You open?"

"Look like we're open?" she demanded. Her response was more aggressive than jocular, but I went in anyway, sitting myself down in a corner she'd already wiped. The dust of my footprints slowly dissolved on the damp floor.

She didn't take any more notice of me, continued scraping chairs and knocking the mop against skirting boards.

"Is there a phone I can use?"

She jerked her head towards a scratched wooden door at the end of the counter, her elbows still pistoning away. I investigated the booth, it was a wooden box a little larger than a coffin stood on end, dark varnish flaking at the edges of etched, opaque windows and around the corrupted brass knob that served as a door handle. The telephone itself sat on a shelf—a standard domestic type, black, with a rotary dial and no coin box.

I dialled the number and listened to the ringing at the other end. A woman's voice answered after the fourth ring, not giving a name, just a curt *Ja, bitte?*

"Burratino with an urgent contact request."

"Urgent?" The R was trilled, betraying Russian origins.

"Before midday—same subject as previously reported. Matters have escalated."

"Current location?"

"Pankow in Berlin."

"Call back in twenty minutes."

I returned to my table, leaving a twenty Pfennig coin on the counter as I passed. The woman had finished mopping, was filling a coffee machine with water.

"Can I have some of that when it's ready?" I asked.

Again, there was no answer, but she leaned down to pick up a cup and a saucer. She slammed them onto the counter, years of practice telling her the exact amount of force necessary to maximise drama without actually breaking the crockery. She turned away and began to count the float money in her purse.

"Any ice cream?"

"It's an ice cream parlour."

"What flavours are there?"

"None." She sighed and started counting the stacks of coins on the counter again.

"No flavours? Or do you mean no ice cream?" The conversation was like the contact I'd just had with the KGB secretary—short questions and short answers.

"*Softeis*," she said, shoving a stack of 50 Pfennig coins back into her purse.

"I'll have a cone of soft-ice, then."

"The machine hasn't been cleaned," she snapped.

Perhaps it was for the best, cold ice cream on an empty stomach wouldn't be good for my digestion.

★

78

"Burratino calling." Ignoring the pointed stares of the shop assistant, I had taken my time over the weak coffee, waiting the required time until I could call Major Pozdniakov's people again.

"Kollwitzstrasse 43 in half an hour. Walk through to the alleyway at the back and turn right. You will be met."

28
BERLIN PRENZLAUER BERG

It was a kilometre and a half to Kollwitzstrasse, and I found building number 45, with time to spare. On the other side of a gap, the kind left behind by the bombs that had fallen on the city forty years ago, stood number 41. But the building I was looking for was simply absent. I stood in front of the break in the row of houses and decided I was where I needed to be, despite the lack of a neat enamel plate with 43 painted on it.

Before taking a closer look at the vacant lot, I lit a cigarette and developed an interest in the local scenery.

A nursery teacher dragged a handcart over the uneven paving stones, each bench in the cart filled with tired toddlers, bickering or dozing under the brutal sun.

Once they had passed, I watched an old lady with a shawl over her head. She had a shopping bag in one hand, a stick in the other and was teetering along the curb, not looking so much where she was going, but concentrating on her feet. I flicked what was left of my cigarette into the gutter and climbed over the rubble that lined the front edge of the old bomb site. Picking my way through sunburnt weeds and fly-tipped rubbish I found a ginnel at the back. It ran behind the houses, bordered on the other side by a high, ivy-blanketed fieldstone and brick wall. It took a moment for me to work out what lay beyond this untidy wall—the old Jewish Cemetery on Schönhauser Allee. I was standing in the Judengasse, a redundant back entrance to the abandoned graveyard.

Turning right, as instructed, I picked my way around vegetable patches and crooked garden sheds that were trespassing on the ginnel, glad of the intermittent shade provided by pioneer trees and shrubs that had somehow rooted in the bricks and stones of the wall.

I could smell the acerbic black tobacco long before I reached the source—Major Pozdniakov himself was a couple of houses further along, his shoulder providing support to a warped shed of rotting window frames and flaking asbestos sheets.

"Burratino!" The warm voice, the cold smile.

"Comrade Major," I replied, keeping my distance from his little black cigarette.

"Still interested in the comrade from Foreign Intelligence?"

"A known associate of his attracted attention during an operational procedure. I was investigating a matter I now believe our mutual friend may be involved in."

"You told my adjutant. Do you have anything new?" He took a starched white handkerchief from the pocket of his brown civilian suit jacket and used it to wipe the damp from his forehead.

I stepped out of the shadow of the shed long enough to look back down the alley. The only movement was of dust drifting and flies swaying in the leaden sunlight.

"Nobody will disturb us," Pozdniakov said, a smile playing at the corner of his lips as he stowed his folded hankie. When he looked up again, a stray beam of sunlight reflected off a cracked window and caught his glass eye. He didn't blink.

"We noticed a West German subject because of his unusual patterns of movement. That subject then made contact with a member of Department XV in Rostock, the associate I reported to your staff." I remained alert for any signs of impatience or displeasure in Pozdniakov's face, but he was examining the ash that was forming at the end of his cigarette, betraying no reaction to what I said. "This morning, the subject was tracked to the Operational Area and we have provisionally linked him to the BKA, the Federal Crime Agency in Wiesbaden."

I didn't need to remind Pozdniakov that I had also linked Sachse to the same reactionary agency—the major was well aware of my suspicions. He had, after all, confiscated the evidence I'd gathered to prove Sachse was providing material to the West Germans.

"Anyone else know about this?"

"Only if the operative in Rostock reported the contact. I've withheld this information from my department. Of course, there'll be further investigations into the subject's links to the BKA and I'm not in a position to prevent or divert any enquiries."

Pozdniakov dropped his papirosa and watched the smoke curl up from the still-live tip for a moment or two. "So other than you, nobody else is aware that our mutual friend has conceivably been within a thousand kilometres of this West German subject?"

I shook my head but waited for Pozdniakov to look up again before responding verbally: "HA II have already begun tracing the subject's contacts in Rostock. I've tried to keep Lütten, the operative in Rostock, and Sachse out of it, but no matter how far Sachse is from the action, if he's involved at all then he will be found and will become a subject in the operational procedure. I thought I should bring this to your attention."

Pozdniakov stared at me with his good eye. I was sweating, even here in the shade of the shed. The smell of the smoke from his cigarette, still smouldering at his feet, made my stomach tighten.

The major turned his gaze elsewhere, his eye sweeping the old wall of the Jewish graveyard. He was thinking.

With a sudden movement, he lifted a foot, drove the heel of his boot hard onto the cigarette, extinguishing it in the sand.

"Do what you need to," he said as he bent down to excavate the cigarette butt. "Sachse has been very useful to us in the past, but if he's involved then he'll have to take his chances."

29
BERLIN LICHTENBERG

Somehow, no one in this select group of officers had thought to throw me out of the meeting. Not a single one of the caterpillar carriers around this table was prepared to admit to the oversight, and so I was allowed to remain in my seat—even though the topic of conversation was me.

"We have *Perspektivagenten*—dedicated operatives with years of preparation behind them, sleepers already in place in the target organisation itself. We have Romeo agents to woo secretarial employees in the operational area, each and every one of them waiting for the call." My superior, Major Kühn, spoke forcefully, focussing on the scratched grey metal of the table rather than the other officers' faces. "The operational plan in its current form goes against the Minister's guidelines —never before have agents with such high security clearance been sent on political-operational missions requiring direct enemy contact in the operational area."

While Kühn was carefully measuring out his words, attempting to express himself clearly without trampling too heavily on Lieutenant Colonel Schur's feet, I remained quite still, enjoying the reactions of the brass. Schur's eyes were hard with impatience, he was waiting for Kühn to finish so he could have the final word. Ewald, like Kühn, preferred to keep his eyes on the table—maybe he was embarrassed about telling me that my West Confirmation was being weighed on the Ministry's internal scales. Perhaps it was my uncertain status that had sparked Kühn's unexpected challenge.

Leaving the question of whether or not I was still West

confirmed to one side, I actually agreed with Kühn. The proposed operation wasn't without risk, someone with as many state secrets in his head as I should really avoid contact sport in the Operational Area, particularly when something like this was going down.

Lieutenant Colonel Schur finally stirred, his hand rising to stroke the grey goatee beard that he'd probably been wearing since the days of Ulbricht. Kühn, sensitive to the superior officer's movements, lost his thread, his sentence waned into silence.

The three of us waited for Schur to speak.

"It has come to my attention that the imperialist agent Weber Anna has been added to the shopping list." This was news—it meant West Germany knew Anna Weber was being held and was prepared to pay to get her back.

Still listening to Lieutenant Colonel Schur, I allowed part of my mind to consider this fresh information. Anna Weber was the agent I'd met in Rostock last winter, the one who'd helped me communicate with the BKA officer, Codename Merkur, who was trailing his coat at us. But in return for her assistance, I'd handed her over to the KGB.

I didn't worry too much about what I'd done to her, felt neither pride nor shame. It was just part of the job.

"There are ongoing negotiations over the fate of several Western agents currently in our care, the West Germans have their priorities, we have ours. If we decide to release Weber, one of the conditions will be that we can throw in a few more names—a few hardened criminals who have forfeited the right to live in a socialist society—and we will make sure our operative is one of the supernumeraries." Schur didn't look in my direction as he said this, but I didn't need too much nouse to understand he was talking about me.

"We need them to value our offer—we'll change our minds a few times, take names back off the list and insist there's been a mistake, that unfortunately it won't be possible for them to have the extras we promised. They won't like that, they won't want to miss an opportunity for a few more prisoners to be released. We'll drive a hard bargain—more money, resources and agent swaps than ever before. The higher the price they have to pay, the more they'll value their purchases. And if we handle the negotiations right, the West Germans will congratulate themselves on outsmarting us, and we will have successfully infiltrated our man."

Major Kühn had stood up halfway through Schur's long explanation, was biding his time until he could politely interrupt the lieutenant colonel. "If I may, Comrade Lieutenant Colonel Schur—I believe my input is no longer required in this meeting. I see no need to be privy to further operational knowledge of the procedure being planned and would be obliged if you could confirm my orders in writing?"

Schur's face darkened as he watched Kühn leave the room.

"So that's confirmed—you're seconded to my department for the duration," he said to me, his narrowed eyes still on the doorway my superior had just disappeared through.

"Jawohl, Genosse Oberstleutnant," I answered, as if I'd had any choice in the matter.

I only had myself to blame for finding myself in this position: it was I who had let slip that I knew Anna Weber was still in our half of the world.

It happened after our two operatives had followed Heller to Mainz, when Ewald and I discussed the possible next steps for the operation in the safe house in Bernau. He had played his part well—by telling me about the memo on my file he had primed me to watch out for more indiscretions, and I hadn't been disappointed.

After reviewing the notes Matse and I had produced in our cubby hole in the cellar, Ewald sat back and lit a cigarette. "The fact we've linked the subject to the West German BKA provides collateral for other pieces of indirect evidence."

"You think the BKA is involved in the leaks we're trying to trace?" I asked, keeping my voice steady, careful not to scare the horses. I pulled out another sheet of notes for Ewald to look at.

"That case you worked in Rostock back in February. The walk-up, Merkur—he was BKA, wasn't he? And the second hostile agent too? Did she make it back to the West?"

"Our friends have her," I answered, my brain catching up only as the words left my mouth. As far as I knew, the files stated that the KGB had taken Codename Merkur, but the fate of his assistant, Anna Weber, hadn't been mentioned, at least not in any of the reports I'd written.

But other than a moment's irritation at my own indiscretion, I'd not thought about the incident again. After all, it didn't matter, Anna Weber was history. If she was still alive then she'd be in a Gulag on the other side of the Urals, felling timber.

But I'd underestimated Ewald, because a few days later, in this meeting on the top floor of House 2 at Berlin Centre, Lieutenant Colonel Schur not only talked about resurrecting Anna Weber, but also of his plans to turn her and send her back to the West—with me at her side to make sure she didn't leave the straight path of righteousness and socialism.

"You're looking healthy," said Schur once he'd formally ended the meeting. He stared at me for a moment longer, then stood up to leave "See to it will you, comrade," he instructed Ewald as he passed.

"See to what?" I asked once we were alone.

"Intensive briefing," replied Ewald, putting his papers in his briefcase.

"Another trip to a half-built military base?"

"A little closer to home this time," he replied. "But turn your gas and electricity off—you might be away for a few weeks."

30
MAGDALENA

Apparently, I needed a prison pallor, and simply avoiding the sun for a few weeks wouldn't do the job.

So at six o'clock the next morning, I knocked at the gates of UHA II, otherwise known as the Magdalenenstrasse MfS Remand Prison. Or, by its ex-occupants, simply as *Magdalena*.

Books and songs have been written about that place, but not by the kind of people I'd choose to read or listen to. I'd passed the prison on my way to work nearly every day for the past eight months yet had never actually thought much about the place. You see, the walls are five metres high, and I don't live in the kind of country where you ask what's hidden behind high walls.

So, after looking at, but not seeing the place for so long, I was going to find out what lay on the other side of those gates.

If I was entitled to special treatment at Magdalena, the memo hadn't made it across the road from Berlin Centre. The screws from Department XIV, commanded by an *Uffzi*, first confiscated my personal items then stripped me and bent me over for a cavity search. Without a word, I was issued with a blue tracksuit, check bedsheets and a grey blanket, all stinking of baked-in sweat and institutional disinfectant, and led to the four-storey block on the south side of the site. There I was assigned an en-suite cell all to myself. The heavy wooden door banged shut and the steel hatch clanged open in the same movement as the runner who had brought me here looked through the gap. "No sitting or lying on the bed during the day!" He slammed the hatch shut.

I sat on the low wooden stool, turned my face to the thick glass blocks high up on the outside wall and started working on my prison tan.

I was familiar with the rhythms of remand prison, having spent a few weeks in Hohenschönhausen after an unfortunate misunderstanding involving the disappearance of my superior officer, a Prussian bastard named Fröhlich.

So when the hatch clanked open again, I didn't bother to stir from my stool, and wouldn't do so unless told to stand by the back wall of the cell. The hatch slid shut behind my back without any commands being issued—they'd merely been hoping to catch me lying on the bed.

Further along the corridor, I heard the rasp of a key turning and the scrape of a door. Footsteps, followed by a second scrape, then further footsteps fading into the incessant undertones of prison. At some point, they'd come for me too and the promised intensive briefing would begin.

In the meantime, I still had some stains on the ceiling to count.

31
MAGDALENA

It must have been late afternoon when they came for me. The hatch opened to allow the routine order to stand against the back wall to be bellowed in my direction, then the key turned in the cell door and we began the march down the corridor. Eyes lowered, steered by the curt commands of the runner who always remained a few steps behind me.

Back down the stairs and through corridors and yards until I was told to face the wall while the door to a single storey building was opened.

Whatever I'd expected to see beyond that door, it wasn't a living room. Sofa and chairs in a soft, green material. Shelving and cupboard unit covering the end wall. A table with a lamp and a telephone. Everything you'd expect to find in a hundred thousand living rooms across the Republic.

Cosy. Except, that is, for the stack of files on the coffee table and the grey uniformed soldier standing to attention just inside the door. Not to mention Captain Ewald watching me from the comfort of an easy chair.

"Coffee?" he asked the uniform by the door, my runner having already disappeared.

The soldier's head jerked back a little, his eyes widening in surprise at the request. "*Jawohl, Genosse Hauptmann.*"

He opened the door to signal to someone outside, but Ewald heaved himself out of his low chair and stood behind the uniform until he took the hint and left us alone in the room. Ewald pushed the door shut behind him.

"Comrade Reim, everything to your satisfaction?

Accommodation comfortable?"

I didn't bother replying, there was no humour to be found in a prison cell, even if you know you'll be out soon. I sat down to wait for the coffee.

Ewald placed several files in front of me and I leaned forward to read the top title: *Site Plan and List of Buildings at the Central Headquarters of the BKA in Wiesbaden, Federal Republic of Germany*. Curious, I reached out to open the cover, but stopped when the uniform returned, holding a thermos of coffee. I put my hand over the title of the file as he passed me, watching as he deposited the jug on the table next to the telephone.

"We can manage, Comrade," Ewald growled as the soldier stopped by the cupboard to take out cups and saucers.

The screw turned smartly and stiffened to attention. "With permission, Comrade Captain, a member of Department IX is to be present at all times during a visit."

"Thank you, Comrade," Ewald repeated, turning to stare at the nervous kid. He was quicker at catching the message this time and slid out of the door without another word.

I stood up and rolled my shoulders, relieved to be free of prison staff, even if only temporarily.

"Is this the point I find out why I shouldn't look too healthy?" I asked, handing Ewald his cup. I already had an idea—it wasn't that difficult to work out, not after Schur's talk the previous day about selling prisoners to the West. But I wanted to know how long I'd be staying at the Hotel Magdalena.

"Let's start with the files—there are a few things we need to put in place before you begin your big adventure."

32
MAGDALENA

The laws of the German Democratic Republic are nothing if not humane, and one of those laws ensures that every detainee has the right to a daily period of exercise in fresh air. To that end, one of the yards at Magdalena has been subdivided by high walls. A guard paces a catwalk, he peers through the wire mesh stretched over the top of each of these roofless cells to ensure that prisoners are making the most of their exercise time.

But just as I was taken down for my exercise the next afternoon, a thunderstorm broke. The heavy raindrops ricocheted like jacketed rounds off the crudely rendered walls, and perhaps that accounted for the guard's neglect—instead of stalking the high walkway, he sought shelter. But the mere fact of the storm didn't explain how a second detainee came to be thrust into my tiger cage.

I was squatting in the corner of the tiny exercise yard, out of sight of the runner who opened the door and allowed her to enter. She began measuring out the perimeter, neither looking up at the catwalk above, nor around at the rough walls, and she didn't notice me until she'd turned two corners. Seeing me out of the corner of her eye, her head snapped around, shocked that such a mistake had been made.

Her wide eyes darted upwards, checking for the patrolling guard, but all she could see was the wire mesh and the heavy clouds that threw bucketfuls of water at us.

I waved her over, and she splashed towards me, her synthetic-felt slippers sodden, her hands clasped in front of her. If I hadn't been expecting her, I wouldn't have recognised Anna Weber. Her long, shining hair had been cropped, but was already growing out, forming a close, greasy cap. Her blue eyes were clouded and dull, and her mouth looked like it had forgotten there was, somewhere, still a world of joy where she could smile. For her, there had been nothing to smile about since I'd handed her over to the KGB six months earlier.

Perhaps she didn't recognise me—there was no curiosity in her face, only the fear she'd be caught breaking the rules. I gestured her down to my level, but she remained standing, so I stood up, took a step towards her, guiding her to the lee of the wall, where a little less rain fell.

"Anna," I whispered in her ear. She flinched, looking upwards again to see whether the guard was watching. "Anna, is that you?"

I got a nod, but she still looked away, anywhere but at me.

"It's Reim, remember me?"

For the shortest moment, her eyes rested on me. Perhaps it was imagination, but I was sure that Anna Weber's eyes cleared, just for that second or two.

"I tried, Anna, I really did—that's why I waited for you in Rostock-Lichtenhagen, I wanted to warn you. Sorry, I'm so sorry, I tried to get you away from the KGB—they made me, they forced me to hand you over. And now I'm here too ..." It was my turn to look away. I didn't wipe away the rain that dripped onto my face, I looked down at the cement floor, ashamed. "Sorry, Anna, I failed you."

Her eyes lifted, met mine just as the door to the tiger cage was thrown open. A guard came in. He looked from Weber to me, back through the open door.

"There's two of them in here!" He grasped Anna's shoulder and dragged her through the door. "Against the wall!" he shouted at me as he went.

I turned to face the wall, smiling as I heard the splashing of a second runner come to take me back to my cell.

33
MAGDALENA

"All go according to plan?" We were back in the visitor's room, and this time Ewald had brought a couple of packets of cigarettes and a bottle of *Doppelkorn*.

"Better than we hoped. The guards interrupted at just the right moment, just as I got through to her," I replied.

"Let's celebrate our first step." He passed me a glass.

We downed the schnapps, and I reached over to top up my glass again. Celebration indeed.

"So now she thinks you're in the same boat—did you tell her why you were arrested?"

"I didn't think she'd take it in—she wasn't in a good way."

"She's the class enemy, a saboteur—no sympathy for the hostile-negative forces and their agents!" Ewald gave me a sideways look.

I swallowed another mouthful of alcohol. "If we're going to use her, then we need her in good condition."

"Don't worry about that, we'll get her back in shape."

And then it was back to the files: genning up on known senior personnel at the West German BKA.

When it was time to go back to my cell, I had a question for Ewald.

"What's her real name?"

"Who?" Ewald was making a tidy stack of the files, ready to slide them into his briefcase. He didn't look up.

"Weber? Anna Weber is a cover name—do we know her real name?"

"There's no operational necessity for you to have that

information." He looked up from the files, followed my eyes to the half-empty bottle of *Doppelkorn* on the table. "Why don't you take that with you?"

My hand was already stretching out to take it, but I hesitated. I wouldn't get it past the guards.

"Go on, Reim. You've earned it."

"Maybe we'll take a glass when you come tomorrow?"

"You worry too much! Put it under your tracksuit top, bring the empty back in the morning. If the screws find it, I'll square it with them."

I took the bottle, my mind setting the scene in my imagination: Reim in his cell, back to the door, drinking schnapps out of an enamel cup, the bottle hidden under the covers of his hard and narrow bed.

I brought the empty bottle back the next morning, as arranged. As I handed it over, Ewald held out a full one. I took it and stared at the label for a few seconds, wondering when the brass had worked out that I had a thirst. Or was it just Ewald being both astute and generous?

I should have refused the *Doppelkorn*, proved to both him and myself that I didn't need it. Instead, I put it on the table so I could stare at it while I read the files.

The briefings continued day after day—reading files and discussing the operation during the day, a bottle to keep me warm at night. We worked well together, Ewald and I. He knew the files even better than I did, and again and again we went over the death of Source Bruno in Bonn and the pursuit of Codename Merkur in Rostock and Berlin. We looked at the events from every angle, working out what could be safely divulged, and what was better kept to ourselves.

"The interrogation of Codename Merkur in Bad Doberan," Ewald said, tapping the file. "Let's make that level 2, along with your visit to Warnow shipyard—Merkur will have filed reports, we can assume they know all about it. As for the clandestine meet with Merkur in Berlin, we don't know whether he had a chance to report it, so I think your chat by the Müggelsee should be top tier—only give it to them once they're on the verge of accepting you. If Merkur didn't report the meetings then that's all to the good—you'll have brought them something they don't know and that'll help build trust."

I agreed with his assessment of what to give up during questioning. We'd been over it all before, but I didn't mind the repetition—I couldn't afford to get this wrong.

"Any thoughts on what we should charge you with?" asked Ewald in between sips of coffee.

"Paragraph 99, section 1 of the criminal code: treasonous communications," I answered immediately. I had thought about it, and there wasn't a huge amount of choice when it came to the laws I'd supposedly broken. "Say the judge agreed to mitigation for handing over the imperialist-revanchist agent, Anna Weber."

"Two to ten years imprisonment. We'll say six then, shall we? That'll make you interesting enough to the West."

We were making progress, but I didn't reach for the bottle to celebrate. After that first one when I'd met Weber in the exercise yard, I'd tried to hold back, only cracking Ewald's supply once I was in my cell. The bottle was usually dead shortly after lights-out, leaving me dry in the morning, but I could handle that, it had been my way for years.

I took the coffee cups to the wall of cupboards at the end of the visiting room, catching sight of myself in the mirror on the back of the door that screened the sink. I stopped and looked again at the bloodless face, the dirty, thinning hair and the bloodshot eyes that stared back at me.

"How long have I been here?"

"Nearly a month. Why?"

"No reason," I replied, giving the crockery a rinse.

★

A few days later, Ewald turned up with a bottle of Rotkäppchen sparkling wine.

"That looks familiar."

"It's the bottle you brought to Bernau that day. We didn't get a chance to drink it back then," he said. "But I'd say we've got something to celebrate now."

I held out the coffee cups and he poured the frothy wine. A delicate *Prosit!* and a sip while I waited for him to tell me what the occasion was.

"Negotiations with the West Germans have been concluded. Tomorrow, we'll take you to Karl-Marx-Stadt for some decent grub, new clothes and a hot bath. Everyone on that list will be getting the same treatment, we have to make sure you all look presentable for your trip to the West. After that you're on your own, although your friend Weber will look after you."

I got the joke, it wasn't a very good one—we both knew I'd be looking after her—but neither of us wanted to spoil a good toast.

34
UHA KARL-MARX-STADT

The coach seemed to fill the prison yard, oversized, gaudy and obviously from the West. Yet the dozens of prisoners standing around didn't feel the need to comment on the fact. Nobody seemed to have any need to talk at all.

We waited to board, most of us with a bag or suitcase or two, but I had nothing more than the clothes I'd been wearing when I entered the Magdalena. A screw with clipboard and pen stood next to the coach, checking each prisoner's name as they reached the head of the queue. Finally, it was my turn.

"Borchert, Wolfgang," I told him, handing over my blue *Ausweis* and my release papers. Borchert was the cover name I was using when I first met Anna Weber up in Rostock, and for some reason it had been decided that I should take the same name for this part of the operation, perhaps because the Western intelligence agencies would have it on file.

With a nod, I was allowed to board. I walked down the narrow aisle, trying not to look at the drawn faces to either side. Each and every person I passed was sitting upright in their seats, eyes cast down at luggage or knees. Nobody talked to their neighbours, nobody looked out of the windows. Everybody wanted this journey to be over.

I found Weber sitting by herself near the back. She had a small vinyl sports bag on her lap and an empty look on her face. Seating myself next to her, I did as the others did and lowered my eyes.

We remained that way for twenty minutes or so until the rumble of the engine broke the hush that hung over every seat. I looked up briefly as the driver swung the heavy vehicle through the gates of Karl-Marx-Stadt MfS remand prison, following a black BMW with GDR registration plates onto the street. This was my first view of Karl-Marx-Stadt—the short trip a week ago from the train station to the prison had been in the back of a windowless Barkas panel van—and I now turned my gaze far enough to see past Weber and out of the window. Along the main road out of the city, past piebald houses and dull shops flaking paint from windows and doors, around the sharp curves of the approach road to the motorway.

Places printed white on blue signs slid past, my lips shaping the familiar names. I wasn't the only one doing that, others on the bus were also peering out of the windows, wistful, maybe relieved, that this would be the last they'd see of any of these towns.

But that wasn't the case for me, I'd be back before too long. Still, it was part of my cover to behave the same way as the other passengers, to persuade myself that this was for real— that I'd been stripped of my citizenship and was being thrown out of the country. My life bartered for a truckload of goods and raw materials.

I lifted my hand off my knee and inspected it. Fairly steady, the slight tremble could be put down to the shuddering engine. The rest of me didn't feel too bad either, I was over the worst. Not that I'm saying the last week in UHA Karl-Marx-Stadt had been easy: high temperature, tachycardia, the sweats, nausea and vomiting—I'd had the lot.

But I'd been there before, I knew I could cope, although the prison surgeon had been less certain. He'd phoned Berlin, tried to have me taken off the travel list—I knew he was doing it because he told me all about his efforts. I could imagine the conversation he'd had with Berlin: *The general constitution of the patient is such that the authorities and press in the West may seek to make adverse and public inferences regarding conditions in GDR penal institutions.*

But Berlin would have told the surgeon to get me on that bus, even if he had to dope me up and tie me down to do it. I had a rendezvous to keep, and a minor case of cold turkey wasn't a valid reason to miss it.

And it was only then that I realised why Ewald had been so generous with the fusel back at Magdalena. I'd been unforgivably naïve, I'd trusted him. But Ewald was only interested in making sure I looked like I'd spent the last six months in Bautzen—and given the withdrawal symptoms I was still experiencing, I had to admit he'd achieved his goal.

While I'd been staring at my hand, Weber had begun to take an interest.

"Was it bad?" she whispered, her voice barely audible over the heavy engine and the thrup-thrup of wheels on concrete.

I turned, just enough to see a little of her face, to get an impression of her appearance. She looked better than when I'd last seen her in the exercise cell at Magdalena. They hadn't done a bad job of tidying her up—her hair and skin were clean, she even had some colour in her cheeks, but her eyes were still dull and her fingernails were ragged from chewing.

"They're not going to let me go," I said, my voice croaky. "They'll stop the bus, take me off ..."

She slid her hand from beneath her sports bag, bridging the narrow gap between our seats. She touched the palm of my hand and I slid my fingers down to close around hers. She squeezed back.

Our hands remained that way until we reached the border crossing point at Wartha three hours later.

35
EISENACH

The coach curved high above Eisenach until, at the end of the motorway, it was forced to nudge its way down the steep valley, part of a stream of cars and trucks heading for the West. A *Volkspolizei* radio car skulked in the verge, while on the hillside above us, heavily guarded West German construction firms—paid with West German money in the hope of bringing the two German states physically, if not politically, closer—were spanning a ferro-concrete bridge across both the river Werra and the border.

As the vehicles around us filtered into the various lanes at the border crossing point, the black BMW that had accompanied us from Karl-Marx-Stadt pulled to one side, and a member of the PKE left his hut to wave us past the red and white-striped barrier.

It was another kilometre to the actual border, and as we neared the white line that demarcated the meeting of the Socialist and the non-Socialist worlds, the silence on the coach thickened. Our eyes traced the metal fences crowned with barbed wire and sensor wires, we couldn't help but count the searchlight-topped towers, and we held our breath until the coach drove beneath the final inspection gantry and rumbled over that line. The wheels smoothed as they hit West German tarmac and with a shout—not quite a cheer, more a cough of relief—from one of the seats at the front of the coach, the tension that had clamped our muscles was discharged.

Weber gave my hand another squeeze as the coach slowed to pull into a quiet corner of the West German checkpoint.

Brakes hissed as we came to a stop and the door concertinaed open. A couple of suits climbed aboard, one exchanging a few words with the driver while the other, the one wearing a dark grey woollen car coat, threaded his way down the aisle, looking closely at each face he passed.

"Welcome home!" said the suit at the front, trying to divert the passengers' attention from his colleague who had already covered half the bus. "You're in the Federal Republic now, we're going to take you to Giessen where you'll be able to stay until you can find a more permanent place." He continued with his little speech, warm words polished thin from overuse.

The colleague had reached our seats. He stopped to take a closer look at Weber and, finally satisfied, spoke to her.

"Frau *Kriminaloberkommissarin?*" he held out his hand for her bag. I stood up to let her out of the window seat.

As I shuffled into the aisle, the suit took a step towards me, forcing me further towards the back and placing himself between me Weber. He waited by the seat, ready to shepherd Weber up the aisle towards the door at the front, but she didn't move.

"Not without him," she said.

The suit thought Weber might be disorientated by her ordeal, he leaned forward a little to encourage her onwards. But she refused to be shunted into motion, steadily staring over his shoulder at me.

The suit turned around, his eyes swept me from sweaty forehead via synthetic-fibre suit down to my unsteady legs. Finishing his assessment, he turned back to Weber. She waited until he nodded assent before allowing herself to be eased forward, myself and the suit following in her wake.

We passed the other suit, still reciting his spiel to the exhausted passengers, down the steps to the tarmac. The air was sharp with fumes, clouds slithered overhead, hesitantly letting off faint drops of rain.

Weber turned to the suit, who had again placed himself

between us.

"You're here to take me to Wiesbaden?"

"Yes, Frau *Kriminaloberkommissarin*. A flat has been arranged, somewhere comfortable for you to recover before debriefing."

"Good. He's coming with us." She nodded in my direction, just in case the suit was a little slow on the uptake.

"There's nothing in our orders about a second body, Frau *Kriminaloberkommissarin*."

"I'm giving you the order now." The suit hadn't introduced himself, but from the way he talked it was clear to everyone present that he was junior to her.

He signalled to a dark blue Mercedes 190 parked fifty metres or so away. It nosed its way across the concrete apron towards us, followed by a white Opel Kadett.

The suit held the rear door of the Mercedes for Weber, shutting it once she was safely stowed then turning to briskly pat down my sides and legs, reaching under my jacket to feel my armpits and back. Satisfied I wasn't carrying anything I shouldn't, he climbed into the front passenger side. I was left to manage the door by myself.

The car curved out of the checkpoint, the engine barely audible. I leaned into the soft leather seats, feeling my shoulders and neck slacken. The minor power struggle I'd just witnessed between Weber and the suit had impressed me—I'd known what Weber was capable of in the field, but she'd just shown she was also able to boss the troops.

But a glance to my right told me that Weber herself wasn't feeling so comfortable, despite her minor victory. Her back was rigid, her chin held high and her eyes taking in only the Autobahn that unfolded before the windscreen.

36
WIESBADEN

With two goons sitting in the front seats of the car, I couldn't ask Weber why she'd let me come along for the ride. Not that I was complaining—her intervention had saved me from having to blag my way into the car, because my orders were to stay close to Weber no matter what—she was my ticket to being accepted by the BKA brass. If I'd lost her at the border, I might as well have packed up and gone home.

But now I was on my way, and given that I couldn't talk with Weber, I did what any good soldier does: eat when you can, not when you're hungry; sleep when you can, not when you're tired. And since I hadn't noticed any offers of food, I pushed my legs out as far as they would go and put my head down for a snooze.

I woke when the texture of the road beneath the wheels suddenly changed—the ticking of the concrete surface had given way to the hum of tarmac as we left the Autobahn. I sat up and looked out of the window, trying to get a handle on our surroundings. A glance at my watch told me we'd been underway for just over two hours, which put us anywhere between Hannover and Heidelberg.

We were on a fast road, brightly lit commercial buildings to the right, dense trees and bushes shielding the view to the left. Traffic was light, but much of what I saw on the road was wearing American military plates, army vehicles and civilian cars alike. That put me in the southern half of West Germany, I decided, and given the density of those white US plates, I made a wild guess that we were near Frankfurt am Main, where there was a concentration of bases.

But I couldn't make out the overhead road signs from my position in the back seat, and I cursed myself for sleeping instead of paying attention to where we were heading.

"We're in Wiesbaden," said Weber, noticing my confusion.

I gave her half a smile in thanks and at the same time, clocked the fact that the suit in the front passenger seat had pinned his ears back, determined to hear every word Weber and I might exchange.

The road narrowed into a residential street, modern blocks of low-density flats alternating with large villas that pre-dated the war. We passed bus stops—the green H on a yellow background was familiar enough to set up a disorientating echo of déjà vu—we were in Germany, but not my Germany. I missed the tang of dust and partially burnt hydrocarbons, the homely sight of soot-clogged rendering on grey and brown buildings.

The houses to either side of the road swelled to ever greater opulence as we neared the town centre, the villas had evolved into small palaces, the low-rise flats into free-standing *Gründerzeit* apartment buildings.

Formal parks flanked the road, their edges nibbled by widely-spaced mansions. We slowed to a halt beside a relatively modest example, the gardens and ground floor hidden behind a high box hedge. As the driver turned off the road, an elegant wrought-iron gate slid aside to allow us access.

37
WIESBADEN

The Mercedes came to a halt in a sterile garage under the villa. The shutters rolling down behind us and the steel-lined door in the corner were the only features in an otherwise blank space made of raw concrete and skeins of electrical cables.

The suit opened the rear passenger-side door to allow Weber to alight, the driver went to unlock the internal door and I saw myself out of the car. By the time I'd made my way around the long hood of the Mercedes, the driver was standing to one side as Weber passed through the doorway. The suit remained close on her heels, but the driver waited a little longer, impatient for me to get into gear and follow the others.

And follow them is exactly what I did—up a cement staircase and through another door, this one of heavy, varnished wood embellished with quaint flourishes. The hallway beyond was long and wide enough to drill the honour guard for duty at the *Neue Wache*.

An over-elaborate bureau squatted next to a row of coat hooks that glittered with brass and semi-precious stones, and a trompe l'oeil fresco glared at a mirror set into a gilt frame heavy enough to sink a customs patrol boat, while the marble floor was so polished I regretted not packing my ice skates.

My admiration of the surroundings was interrupted by the driver, who gave me a shove in the back to encourage me to move more and gawp less. The suit and Weber had already entered another room, and I slipped and slid across the hall as I tried to catch up.

We'll call the next room the drawing room—I don't actually know what a drawing room is, but a battery of artists must have been enlisted to paint-bomb the place because the fresco in the hallway was a mere miniature compared to the ceiling and walls in here.

I decided to keep my eyes down, focussing on the worn Turkish carpet—it was the expensive kind, the kind that costs kids their eyesight—but at least it didn't hurt to look at it.

Temporarily blinded as I was by the loud ornamentation, it took me a moment or two to notice we had company. Unlike the suit and the driver, both now positioned between myself and the door, this man was a policeman, or if you were of a mind to, you could persuade me he was a senior officer in the military. Either way, he was definitely not your standard issue intelligence goon. His posture gave him away: upright, proud and ostentatiously unconcerned about any sudden moves that might come his way—there were always other people around to take care of that kind of thing for him.

"Ingo, good to see you." Weber was shaking his hand, her eyes dancing in her tired face.

"And you too, Anna. Here, let me get you a drink—you'll appreciate this one after your little adventures."

"I'll have what she's having," I said from the background, but when nobody reacted, it just felt like weak heckling. Nevertheless, when Ingo poured the brandy from a cut-glass decanter, Weber put another glass on the tray for him to fill.

The drink, when it arrived, was fine cognac—or what I took to be fine cognac. It was as smooth as the marble floor I'd just skidded across, and it made me feel a lot more like myself. A sip of that stuff and I no longer needed to put any effort into repressing the slight tremble evident in my tired hands.

So it was with a calmer eye that I now studied the hideous room and its only marginally less intimidating occupants.

"Glad to have you back," Ingo toasted Anna, and I joined in, raising my glass in her direction, even though nobody was interested in my contribution.

"I'm sure you have lots to tell us, but let's not hurry things. Are you hungry? I thought we could eat together—the kitchen has prepared a light meal," he continued speaking, even as Weber flapped her free hand to signal her lack of appetite. "But before we sit down, perhaps you could introduce us to your guest?"

Anna took her eyes off Ingo long enough to glance in my direction. Our eyes met, but I didn't understand the message she flashed my way. "This is *Unterleutnant* Reim. Without his help I wouldn't be here."

"*Unterleutnant*, eh? What are you, a border guard who assisted our colleague to escape?"

"Unterleutnant Reim was with the Ministry for State Security."

Ingo raised a single eyebrow and took another look at me. I nodded to confirm what Weber had just said. "And you helped Anna? Just how did you help?" His tone wasn't exactly aggressive, but he certainly didn't sound grateful either.

"He tried to warn me before I was arrested." Anna still seemed happy to do all the talking, and I saw no reason to intervene—the pair of them looked so cosy chatting together. "And by trying to protect me he lost everything."

"I see. What was the name on the manifest?" Ingo asked the suit who, while I'd been standing there drinking aged cognac, had been murmuring into a telephone receiver.

"Wolfgang Borchert, sir."

"Wolfgang Borchert like the dead writer, or *Unterleutnant* Reim like the Stasi man? Which is it to be?" He did the eyebrow trick again, and I decided it was time to speak for myself:

"My name is Reim, Hans-Peter. But I was ordered to use the alias Borchert—I was provided with papers for that identity." And without any form of advance notice, I dipped into my pocket, acutely aware of the effect such a risky manoeuvre would have on the two goons behind me. Even though they'd already frisked me, I could imagine their stiffened muscles, the preparatory step forward, ready to pounce if anything lethal appeared in my hands. Ingo, though, remained relaxed and I followed his example, also taking a step forward to hand him the birth certificate and various other official pieces of paper I had in the name of Borchert.

"No *Ausweis*?"

"They took it off me before I left—said this would be enough to establish my identity once I reached the West."

Ingo shuffled through the documents again, not really reading them, just using the action to obscure the fact that he was thinking.

"Whatever you're doing here, I'm sure you'll appreciate that we need to be careful, Herr Reim. We'll find somewhere comfortable for you to stay while we make a few enquiries." He flicked his fingers at the suit, who took a step towards me. Close enough for me to feel his breath on the back of my neck.

I took the hint and followed the driver through the door, trying and failing to catch Weber's eye as I left.

38
WIESBADEN

While Weber was enjoying her welcome home meal in a rococo villa, I was shown rather less generosity. A short trip in the Mercedes and then I was shunted into a sparsely furnished windowless basement in a modern block of flats.

I had a hard chair to sit on and a naked light bulb to entertain me. At the other end of the room a couple more chairs waited behind a desk, its surface empty except for an adjustable lamp—just your typical interrogation room. It felt like home.

The cellar may have been familiar enough, but I was tired and beginning to doubt the grand plan—yes, that grand plan which had sounded almost reasonable while I was being briefed in Berlin. In that moment I was more than glad of the cognac Weber had passed my way, even though I would come to regret it, and not just because it was far too fine for the likes of me.

But for the moment, I thought I knew what was coming my way. The familiar rituals: sit on that chair and tell us your legend. We won't believe you, but we'll ask you to repeat the story until it's so crumpled and worn we can see through the holes.

And of course, first, the wait. Perhaps they needed the time to find a couple of qualified interviewers prepared to work at no notice and with zero preparation, but it was more likely they were hoping to make me sweat a little.

When the two interrogators arrived, I didn't get any kind of look at them because my driver came in first to switch off the main light and angle the desk lamp at my face. But when the two grey figures came into the basement it was finally time to get down to work. Level 1: the get-to-know-you cover story, the *Katzendreck* that would establish that I was willing and able to talk.

I told them about my department, ZAIG/II, and the location of my office in Berlin Centre. I gave them outdated information about my previous department, HA VI, and about the operation to locate Merkur, better known to these guys as *Polizeirat* Dr Andreas Portz of the BKA branch in Bonn.

All the material I gave them had been sanctioned in an off-the-record meeting by Lieutenant Colonel Schur himself. In order to help establish my credentials, most of it was not only true, but easily verifiable.

I don't know whether the two guys in the room with me thought they were getting enough to justify their overtime, but after three hours or so, one of the dim figures behind the lamp turned to the other. I couldn't see what they were up to—a short whispered discussion, perhaps, or the exchange of a prepared signal—but as one, they packed up their notes and left the room.

I stayed in that cellar for a while, all by myself, before the driver returned to collect me. He pointed me at the stairs and we climbed the modern, featureless steps to the top floor where he unlocked a door and showed me into a small chamber—more of a broom cupboard, really—with a sink and a narrow cot under thin curtains that were drawn across a barred window.

"Nice room, I'll take it," I said, but he wasn't in the mood to appreciate my wit.

He shut the door as he went and I heard the key turn in the lock.

39
WIESBADEN

When the suit tried to wake me the next morning, I rolled over and vomited on his perfectly shined, handmade shoes. The brandy the night before had seen me right for the interrogation that had followed, but it also set my cold turkey treatment back a week: dry mouth, palpitations, no appetite, pupils shrinking from whatever vague light bled through the curtains. I had them all, along with the nausea.

The suit leaped back, the look on his face telling me I may have avoided a beating this time, but it was a one-time offer and I'd better not vomit on anyone's shoes again.

"Get yourself out of bed," he rasped as he left my cupboard.

With an effort I swung my legs to the floor and sat up, staring at the closed door. I couldn't deal with another interrogation without a drink inside me, and since no drink was in sight, I let myself flop back onto the bed, not bothering to pull the eiderdown over my shivering body.

The suit came back, he'd wiped his shoes, but streaks of sick still decorated the cuffs of his pressed trousers.

"I told you to get up!"

I groaned a little, then moved my face within vomiting distance of his legs, tightening the muscles around my mouth to stop myself from smiling as he took a hasty step back.

He reached over to place a hand on my brow. I must have been running a temperature on top of everything else, because, in a different tone, grudging, he announced he'd be back with the physician.

They must have had a tame doctor on hand because it

didn't take long for a lanky fellow with a thick moustache and thinning hair to step into the room. I could tell he was a professional because of the white coat and his habit of speaking to me in the first person plural.

"How are we feeling?"

"I'm lousy, doc. Couldn't say how you're doing, though."

He shut me up with a thermometer in my gob and put a cold stethoscope on my chest, moving it around to listen to my heart and lungs.

"Much of a drinker, are we? We see a lot of that in those coming over from the East."

He had my number, there was little point denying it, so he stuck a needle in my arm and stole some blood for good measure.

That was when I discovered that military doctors are pretty much the same, no matter which side of the Wall you happen to find yourself on. If your leg isn't hanging off then you're fit for duty. If it does happen to be hanging off, well, there's nothing that won't be cured by a pill the size of one of those dinky bars of soap they lay out in the Interhotels.

The medication the doctor prescribed was brought to me by my guardian in the suit. I couldn't disagree with the treatment, a slug of vodka on top of the horse pill, even though I knew my interrogators would use the alcohol against me. I knew that if at any point they weren't happy with my answers, I wouldn't get my dose.

But as a way of getting the patient back on his feet, you couldn't knock regular applications of ethanol as the best and most expeditious therapy available.

So, one glass of fusel later, I was ready, if not quite steady on my feet, to head downstairs and face more questions.

I optimistically calculated that I could hold out until the afternoon before I needed another pick-me-up, but what did I know—the effects of one tiny cognac the evening before had knocked me sideways. I thought I understood how my body reacted to alcohol withdrawal—after all, I've been drinking on the job without it affecting my work for years—but I hadn't taken into consideration the amount of *Doppelkorn* Captain Ewald plied me with during the briefings at Magdalena. Best not to think about that, nor what a schmuck I'd been to gleefully cane whatever he handed over.

When I got back to Berlin, I'd have words with the good captain. But for now, I had an interrogation to get through.

While waiting in the cellar, trying not to let the bright light bother my sensitive eyes too much, I thought back to what I'd told them the night before. Had I really been as careful as I thought, or had alcohol withdrawal already begun to cloud my judgement?

Maybe, maybe not. But I had little choice but to continue with the plan that Ewald and I had worked on so carefully for so long.

So when the two shadows came through the door behind me, and slid along the wall to their side of the lamp, I was ready to serve them more *Katzendreck*.

40
WIESBADEN

They didn't get round to asking about Anna Weber until sometime in the late afternoon—it was a few hours after we had stopped for lunch, which in my case had been a selection of cold meats, pickles, bread and a sweet pastry. I still had no appetite, but managed to jimmy a little food between my clenched teeth—I told myself I needed my strength.

And finally, after a few hours of repetitive questioning, they popped the question: "Why did you help the person known to you as Anna Weber?"

"Initially, I thought she was on our side—an IM run by a local handler. By the time I was aware of her status, we'd had some interaction. In that time I'd assessed her skills, I respected her abilities."

"But why did you help her?"

"I've known for a long time that my country in general, and my employers in particular, are on the wrong side of history, but couldn't see any way to extricate myself from the Ministry. Meeting Weber opened up the possibility of making contact with the authorities in the West, I saw a chance to negotiate through her-"

"For what? What did you intend to negotiate?"

"My defection."

There it was. The biggest lie in the whole pack. The only lie they needed to swallow—if they believed me, then I'd be halfway towards completing my mission.

My interrogators gave my statement its due, and we sat in silence for a minute or two before they moved onto unrelated questions.

"Tell us more about Captain Dupski's bowling team."

So I told them, knowing that sooner or later, probably after a series of repetitive and trivial questions designed to break my concentration, they would question me about my intention to defect. I had my answers waiting. So long as the shivers didn't overtake me, I'd be ready for them.

The days went by, always with the same interrogators, and usually with the same questions. The atmosphere in that underground room didn't get any warmer, but it did become familiar. At the start of each session, I noticed how the lamp was pointed a little lower, the focus of the light slowly moving away from my eyes. I didn't know whether it was gravity doing its work, pulling the head of the angled lamp down, or whether it was intentional, part of their interrogation plan, but on the afternoon of the third day, I took my chair after a short break in which I'd been allowed a half-glass of vodka, and realised that I could keep my eyes out of the glare if I moved my head back just a centimetre or two.

I was still alone in the room, so I took the opportunity to shift the chair back a little. The position of the chair was marked on the floor with chalk, but either nobody noticed the move, or nobody cared. Perhaps it had to do with the fact that we were pressing forward, into the trust phase of the interrogation, when the questioners try to build rapport with me. Nevertheless, I knew that if they didn't get the results they needed, my privileges would be cancelled. No more friendly questioning, the unrelenting light would be focussed directly in my eyes again.

Sitting out of the direct beam of the lamp, I could finally see my interrogators. They were both in their mid-thirties, and both smoked Lucky Strikes. They were dressed alike, too—jeans, shirt and suit jacket—and both were approximately the same height, clean-shaven with shortish blonde hair parted on the left. They spoke practically accent-free high German and at times they had (or pretended to have) problems with my Berlin dialect.

We'd come far enough for them to share their cigarettes with me, and with a plentiful supply of nails along with my ration of alcohol, I was comfortable enough. Nor did the interrogations present any difficulties—I'd faced worse from my own side.

"Comfort break," announced the interrogator on the left after a particularly easy session. "Fancy joining us?"

"I'll stay here," I replied taking out a nail. They'd given me my own deck of cigarettes now, and a lighter to go with it, but they knew they could safely leave me down here—other than the table and chairs, there was nothing that would burn. If I tried my hand at arson, the worst I'd manage would be to give myself a nasty dose of smoke inhalation, and I'd rather get that from the Lucky Strikes.

The twins left the room and I heard the bolt slide home. Sitting quietly in that bare room, I waited for their footsteps to fade, then went over to the desk they'd just vacated. Usually so meticulous when it came to clearing up, this time they'd left their things behind: a travel alarm clock stood in the centre, along with a piece of paper on which the timings of our sessions had been recorded. But in front of the seat to the right lay a piece of A3-sized cartridge paper. It was a portrait of me.

Fischerklause, I thought. The first week in February. Anna Weber and I in a cosy bar up on the Baltic coast while she drew a portrait in charcoal. That was the picture in front of me—except the portrait Anna Weber had done for me was gathering dust in my flat in Berlin. And the drawing I had in front of me was done in soft pencil rather than charcoal.

I turned it over and read the short note written in the same soft pencil: *Wolfgang Borchert, Warnemünde, 7. Feb. 1984.*

Not a bad trick, she'd got the better of me that time. I closed my eyes and allowed my thoughts to go back to the *Fischerklause* bar in Warnemünde. I could see Weber doing a sketch in pencil before working with the charcoal sticks. And here was that first draft.

Angry at myself for my own past negligence, I left the portrait on the table and went back to my chair in the middle of the room. It had been a mistake not to take that draft portrait from Weber, even if I hadn't suspected her of being a Western agent at the time. But what other mistakes had I made back then? What other slip-ups would surface?

Aware that the room was probably spiked with one or more hidden microphones, I restricted myself to an internal rant, soundlessly venting my self-reproach. But even that was interrupted by the sound of the bolt being pulled back.

It was the twins returning for the next round.

41
WIESBADEN

We'd reached level 2 information—I was telling them how I had interrogated their officer Portz alias Codename Merkur in a safe house in Bad Doberan, all the while mentally rehearsing whichever portions of *Katzendreck* I'd be serving up next and considering whether it was time to begin dishing out material that could be potentially harmful to Berlin Centre yet deemed worthy of disclosure if it helped persuade the West Germans I was serious about defecting.

They wrote down the details of the spy network at the Warnow shipyard that their man Portz had tipped me off to. I wondered whether his treachery had been choreographed, much as mine was now, or whether he would be in trouble if the Russians ever let him come back to the West.

There were a few questions about what else Merkur had told me about, a few details to clarify about the network in the shipyard, then they moved on, keen to gather as much fresh material as I was willing to give them.

So I told them about the marking of passports and other documents at the border by the Passport and Control Units, visible only under UV light. I didn't doubt they already knew about that particular trick, but I was able to provide them with up to date information on what each mark actually meant: whether entry to or exit from the GDR should be allowed with no questions asked, only after a thorough search, delayed or refused.

It hurt to give up that information—I was no longer posted to the department responsible for security at the border crossings, but that particular revelation was what, so far, had felt most like a betrayal of my colleagues.

Nevertheless, it was good material, material that the Westlers could easily verify by cross-referencing their own records with the results of a simple experiment with a UV lamp.

Satisfied with what I'd just told them, the interrogators decided to wrap up for the day. We left the cellar, the twins destined for their own debrief, myself heading upstairs for the little bedroom and a shot of medicinal vodka.

Once I'd been locked in, I took the waiting glass of alcohol and without looking at it or smelling it, I poured it down the sink. Every night, it was a struggle, but I knew I had to reduce my need for alcohol. I was continuously shaky and nervous, but determined to get myself to a position where I could still function if they decided to turn off the tap.

After a week, the original suit who had accompanied me ever since I'd crossed the border was replaced by a clone of himself. Come to think of it, both suits, the driver and the twin interrogators were all cast from the same mould—it was as if West German intelligence staff were modelling themselves on their American masters.

42
WIESBADEN

A few days after my guardian had been replaced, the twins decided it was time to start the train of questions from the beginning again. I climbed aboard, and we all enjoyed the familiar view for the third, the fourth, even the fifth time: my own biography, the location of my office and that evergreen, Captain Dupski's bowling team.

I recognised the attempt to erode my concentration, and was ready and braced for the train to jump the rails and speed off in a new direction.

"Was there a particular reason for your decision to defect? Did something happen?"

They'd stayed away from the topic of my defection, it hadn't appeared on the timetable since the second day of interrogation, but here we were, they had decided it was time to talk *Tacheles*.

So I didn't reply. I looked down, at my hand, clasping a cigarette. Watched the smoke curl up to join the smog hanging below the low ceiling. I waited them out.

It took a minute or two for one of them to clear his throat.

"Well?"

"I'd like a break."

"A couple more questions, then you can have a break."

Another moment of silence, I looked up at them, almost immediately lowering my head again and stubbing out the Lucky Strike. I reached into my pocket for another nail and lit myself up, not bothering to suppress the shaking of my hands. I twisted the tip of my cigarette in the little foil ashtray, shaping the spent ash into a cone. Unable to postpone the moment any longer, I began:

"On the sixteenth of September last year, I was detained at the Firm's main remand prison in Berlin. The head of my section had been found with a hole in his chest and I was the one with the weakest alibi, having been seen in the area around the time of death."

I took a deep breath, then a deeper puff on the nail. The fingers of my left hand clawed at the material of my trousers.

"I spent two weeks in that place. Round the clock interrogations, sleep deprivation, food deprivation. The usual." Another gasp of the Lucky Strike, a furtive glance to check the twins were writing all this down. "Fourteen years I've given to the Firm, given them my all. Screwed up my marriage working every day and most nights—and they treat me like that ..."

"You haven't mentioned your time on remand before. Why not?"

"I don't like to think of it."

I lapsed into silence. If they wanted more details, they'd have to dig for them—nobody values a product they haven't paid for.

Instead, they jumped the tracks again: "Do you know anyone here in the West?"

I hesitated, why did they ask that? But I couldn't wait too long, if I didn't answer soon it would feed their suspicious minds. And since I calculated that they already knew the answer, I told them the truth.

"My wife. She's here in the West."

"When did you last see your wife?"

"Fifteenth of September, 1983."

"You know the exact date. Why is that?"

I didn't answer.

"Is that because it was the day before you were arrested?"

121

I smoked my cigarette, nodded.

"Was there a connection? Do you think the two events were related—your arrest and the disappearance of your wife?"

Disappearance? I hadn't mentioned any disappearance. Which meant they already knew how my wife had left the GDR—I congratulated myself for making the right call, admitting I knew she was over here.

"I told you, I don't like to think about what happened at that time."

I thought they'd push me on that, it was the obvious line to take. Instead, the twins shuffled their papers around the desk for a bit.

"What's your wife's name?"

"Renate Vera Reim, née Kubzyk, date of birth: fifth of September 1951."

One of the interrogators passed a sheet to the other. They put their heads together and murmured for a while.

"How was your relationship with your wife?"

What did they know about my wife? Not knowing how much information they had, I decided to hedge my bets. I rejected *acrimonious* as a description of our relations and opted for the middle ground: "Estranged, but not divorced."

"We have here a statement by Renate Vera Reim. She says that without your help she would not have been able to reach the West."

I lit another cigarette. What was she thinking, saying a thing like that? Did she think she was helping, or had she said it in the knowledge that if word got back to the Firm, I'd be a prime candidate for a short stay in Leipzig prison followed by a shot in the back of the head?

43
BINGEN

I didn't understand why my wife had said what she did, but my interrogators showed no such doubts—they seemed to consider her testimony enough to bring me over the line. I was packed into the Mercedes the very next morning and driven out of Wiesbaden.

This time, I paid more attention to where I was being taken: over the Rhine on the Autobahn bridge, then west for ten minutes or so before leaving the motorway half a dozen exits later.

My new accommodation was on a hill above the small town of Bingen. A crooked, half-timbered house surrounded by woods on three sides and a vista of the Rhine valley on the other.

On the terrace, I paused to take in the view. A lonely crenellated tower watched over the Rhine from the tail of an islet and a ruined castle squatted halfway up a cliff on the far side. The broad river valley was open to the sunlight I had barely seen since high summer.

Gripping the balustrade, taking in the scenery, I had the urge to sit myself on the manicured lawn and call for a cigarette and a glass of the local wine. But before my fantasies could take full flight, I was interrupted by the current version of the suit.

"Would you come inside?"

A final look at the Rhine and I entered the house, stooping to pass beneath the drunken lintel.

★

Anna Weber was waiting for me in a white-tiled kitchen, standing by a coffee machine that dripped boiling water into the filter, filling the kitchen with welcome. Bread rolls and pastries had been arranged on a tray, along with apricot jam, butter, cheese, chopped herbs and sausage.

"You've arrived." She gave me a smile, the first genuine greeting anyone had offered me since I crossed the border. "Breakfast is ready."

She carried the tray past me and out of the house and I gladly followed her to the terrace, checking cupboards and corners as I went in case Ingo, the officer from the opulent villa in Wiesbaden, happened to be lurking. I watched as she set the contents of the tray on a lace tablecloth-covered table.

Her movements seemed fluid, she had more colour in her face and the overall impression of health was enhanced by her hair—the gelled spikes told a story of a confident woman choosing to wear her hair short, rather than one who had lost her locks to prison shears.

But looking more closely, I couldn't overlook the prominent cheekbones that served to darken the rings around her eyes, the ragged nails and cuticles that told of undefeated nervousness.

While Weber set the table, the suit stood to one side, trying not to look like the spare wheel. Weber turned her smile on him.

"Thank you, I'll take it from here."

He gave a stiff little bow and scrunched across the gravel to the black Mercedes. I watched him reverse down the long driveway and Weber fetched the coffee.

"Come now, eat!" she said, unnecessarily repositioning the cups and saucers. I pulled up a couple of chairs, placing them side by side so we could both enjoy the view of the Rhine gorge.

I wasn't hungry, but I spread a little butter on half a bread roll and sipped my coffee.

"What am I doing here?" I asked once I'd taken a token bite.

"Somebody will come to see you soon, they'll let you know what they've decided to do with you. I haven't been told anything, so there's no point asking, just have your breakfast and take in the view."

I watched her eyes, the way they peeked sideways, drawing my attention to the little house. I tapped my ear and she nodded. The place was bugged.

"Thanks for breakfast," I ventured, trying to think of safe topics of conversation.

"You're welcome. Apparently they're looking for a neutral role for me, they say I've played my part and should take it easy for a while. But I'm not having any of that, told them I was too young for early retirement and if they didn't have anything else for me to do then I'd play nursemaid, make sure you stay out of trouble."

"You're wasted on a babysitting job," I said, truthfully enough. Weber was owed an easy number after what she'd been through, but she was still too good an agent to be looking after a defector.

"Well, they wouldn't listen to me, maybe you'll have more success in persuading them."

"I doubt a recommendation from me will be worth much."

She laughed at that. It was the first time I'd heard her laugh, and it surprised me. Not many people can go through months of KGB and Stasi interrogations and find something to laugh about just a couple of weeks after being released.

44
BINGEN

I stayed on the terrace for the rest of day, waiting for someone, anyone, to come and talk to me, but nobody bothered to show up. I didn't mind, I told myself, I appreciated having all that space around me, it did me good to just sit in the fresh air and sunlight after weeks of incarceration. I appreciated being able to allow my concentration to lapse, to watch butterflies visit the open flowers dotted around the tidy borders of the garden below the terrace, the tugs pushing endless trains of dumb barges up the river, the circling black specks of rooks surrounding the tumble-down towers and walls of the ancient castle standing proud of the vines on the opposite side of the Rhine.

As the shadows dialled around the terrace and the late afternoon sun moved behind the house, Weber brought out a tray—the smell of baking had been tickling my nostrils for the last half hour or so.

"*Zwiebelkuchen und Federweisser,*" she announced as she set the feast on the table.

Weber was already pulling the loose cap off the bottle and pouring cloudy, sparkling wine into two glasses. My heart beat faster in anticipation of the alcohol heading my way.

I consumed more of the young wine than the onion tart, but the pair of us sat there in companionable silence, unable to talk about what connected us for fear of being overheard.

We were in the shade now, and a cool breeze had followed the broad river down from the Alps, making me shiver. One of the suits had given me a pullover before I came here, and I got up to fetch it from my room.

When I returned, Weber was no longer alone—Ingo had joined us, had taken the seat I'd just vacated. I took the bench on the other side of the table, my back to the view, but in a good position to see both Ingo and his driver, who was standing on the gravel drive, smoking a cigarette. Behind him gleamed a Mercedes 280 SE—a larger car than the one that had brought me here, it was the same model as the one that had picked up Heller when our operatives followed him through Denmark and down to Mainz.

Ingo himself was a little different from how I remembered. Of course, he still had those eyebrows, but I realised that I wouldn't have been able to describe him adequately, not without seeing him again. To compensate for earlier lapses, I took a closer look now, noting his distinguishing features: around one meter eighty, mid to late forties, slightly built but with a discreet belly overhanging his snakeskin belt. Thin mouth suspended between a receding chin and a pair of flaring nostrils. Tops of his small ears covered by fine, greying brown hair swept into a parting in an attempt to disguise his developing widow's peak. Narrow shoulders, as if he'd always skived sports at school, slender wrists barely strong enough to support his heavy gold watch.

"*Guten Tag, Herr Reim.*" It was more of an announcement than a greeting. He had a southern accent: Bavarian? Swabian? Not strong, merely an unobtrusive lilt to let you know he was proud of his *Heimat*.

I nodded in return.

"Thank you for being patient with us—I'm sure a man of your experience appreciates the necessity of caution in cases such as these-" But I didn't hear what they had to be careful about—a couple of jets darted into the periphery of my vision, already out of view before the howl of their engines could overtake Ingo's words.

When I turned back, the corrugated scream of the jets was

still bending the air.

"Phantom F4s," Ingo informed me, although I'd already made the identification—the wings were so much stubbier, the noses sharper than our MiG-21. "Our American friends like to make use of whatever good weather we have. Our French guests, on the other hand, prefer to do their low-flying in misty conditions. If you're up early enough in the morning, you may be lucky enough to see their new Mirages."

"What are your plans for me?" I asked, holding my glass up for a top-up of *Federweisser*. It was sweet and bubbly, the alcohol rising quickly to the head. Perhaps I should wait until Ingo had gone before drinking any more.

"We still have a few questions for you, nothing onerous, just a little follow-up. Once we've got that out of the way .... well, you could say we have a proposal for you. You wanted to come to the West, and you have done—congratulations. But we wondered whether you'd like to use your skills and knowledge in a different setting."

"A different setting? There's no way I'm going back to the East-"

"No, no." Ingo waved his hand as if my objection were a nasty smell to be wafted away. "We want you right here in Wiesbaden, we're interested in your experience in analysis. What do you say? It would give you a start in the West, a chance to pay us back for the trust we're showing in you."

"I'd like that very much—I want to make myself useful, and if you think I can do that ..." Don't show too much enthusiasm, Reim, I told myself. But I held up my glass for the others to toast.

"To trust," I proposed, and Anna Weber and Ingo leaned forwards so we could all touch glasses.

45
BINGEN

At breakfast the next morning, I asked Weber whether I was allowed to leave the safe house. My general fitness had deteriorated over the summer, and I knew I'd need to get my stamina levels back up before the next stage of my mission.

"We can go for a walk together," she answered. "I'll just phone it in first—where do you want to go?"

"You decide." Clearly, I wasn't at liberty to leave the grounds by myself—my keepers were being sensible, they didn't want me disappearing or getting up to any mischief. But I didn't fret about the restrictions, and I wasn't averse to Weber tagging along for a walk. After all, we had a few things to talk about.

She went to phone whoever it was she needed to check in with and I leaned against the railing at the edge of the terrace. The rumbling of a long goods train reached me and I scanned the valley until I saw it snaking along the far bank of the river, below the ruined castle.

On the river itself, a KD cruise ship emerged from the low morning mist and overtook the ponderous freighters as they hooted and beat their way against the current.

"That's all settled," said Weber, re-emerging from the house. "We have an outing booked for this afternoon."

"Where to?"

"See that little thing there?" She pointed to a narrow boat with a free-standing bridge that was coming alongside near Bingen old town. "We'll take that ferry over to the other side."

★

I dozed in my room until it was time for our excursion. I shouldn't have been surprised by how exhausted I was—I hadn't slept properly since coming over the border, always keeping half an eye open in case my interrogators decided the early hours of the morning would be a good time to ask difficult questions.

Even now I could be taken to the nearest cellar at any time and asked whether I wanted to change my story. I knew that while I was in the West, I would never truly get a decent night's sleep.

But the morning passed uneventfully, no grey suits put in any sudden appearances, and when Weber knocked on my door to tell me it was time to go, I was more than ready to leave.

She was dressed casually in white trainers, tight blue jeans, a grey sweatshirt and a bright cap, whereas I had on one of the cheap suits they'd left in the cupboard for me. I'd left the ties in the drawer and the day was warm enough to allow me to carry the jacket hooked over my shoulder.

We took the rough path through the trees to the public road below, and even though I used the opportunity to look around, I saw no sign of sentries watching me or the property.

Once on the road, a mere lane that meandered up the side of the hill to the wooded plateau, Weber steered me to the right before taking another hiking trail that zig-zagged down to the railway line on our side of the river.

We crossed the railway and followed the water as far as the jetty I'd seen earlier. The little ferry was already on its way towards us, cutting across the wake of a long tug train and coming around for the approach to the pier.

A small crowd of tourists had already gathered at the railing, and an American family joined the queue shortly after we arrived. None of them looked anything like the suits I'd been interrogated by in Wiesbaden, none of them looked even vaguely fit enough to be employed by the BKA or any other police or intelligence agency. Could they really be trusting Weber to babysit me all by herself?

On board the ferry I insisted on sitting at the stern, where the noise from the propeller wash would make it hard to overhear anything we might say to each other, but I left it to Weber to decide when to start the conversation.

Weber, however, had other ideas. She spent the crossing pointing out the various sights: the white Mouse Tower on the islet, in which an archbishop was eaten by mice after he'd burned his starving tenants alive; the Niederwald monument at the top of the slope on the other side of the Rhine, built to celebrate Kaiser Wilhelm I and the German Empire of 1871; the ruins of a railway bridge, blown up by the retreating fascist German army in 1945. A snapshot of German history from just one viewpoint, a history that the West German state was content—no, keen—to enlist in a doomed quest for a *raison d'état*.

I half-listened to Weber's history lesson as I watched the other passengers. Even though I couldn't find it in me to suspect them of being anything other than what their appearances suggested, I still noted their clothes and features.

We docked at Rüdesheim and walked down the banks of the river with the crowds of tourists, tunnelling our way through the centre of the long queue outside the KD river cruises ticket office.

I used the elevation from a footbridge over the railway tracks to look back the way we'd come—the American family that had joined us on the ferry were now in line at the ticket office. Otherwise, I didn't recognise any faces.

A goods train rattled beneath the bridge, shaking the structure. I leaned in to Weber and half-whispered, half-shouted into her ear. "Are we by ourselves?"

Still holding on to her cap, she looked up from the dusty containers swaying past and gave me a short nod.

46
RÜDESHEIM

Weber led me up a steep cobbled alley fringed by wine taverns, each boasting loudspeakers at head height. Pushed onwards by the swell of holidaymakers, we passed from one imperialist, revanchist tune to another: The Westerwald Song, Lili Marlene, The Watch On The Rhine.

I shook my head in bewilderment, but could do little but follow my guide—the stream of ageing Germans and Americans in check shirts and knickerbockers was relentless, each hauling their hiking sticks and generous waistlines up the slope, pushing all who went before them.

Weber looked around every so often, checking I was still in her slipstream and peering into each of the wine gardens that seamed the narrow lane.

She jerked her head to one side, not attempting to making herself understood above the amplified tootling of a worn-out record, and entered a wine garden. She made for the corner where two long benches met.

We sat in relative seclusion beneath fading vine leaves that trailed along a brightly painted wooden pergola. The rest of the garden was occupied by thirty or forty Japanese tourists along with a smattering of middle-aged German couples who kept themselves apart from the other guests, sitting near the free-standing bar where waiters poured drinks and made up the bills.

As full as our chosen hostelry was, it still provided sanctuary from the unremitting flow of superannuated humanity that edged its way up the lane beyond the low wall.

Although there were no loudspeakers here, the Loreley song still oozed its way into our hearing.

"Welcome to the Drosselgasse, the biggest tourist attraction in Rüdesheim," said Weber, trying to catch the eye of a passing waiter. He paused in mid-stride, checked her out and decided she was worth bringing a couple of menus, but Weber stalled him with an order.

"A bottle of your house Riesling and two plates of *Sauerbraten*."

But I took the proffered menu and flicked to the back while Weber talked to the waiter. Seeing what I wanted, I added my own request: "And an Asbach Uralt."

The waiter looked like he was considering whether to argue with her about the order, but seeing her look, he nodded and drifted away to another table.

"How did you know *Sauerbraten* were available?" I asked.

"Local speciality, tourist trap—of course *Sauerbraten* are available. And if they'd run out, we could have had the Schnitzel."

The drinks arrived before the food, and Weber and I clinked glasses, looking into each other's eyes as we did so. Sweeter than I'm used to but a reasonable body nevertheless.

I put the wine glass down and tried the brandy. That was stronger than expected—as the alcohol burned its way down my chest, I held the small glass up to the light and smiled at it.

"Is that what you wanted?"

"Just what the doctor ordered," I answered.

We sat for a moment longer, watching the coach-load of Japanese guests enjoying their meal and taking pictures of every dish, the waitresses and each other.

Finally, Weber spoke. "We can talk here."

I agreed—other than the waiter slipping past with orders for nearby tables, I couldn't see much danger of being overheard. Unless Weber was wired. But I dismissed the thought—if she'd gone back to her own side, then this mission was doomed anyway, and me with it.

Now I had a chance to speak a little more openly with Weber, it was hard to know where to start. My priority should have been to establish whether Weber was going to keep her word about supporting me in my mission over here in the Operational Area, but I asked about her relationship with this officer Ingo.

I watched her stare out of the gateway that separated us from the torrent of tourists. Her face was still pale, as if she'd spent all summer locked up inside, which of course she had.

"I wanted to thank you," I said simply, deciding the gentle, understanding approach was necessary. And that meant giving her some prompts and paying attention to how she responded.

"Thank me? What for? Getting you out of that hole you managed to dig yourself into in that orchard back in February? Not to mention patching up your arm?"

I swallowed. I hadn't expected her to go that far back. But if our little adventure in Berlin was what was most important to her then I could work with that.

I let my memory slip back to a dull, cold morning in Lichtenberg. The garden of the *Station der jungen Naturforscher*, three pistols pointing at me—two held by men I'd been working with, the third by First Lieutenant Sachse, who was in command of the hold up. He wanted me to hand over the package of evidence that would prove his treachery, but I hadn't even found it at that point. Since he didn't believe me, the situation was set to rapidly escalate.

That was when Weber stepped in, holding what everyone present assumed was a machine pistol, but which turned out to be just a toy Kalashnikov.

Long story short: Weber saved my skin, and in return, I handed her over to the KGB.

47
BINGEN

The next day Weber was called in for a meeting in Wiesbaden and while she was away I was confined to barracks. I sat at my bedside window for a while, trying to catch the sideways slip of human movement between the trees. They were good, I'll give them that—it took me half an hour to be sure I'd spotted the two sentries discretely doing their rounds in the woods below the house.

Weber and I ventured out from the house on Wednesday, once again returning to Rüdesheim. Allowing ourselves to be shunted up to the top of the Drosselgasse, we switched into the queue for the cable car that linked the town with the Niederwald Monument two hundred vertical metres up the side of the gorge.

As the cable car, an aluminium pod barely large enough to contain its two seats, shuddered out of the base station and along the wire, I asked a question which, in operational terms, was completely unnecessary but had bothered me ever since I'd spoken to Weber in the exercise cell at Magdalena prison.

"Will you tell me your real name? Or do I have to continue using your cover name?"

She didn't reply immediately, and I waited patiently for her to decide to trust me. But after a while I realised she wasn't going to answer, so I tried another question—one that felt equally important to me, even if it was just as operationally irrelevant as her name.

"Why are you helping me?"

Again Weber didn't answer. She stared instead at the strakes of cirrocumulus clouds heading down the Rhine.

The car scraped and shuddered as it cleared a pylon, it rocked in the slow wind.

"You mean, why am I helping you, even though you betrayed me to the KGB?" she finally responded.

I wasn't interested in a discussion about whether I'd betrayed her, instead I tried to find whatever words that would work in this situation.

"I wasn't given any choice. The Russians knew about you— the KGB major we met at Wünsdorf, he knew everything. If I'd tried to keep you away from him he would have put us both in the glasshouse."

"Yet we both ended up there anyway."

I held out my hand, palm downwards, just as I had on the bus the day we left the GDR. This time it was steady. "Except the KGB didn't lock me up, it was my own Firm. They found out that I'd collaborated with your boss, Portz, when I was trying to find the evidence against Sachse. They're not stupid —once they started looking, they worked out how I'd tried to warn you about the KGB." The best lies are based on the truth, they're the only kind that will stand up to any kind of scrutiny. "They let me out to do this job. If I do it right, if I meet the operational objectives then they'll drop their investigation into my activities."

I waited to see whether she was going to swallow my sob story, and it looked like she might, because she left the clouds where they were and dropped her blue eyes to meet mine.

"I was allowed home on condition I help get you embedded. They briefed me and prepared me, and now I've done what I said I would and you're almost there. The rest is up to you."

"What's my current status?" I wasn't sure about switching so quickly from apologies to business, but the summit station was already drawing close and our tête-à-tête was about to end.

"Officially, I've not been told anything, but my guess is they regard you as low risk. You could probably escape if you wanted to, I think their main concern is that a Stasi snatch squad will come for you."

I smiled at that thought, and she almost joined in.

"And what are they planning to do with me?"

"You're a good catch, they want to use your operational knowledge to analyse the data they're getting from an asset in the East. Once you've been cleared to work on that material your holiday will be over."

That was good news, my operation was on course.

"You still haven't answered my question: why were you prepared to help me? You could have given me up as soon as we crossed the border—it's treason, what you're doing. You're betraying your own country."

Weber looked surprised for a moment, but her face fell into shadow as the cable car glided below the canopy of the trees that surrounded the summit station.

"This is a one-off. I won't be doing it again, so make sure to tell your people they won't be able to use me again." She was momentarily distracted by the trees, the branches reaching out to the little gondola. "Anyway, we had this conversation all those months ago—in a dive somewhere outside Berlin. Seven Steps—was that what the bar was called? I told you then: I want to see justice done, I want to see your First Lieutenant Sachse suffer. He's responsible for Arno Seiffert's death."

Revenge. That was a motive I understood.

48
BINGEN

When we got back to the house, a large Mercedes had landed on the drive below the terrace. I followed Weber inside, mentally preparing myself for whatever might be waiting.

It was Ingo with one of his cloned operatives. I thought he'd come to see Weber, but when he sent her out of the room, I realised I'd read the situation wrong.

Ingo, his goon and I sat in the living room—a cramped space with low ceilings and small windows. Ingo sat apart, watching while the clone asked the same questions I'd already answered so many times before, perhaps still hoping to catch me out on the basic details, like my name or place of birth.

The fun and games lasted nearly three hours, all without a break or a drink, although Ingo did get up and walk around a little after an hour while the clone and I remained in our seats.

Finally, the interrogator looked up from his sheet of questions and nodded to his superior.

"That'll be all," said Ingo, now standing behind me. He moved around to take the seat just vacated and clasped his hands in his lap.

"You remember my offer of the other day, that you come to work for us?"

"You being the BKA?"

Ingo nodded. "It's taken us longer than planned to talk to you. The Federal Republic is home to every German, whichever side of the Iron Curtain they live—but we have to do all the usual checks. Can't have live operatives from your old company taking advantage of our generosity, can we?"

I wasn't sure whether he was talking in general terms, or specifically about me. Not being in a rush to find out, I moved the conversation on: "You want me to vet people emigrating from the GDR?"

If this was the job the BKA had in mind for me then this mission was going to take a lot longer than expected. I'd have to prove myself, work my way towards the targetted position where I could get my hands on the material being leaked from my Firm.

"No, no. We have other plans for you." He waved his hand in a way that let me know that interrogating illegal emigrants was beneath me. "We want your help with information that we periodically receive. Obviously, we assess it ourselves, but we'd like to use your inside knowledge on cases where we don't yet have enough collateral."

"I could give it a go-"

"Frau Weber told us you have a background in analysis, I think you would be an asset to the BKA."

"And what do I get?"

Ingo looked at his hands, his mouth stretched even thinner than usual.

"You get to pay us back for our hospitality, you get a sense of self-worth by working your passage. I won't talk about fighting the good fight, democracy and freedom—it may be a little soon for that."

"Whatever you say."

Ingo stood up, he was smiling now, holding his hand out for me to shake.

"When I enter into alliances with the devil, I generally like to know who he's being represented by."

"Ingo, *Freiherr* von Horchheimer."

Blue blood. I should have guessed.

I stood up to accept the Baron's hand. As I did so, I looked him in the eyes. "Nothing would please me more than to work with the BKA," I told him.

49
WIESBADEN

The next morning saw me in an office which, if you could ignore the filing cabinet and the suitcase-sized portable computer on its own table in the corner—looked and felt more like an architect's living room than a place of work. Large and airy, floor to ceiling windows on two sides, furniture and décor less about comfort and more about style—basically, lots of glass, brushed steel and stained wood surfaces. The utilitarian metal filing cabinet and the unhappy ficus plant next to it were probably the only reasons this ensemble hadn't been made a regular feature in Office & Lifestyle magazine.

After being admitted by one of the clones, I was left to my own devices. Conscious of the possibility of surveillance, I didn't immediately start peeking into every corner of the room, but remained on the low leather sofa. Moving only my eyes, I scanned first the corners, then the top edge of the windows, paying particular attention to the pelmets that hid the workings of the vertical blinds. Seeing nothing that could point to a hidden camera—no unexplained boxy protuberances or coin-sized holes—I levered myself out of my seat and went to stand by the windows. Turning my back on them, I surveyed the other half of the office, trying to give the impression that I admired the occupant's taste.

The only mirror in the room was hanging on the wall to the corridor, which wasn't thick enough to house a camera—I'd noted the dimensions as I'd entered the office. Which meant that, other than behind or inside the heavy tomes housed on the ranks of shelves, I saw no options for a hidden camera.

I was still considering how to examine the bookcases in an inconspicuous manner when the door opened to admit a short man in his best years. His complexion was pasty, nearly half his face obscured by a pair of heavy glasses through which he peered, as if trying to locate me. He marched over to where I stood by the window, his hand outstretched. I recognised him from the pictures in Sachse's package of evidence that Weber and I had found in Berlin. This was *Polizeidirektor* Jüliger.

"*Doktor* Jüliger," he confirmed in a north German accent as he shook my hand.

"Reim, lately *Unterleutnant* of the Ministry for State Security of the German Democratic Republic," I responded.

If I'd expected him to screw up his face or flinch at the name of my employers, I'd have been disappointed. Jüliger gestured to the couch I'd just escaped from and I sat down again, the *Polizeidirektor* took a more comfortable looking chair to my right.

"I thought I should welcome you personally, thank you for your offer of assistance. Coffee will be here in just a moment, but before we really start, let me ask you-"

A knock at the door, and Baron Ingo skipped into the office, as if in a rush to forestall the proceedings. He was followed by a muscular fellow in a waiter's outfit: tray in hand, white linen napkin draped over his arm.

There was a moment when everyone in the room was looking at Horchheimer, then Jüliger jumped up and pumped his hand. "Ingo, glad you could make it."

He sat down, leaning to the side in order to see around the waiter who was arranging coffee pot, creamer, sugar and cups on the table.

Horchheimer waved the attendant away with his fingers and took over pouring the coffee. He filled Jüliger's cup first, adding a couple of sugar cubes and a heavy dash of cream, then turned to me.

"Now don't tell me—you take it black? Black and bitter as

Stalin's gulags?"

I didn't object, and he shunted cup and saucer over the polished table. It was as dark and heavy as promised.

Horchheimer took his with cream and no sugar, and when finally we each had a coffee in front of us, Jüliger and Horchheimer raised their cups to their lips. While they sipped their coffee, I looked over the Baron's shoulder, still intent on committing the office layout to memory.

"Where were we?" asked Jüliger in his vague way. "Yes, I was about to ask you ... One assumes these things, but perhaps it's better to have it all out in the open—tell me, Herr Reim, are you prepared to help the BKA in its duty to uphold the law and defend the constitution, parliament and institutions of the Federal Republic of Germany?"

I glanced at Horchheimer, who just the evening before had asked pretty much the same question, albeit in simpler terms.

"It is my duty, Herr *Doktor Polizeidirektor*."

Unaccountably pleased with my response, Jüliger squinted at me through his glasses, all the while groping for his cup on the table.

"Are you able to give me more information on the tasks I'll be assigned?"

Cup and saucer safely in his hands again, Jüliger turned his attention to Horchheimer, his glasses reflecting the low October sunlight.

"We'll brief you in the morning," answered Horchheimer. "Nothing too onerous, I promise—at least not to start with. Today you're just here for Herr *Doktor Polizeidirektor* Jüliger to have a look at you."

I was shown the door before I had a chance to finish my coffee —for all his short-sightedness, Jüliger must have seen enough of me. The clone in his standard-issue dark suit appeared at my side to guide me through a series of indistinguishable corridors until we reached the entrance.

At the main gate I was subjected to the same, heavy-handed search I'd experienced on the way in. While I was in the gatehouse, letting the sentries pat down pockets and jacket lining, I watched the regular employees come and go, holding up their passes as they walked through the turnstile or drove through the gate. I was marked for special treatment, and they didn't mind if I knew it.

50
BINGEN

Back in Bingen, Weber was sweating over a frying pan of spitting and brutzeling onions. Another large pan sat by the sink, ready to be drained. I paused by the door, feeling the need to check I hadn't inadvertently stepped into a West German soap opera.

"You like Spätzle? Everybody likes Spätzle—but how was it today?"

"I met Jüliger, he says I start tomorrow."

"That's good. I'll be in Wiesbaden tomorrow, I want to talk to a few people, see if I can somehow salvage my career. Help me carry these dishes through," said Weber.

The high pressure system that had brought us a sunlit autumn had been pushed out by cold air from the north, so sitting on the veranda was no longer an attractive proposition. We ate in the poky living room, listening to the snare of rain on the windows.

Once I'd complimented Weber on her Spätzle and polished my plate to prove the point, I crossed the room to look out of the low window, my hands pressed against the sill, watching the wind and rain thrash the autumn leaves from the trees.

"I like this kind of weather, shall we go for a walk?"

It seemed a phone call was no longer necessary, because Weber picked up her raincoat and headed for the door, but stopped long enough to give my synthetic suit a critical look.

"You don't have a coat?"

I shrugged. I had no rain-wear in my cupboard, and nobody

had given me West German Marks or offered to take me shopping, so it was inevitable I'd get wet sooner or later.

"You sure?" she checked.

I shrugged again and opened the front door.

We padded across the slick concrete of the terrace and slipped down the muddy path. My collar was flooded before we'd even reached the end of the garden, but I insisted we continue along the road and onto a hiking trail that led up the hill.

Ten minutes later, I could feel the cold rain dripping over my ribs and under the belt of my trousers, but we were deep in the woods, out of earshot of any interested parties. Surrounded by the patter of rain on mud, the creaking of bending trees and the rush of wind in the few leaves that still held on to summer, I felt it was safe to talk.

"I'm in position. Jüliger is putting me just where we hoped —analysing the leaks coming from the source in the MfS."

"From Sachse?"

"That's what I'm here to find out—whether or not it's him. And if it's not him, then who it is."

We walked in silence for a few minutes, stepping over exposed limestone ribs and fingers of roots, then: "I need you to tell me everything you can about the material. How it gets here, how it's handled. Everything. Even the rumours."

"I don't know much," she said. "In fact, the little I do know is from a chat I had with Portz back in February. It seems Arno Seiffert—your Source Bruno—picked up some hints that the Red Army Faction are being trained in the East. He cultivated the contact, who he christened Dresden, and the information kept coming.

"When Seiffert died, that information was still coming in and the contact needed a new handler, but neither the *Verfassungsschutz* nor the BND wanted to let the other take over. Doctor Jüliger stepped in. I don't know how he did it, but the BKA remained in control and in return, the intelligence agencies get eyes on the finished product and have input on any directions given to Source Dresden."

What Weber said sounded plausible, and tallied with the protocols I'd read from her interrogations.

"There are rumours that Jüliger keeps copies of the Dresden materials in his office ..." she paused to think for a moment. "I was there once, he was lost in some paperwork—as soon as he noticed I was in the room, he packed it all away."

"It could have been anything—hundreds of files must cross his desk every day."

"No, they weren't the usual, that's why I noticed them—the paper was thin, poor quality. Grey, pinkish, dirty yellow—anything but white, and the folders they were in looked unfamiliar, at least to me at the time. They weren't the kind we use at the BKA, they were a light buff colour, same as the ones the officer in Berlin had in front of him, the one who briefed me before I was allowed to come back here."

"You're saying he was looking at originals from the GDR?"

She nodded.

I reached into my pocket for a cigarette, but the packet was sodden, the cigarettes dissolving into a brew of tobacco and paper. Seeing my predicament, Weber hoisted out her own HBs and flicked a disposable lighter, shielding it from the rain with an open hand. I breathed life into the nail, watching while Weber lit her own.

"We should think next steps," I told her between puffs. "Things have gone well so far—getting access to the Dresden material was always going to be a gamble, even with you dropping hints in the right ears," I said. "But now it's worked, I'm in place and the mission is about to get a little more dangerous. If the source finds out that I'm on the team analysing his material then he'll take action to protect himself, and I'll be the one he's taking action against-"

"But how would he find out? Nobody's going to tell-"

"Weber, I respect you, but not this lot in Wiesbaden. I don't trust shiny pen-pushers like Jüliger not to go boasting about their new analyst. It doesn't matter whether it's the politicians in Bonn they go flapping to, or if they want to show off to the so-called professionals at the BND—word could get back to the source. And if it does, my life is at stake, and since you've been helping me, your life won't be worth much either."

Rain dripped onto my neck from the beech tree above, a line of cool water dribbled down my back. Shadows thickened under the trees, even though it was still early afternoon, and the tip of my coffin nail glowed bright in the dusk.

"But if what you say is true," Weber said, "if they don't observe confidentiality—and I'm not saying that's the case—well, there's nothing you can do about it, is there?"

"We can hurry things along—I really don't plan on waiting around for incriminating material to be handed me on a plate. I've got my own ideas how to identify the source."

"But your orders-"

"My orders are to wait and hope. But I'd rather have a rough reception back at Berlin Centre than a comfortable funeral over here." She didn't think that was funny, so I tried to put it in a more reassuring way: "Berlin doesn't care what I do over here, just as long as I bring them the source. If I have to break my orders to do so, there'll be a session of self-criticism, a reprimand and a pat on the back."

Weber started moving, so I followed her, my smooth-soled city shoes slipping in the mud. "What's the plan?" she asked, coming to a stop again. Behind her, a dark squirrel ran up the trunk of a tree, dodging bullets of rain.

"You're sure he keeps the files in his office?"

"I told you, he was looking them over like they were a valuable stamp collection."

"OK, I need to take a look at those files."

"In his office?"

"Tomorrow morning. And I'll need your help."

51
WIESBADEN

"The information you gave us during your debriefing—useful stuff." Ingo von Horchheimer was trying hard to come across as pally, but his body language was off. He'd shown me to a tiny desk in the corner of a large open-plan office, was now leaning over me, arms propped on the small amount of real estate I was sitting at. "Could we get you to write some of that down in a way such that it can be evaluated by our intelligence assessors?"

"You mean information like the conversations I had with *Polizeirat Doktor* Portz in Rostock and Berlin?"

"No. No, I ... Look, just stick to less complicated material for the moment. A description of Berlin Centre, what's on the menu in the officer's mess—that'll do for starters."

Got it. He wanted me to write up some *Katzendreck*, inconsequential material that at first glance might look interesting, but was of little actual intelligence value.

Horchheimer moved off, leaving me with a pen and a sheaf of virgin-white paper. He'd also told me where to find the clippings binders—heavy tomes containing keyword indexes of articles culled from the *Neues Deutschland* and the other Party newspapers in each district, along with the *Izvestia*, *Pravda* and other major Soviet newspapers—which I could use for collateral and to pad out sparse material with white-source intelligence.

I went to have a look at the binders, Horchheimer was on the other side of the room attempting to flirt with a young woman in a lime green pants suit. As I carried the folders back to my desk, I began to wonder why Horchheimer was interested in *Katzendreck* when he already had a source in the Firm was pulling in material.

My first thought was that they wanted more low-grade material to send back to Berlin so HV A could use it to cause HA II further embarrassment. But then I had the idea they might need it for domestic consumption. Did Horchheimer want something flashy enough to make the government think it was getting good value for all the Deutsche Marks it was pouring into the BKA—yet trashy enough that it didn't matter if the politicians told their secretaries and mistresses all about the top secret material they were privy to?

The idea of creating *Katzendreck* to be fed to gullible imperialists appealed to me, but the first possibility I'd thought of was the one that I found the most intriguing. If they wanted me to produce this dross purely to feed back to Berlin Centre, did that mean their source was no longer producing?

I worked through the morning, documenting the layout of Berlin Centre and some of the other central offices that are scattered throughout our half of Berlin. When I got bored with that, I switched to a paper on sports, avoiding for the time being General Mielke's well-documented enthusiasm for SV Dynamo and writing instead about Berlin Centre's bowling league—it had been a popular topic of conversation during my interrogation, so I thought they might like to hear more.

At midday, numbers in the office dwindled rapidly as the pawns headed off to lunch in pairs and small groups. I remained at my desk and continued writing, regurgitating the scores of each section and departmental team that I'd spent so long memorising during my stay at Magdalena.

Time oozed by, marked by the scratching of my pen and the return of the other workers, until finally my watch showed five to three.

Spotting Horchheimer, now trying his luck with another female at one of the desks towards the front, I left my seat and marched briskly up to him, stopping a discreet five or six metres short. I didn't quite click my heels, but merely standing to attention was enough to attract interest in this place.

Horchheimer looked first at me, then around the room, as if to check whether there was someone else I wanted to speak to. Finally he had to concede that it was him I'd come to see.

"Herr Reim, can I help?"

I closed the gap between us, and stopped again, this time standing at ease. "Herr von Horchheimer, your pardon, but I'm not used to these long hours ... the months in prison have taken their toll, you understand?"

"You've just had lunch."

"No, Herr von Horchheimer, I've been working here since receiving your instructions this morning."

"For heaven's sake, if you need a break then go for lunch, man!"

"*Zu Befehl,* Herr von Horchheimer!"

Having provided myself with an excuse to leave my post, I made my way to the canteen on the ground floor of the next building. The midday rush was long over and the tables were empty except for Jüliger talking with Weber over a cup of coffee and a slice of cake.

Jüliger had his back to me, one shirt-sleeved elbow resting on the melamine surface of the table. Next to the cups and plates lay a folded copy of the *Frankfurter Allgemeine Zeitung*. The presence of the newspaper on the table was Weber's signal that all was going well.

I hovered in the doorway for a moment, wondering whether I'd have to walk as far as the serving hatch in order to attract Weber's attention, but just when I was about to make my move, Weber's eyes lifted to the clock on the wall, then swivelled to the doorway, meeting mine for half a second before returning to Jüliger.

Catching her meaning, I headed around the corner to the toilets and waited.

Weber took only a couple of minutes to appear, and once I saw her coming, I entered the Gents and checked the stalls: all empty. I held the door open for her as she slipped into the first stall, pressing herself to the side to give me enough room to slide in behind her.

"I reckon I can hold him for another ten, fifteen minutes at the outside," she said as she handed over a pick gun and a small camera, a Minox 35—the same model she'd been using in Rostock when I first met her.

"I'll put them in the drop when I'm done." I slipped out of the toilets to check the corridor, then held the door open for Weber to make her escape.

She went left, back to the canteen. I went right, to the side door nearest the block in which the *Bonzen* had their offices.

52
WIESBADEN

I ignored the lifts and took the stairs up to the top floor, cautiously opening the fire door that gave access to a wide lobby that formed a central space on this floor of the building. The place was as empty as a Babelsberg film lot after a propaganda film has been wrapped, so I let myself in and marched down the corridors until I reached the isolated wing where the carpets are deep and the nameplates on the doors are made of brass.

Nearing my destination, I halted and wigged my grandma-ears, all the better to listen to the sounds of the building. No voices carried through open doors, no pulse of footsteps escaped the lushness of the woollen carpet, no drone of lifts going up and down the shaft. Satisfied, I genuflected before Jüliger's door and inserted the metal rod of the pick gun into the lock, followed by the hook of a torsion key. A final look up and down the corridor, then I pulled the trigger. My wrist jerked with the recoil of the rod tapping the lock while my other hand twisted the torsion key.

Using the torsion key, I carefully rotated the smooth lock through 360 degrees and pressed the handle down. The door swung open.

The office looked much as it had the day before, except for the addition of Jüliger's jacket draped over the back of a chair and an empty tea glass placed on the polished wooden desk.

A brief glance at the bookshelves—I still wanted to know whether they might be hiding a camera, but it seemed unlikely, and checking would waste valuable seconds—before I examined the lock on the lonely filing cabinet. Better quality than expected, but still crackable. Sorting through the various rods that came with the pick gun, I chose the most promising option and slid it into the keyhole. I pulled the trigger on the pick gun.

The boom as the pick hit the hollow interior of the metal cabinet was like a Leipzig punk band's kickdrum, it gonged around the walls before settling into a hum I could only pick up through fingertips resting on the surface of the filing cabinet. I'd just sounded the alarm on my own burglary.

Crossing to the door, I eased it open a centimetre—ears rotating like an Alsation's, trying to radar in on footsteps, voices or doors opening. But only the muffled sound of distant traffic reached my ears.

Closing the door, I took another look at the filing cabinet. The pick gun clearly wasn't the right tool for this job, but I could see no other way in, not without lock picks or a hand brace.

My watch told me I'd been here for three minutes, Weber had promised me at least ten—I still had a moment to think this over.

So I took another look at the bundle of rods, wondering whether I could use them, but none of them had any hooks or teeth. As handpicks, they were useless.

Turning on the spot, taking in the whole of the office, searching for inspiration, my eyes landed on Jüliger's jacket, draped over the back of his chair by the desk. A couple of strides took me to the jacket, but as I passed the window, my eyes involuntarily flickered towards the outside world. I had an excellent view of the yard below, and of Weber and Jüliger leaving the canteen building. As I watched, they stopped to shake hands, Weber was talking animatedly, trying to delay Jüliger's departure, but he was already turning away.

Leaving the window, I kneeled next to the jacket and pulled out the contents of the nearest pocket. Fuel receipts, a BKA identity card—I put the latter on the desk to take a snap with the Minox, then returned to the pockets. A packet of Montecristo cigarillos, a few small coins, fluff, a book of matches from Hotel Ress.

Second pocket: more fluff and small coins. A square chew in a colourful wrapper, brand: Maoam.

Breast pocket: a folded handkerchief. I stood up to look out of the window, Jüliger was no longer in sight, Weber was in the centre of the courtyard, staring up at the top floor. Resisting the absurd impulse to wave, I dropped to my knees again, hands now feeling the jacket's inside pocket. A light chain was pinned to the lining, it disappeared into the depths of the pocket. Pulling on it, I fished out a small key. Not the right size for the filing cabinet. My eyes darted around the room, looking for a lock this key might fit and coming up with nothing. No, not nothing—there, right in front of my face: the desk drawer. I slid the key into the lock and twisted. It was a match.

No time for more than a cursory rifle of the drawer's contents, my fingers scuffing past BKA-headed paper, a pot of ink, various fountain pens and a few more colourful squares of Maoam. I rearranged the contents of the drawer to conceal my intrusion and locked it, slipping the key back into its pocket.

Nearly finished, and not before time. A check of my own pockets, anything left lying around? Camera, various rods for the pick gun.

Over to the door, time boiling away, maybe already run dry and I just didn't know it yet. Another glance around the room —did I really have everything I came with? My heart, tapping at the front of my shirt, blood breaking like surf behind my eardrums. One hand already on the door handle, I looked over the room, an impression in the deep carpet next to the filing cabinet caught my eye—a shallow canyon across the base pattern.

I crossed the room in a couple of strides, knelt to feel the carpet. The pile had been brushed to disguise long-formed impressions: three heavy squares in a row next to the filing cabinet, all exactly the same dimensions. Once upon a time, there were four identical filing cabinets here; now there was just one.

No time to wonder about their fate, I was back at the door, opening it millimetre by slow millimetre. No sounds from the corridor, none to be heard above those made by my errant heart—*just get out of here!* I shut the door behind me, pushed the rod of the pick gun into the keyhole. It jammed. Tried to pull it out, it was still jammed, pull harder, wiggle it from side to side. Yanking at it, looking over my shoulder, another tug on the handle of the pick gun until it jerked out. Threading it into the lock again, more carefully this time, coaxing it into the narrow channel, but it still didn't fit. Another look down the corridor, no sign of company yet, was that the moment I should have run for it, left the door unlocked and hoped Jüliger would put it down to his own carelessness?

Then the realisation—I'd swapped the rods to crack the filing cabinet. *Slow down, Reim. Breathe.*

I pulled out the bundle of rods, selected the right one and fitted it to the pick gun. It slipped into the lock, a knife through warm butter. I pulled the trigger. A muted crack as it struck the pins and I eased the torsion key round. The lock twisted a full turn and the deadbolt slithered home.

Up the corridor, around the corner. *Don't run, look like you belong here.* Through the door into the lobby. A glance at the indicator above the lift. Number 5 was lit up, a bright ping, a dull clunk and the scraping of the lift doors as they lurched open.

I was already through the fire door—halfway down the first flight of stairs before Jüliger even left the lift.

53
MAINZ MARIENBORN

That evening, Weber and I met in a small bar in the dull western suburbs of Mainz. There were two species of clientele present: the artistic types from the nearby ZDF studios; and heavyset, ink-stained workers from the large printing plant. Just fifteen kilometres from the BKA Headquarters, but a million miles from where you'd meet any of their kind.

"Get what you needed?" asked Weber, but only after the bar staff had brought us our beers and we'd had a chance to observe the other drinkers for a while. She had a scarf around her neck, was tugging at it as if having difficulty breathing.

"Couldn't get past the lock." I told her about the problem with the rod from the pick gun beating the metal cabinet like a drum.

She tilted her head and narrowed her eyes, as if critical of my ability to pull off a simple burglary. Her hand went back up to the scarf. I noticed her nails were still as ragged as they had been on the bus from Karl-Marx-Stadt, the cuticles around her fingers raw.

"I didn't have enough time—you promised me ten minutes," I pointed out. And not unreasonably so.

"I don't know what that was about," her eyes slid away, towards a knot of women with oversized perms who were giggling into their cocktails. "At first he was polite, friendly even, but I lost him as soon as I steered the conversation around to coming back to work—he wasn't concentrating, you know: tapping his fingers, looking at those black and white portraits hanging above the tables and checking his watch.

Then he announced he had an important phone call to take and left. I followed him, tried to hold him up a little longer, but he wasn't having any of it."

Why would Jüliger grant an audience, then suddenly run out of interest when an able and proven operative asked to come back to work? Did the BKA suspect Weber of being too close to me?

Shunting the question aside for another time, I returned to the immediate problem.

"Did you retrieve the camera and the pick gun?"

"I stashed them—don't look at me like that, I have my secret stashes. Never know when you'll need them."

A stash—who'd have thought Western operatives would feel the need for such thing? And what did they keep in them, apart from burglary tools and micro-cameras? My mind briefly wandered over the contents of the emergency stashes I'd set up in and around Berlin: passports, money, pistols, disguises.

"No worries, I only took one picture. No hurry to retrieve the film—it can wait until I get a few snaps of those files. Talking of which—you need to find out when I can get into his office again."

"You want to try again?" She let go of her scarf long enough to lift her glass of Binding lager. "I don't see how I can help you again—I've no idea when he'll be away from his office—how can I? I'm no longer on the inside."

"Just find a reason to go to the BKA Headquarters, there's always some paperwork that needs a stamp and signature from the personnel office. Once you're there, visit old friends, listen to the rumours. Who knows, maybe something useful will crop up." *And something useful better crop up soon—before Source Dresden catches on that I'm sniffing him out.*

"Final thing," I said, putting my hand on Weber's arm. She was fingering her scarf again, looking around the bar and generally showing signs of wanting to leave. "I need you to make contact, we're already late—a phone number in Munich, just phone up and ask for a certain name-"

"I can't. I won't do that—I'll help with logistics around the core mission, just as I promised, but I can't afford to do more than that. Who knows who's listening in on that number, it might be recorded. If they tape my voice ..."

"OK, no worries," I had both my hands up, palms out, trying to reassure her. I couldn't push too hard, she'd already tried to quit on me once and I'd ignored her. "I just thought it'd be safer if you-"

"Reim, I've got something to tell you—I told Ingo I can't babysit for you any longer. I'm moving out of the house in Bingen, going back to my old flat, here in Mainz."

"If you're no longer my babysitter, who's going to take over?"

"Doesn't matter that much—everything you need to do will happen during work hours anyway. I'll tell you where I've cached the camera and tools on site, and we can stay in contact through dead drops." She was talking fast, still not looking at me. "Listen, I've set up two drop-offs and two pick-ups as well as a couple of reserves ...."

I didn't like what she was telling me, but I listened carefully anyway. If I couldn't persuade her to stay in the house in Bingen then knowing the protocol for filling and clearing those dead-letter boxes—four in Wiesbaden, one in Mainz and one in Bingen—would be critical for the success of the mission. Perhaps even for my own safety.

54
BINGEN

"I'll stay until Monday," Weber told me again over breakfast on Saturday morning. "They've not found anyone to take over yet."

"So what's next for you?" I attempted an empathetic expression, but she was too interested in cutting her bread roll to notice. "If the BKA haven't fired you but aren't giving you work then where does that leave you?"

"Paid leave." She left her roll on the plate, her hands disappearing below the table. From the twitching of her elbows I guessed she was picking at her nails again. "I just can't understand it—Jüliger refused point-blank to talk about when I could come back to work, Ingo tells me I need a rest. It doesn't seem to matter who I talk to, I just get stonewalled."

I'd seen this before, an operative cracking once the operational tension had eased a little. But even if she were no longer in the care of the KGB, she wasn't out of the rough yet. I needed Weber to hold it together just a little longer.

I was also concerned about the operational aspects of her being frozen out. Did her superiors really think she needed some downtime, or were they keeping her at arm's length until they'd worked out how much she gave away during interrogations by the KGB and my Firm?

"Sounds like you did the right thing, asking to be relieved of your babysitting duties. Frees you up for other tasks— maybe if you keep asking around, use your contacts ... Something will turn up sooner or later." I tried to keep my encouragement as general as I could make it, I couldn't speak too directly in this building with its hidden microphones. But Weber got the message: *hang in there, find out whatever you can from your colleagues.* Her elbows stilled for a second, then she got up to refill the coffee maker.

"Actually," she said as she spooned coffee into the filter, "talking about networking, there's a party tonight. Want to come?"

No, was the answer. While I had and would continue to engage with various individuals at the BKA to complete this operation, the more people I met and the more I talked to them, the greater the chance I might slip up somewhere along the way. That's why chummy get-togethers with Weber's colleagues were pretty far down my list of things to do.

But I didn't voice my concerns, and not just because of the microphones. Instead, I raised an interrogatory eyebrow, in the style of Baron von Horchheimer.

"I think it would do you good to meet some of the other people you work with—it's time you stopped being a refugee from the East and started to settle in ... It's a gathering for officers in the higher service." She nodded at me while she was talking, encouraging me to say yes.

A gathering for officers in the higher service—the old civil service ranking system, a constant ever since the days of the Kaiser, surviving the bourgeois Weimar Republic and the Nazis. It was one of the many little ways West Germany flaunted its revanchist ambitions.

"But what shall I wear?"

"Your normal suit will do." Weber laughed—not just a faded smile, but a genuine laugh of the kind she'd surprised me with when I'd first arrived in this safe house.

I thought about the cheap suits I'd been given. I'd worn one of them every day this week and it was already a little shiny around the elbows. Time to try on the other if I was going to a party.

55
WIESBADEN

That evening saw Weber and myself climbing out of a taxi at one of Wiesbaden's classiest restaurants. We were met at the entrance and ushered up a broad staircase.

A set of double doors opened onto a large ballroom, the décor of which owed some inspiration to the overblown villa Weber and I had been brought to when we first arrived from the GDR.

Baron Ingo was standing just inside the doors, dressed up like a penguin and missing only a top hat to make him look like the anachronistic throwback he was.

Predictably enough, he folded his upper half over Weber's fingers and slobbered a little. He took his time over it, postponing the moment he'd have to relinquish Weber's hand.

"Herr Reim, nice of you to join us," he murmured smoothly once he'd finally straightened up, although I noticed he still had hold of Weber.

"What are you doing here, Ingo? This is for the higher service," she said, taking back her hand.

"Well, it is true, I am in the *senior* service," he oiled, making sure everybody around him heard how he outranked the entire gathering, "I thought I'd look in, see how the troops are doing."

Troops? The population of this room was made up of ranks (in terms that made sense to me) between second lieutenant and captain.

"Of course, Ella insisted we drop by, she wanted to see the handsome junior officers," he swung around in an elaborate search for his wife, finally locating a pinched looking woman half his age in a dress reminiscent of a profiterole. In contrast to all the other women in the room, with their hair inflated by perms and hairspray, Ella had scraped her straight blonde hair into a severe chignon. She sensed she had an audience and turned away from a small group of women in short, angular business suits to fix Horchheimer with a theatrical smile. As she swept towards us, droplets of light from the chandeliers tinkled and ricocheted off her bright diamonds and sparklingly white teeth.

The movement of her feet remained invisible beneath the froth of her skirts, the peach silk billowing as she pulled up by Horchheimer. She indulged us with another view of her faultless teeth and extended her hand in my direction.

I may have defected to the West, but I still had my socialist upbringing to thank for the fact that I didn't copy the baron's example. Instead, I grasped Ella's hand, turning it sideways so I could shake it heartily.

The smile faded for an instant while her eyes flickered over my polyester suit, then she withdrew her hand and offered her arm to hubby, who clamped it safely under his elbow.

Having dismissed me, and showing zero interest in Weber, Ella had eyes only for Horchheimer, who suggested we try the canapés then marched his wife off to buttonhole someone more important.

I caught Weber's eye, but she looked away quickly, unsure whether to giggle or defend the baroness.

Weber's other colleagues and their spouses were generally more civil than Ella Horchheimer, but they all shared her discomfort in my presence and I heard the whispers behind my back—*Defector*, and the even less considerate *Pet Stasi*.

At some point, I left Weber's side and navigated my way through sidelong looks and whisperings towards a sideboard laden with exotic foods in doses small enough to guarantee I'd never satisfy my hunger, no matter how many morsels I popped into my mouth. I angled a flute of champagne from a passing tray and surveyed the food, unsure which of the canapés would provide the most calories.

A small pocket of men had somehow lost their wives and girlfriends and were using the opportunity to chat while openly ogling one of the waitresses as she carried a tray of drinks around the ballroom. They were so intent on the young woman's stocking-clad legs that they didn't notice me deciding whether to start with the midget *Rösti* or the salmon mousse-balanced-on-sliver-of-cucumber.

"We should call her over, get a glass of *Sekt* each," said a tall, middle-aged man with a bald head and a heavy moustache.

"We should call her over and get her phone number," joked a younger man by his side. Then, still ogling the waitress, he changed the subject. "You heard the old man is pretty much insisting on going to the TREVI prep in Strasbourg?"

"Thought that particular baton had long since been passed onto von Horchheimer?"

I decided to start with the *Rösti* but the plates were a few metres further along the table. Not wanting to move away from the indiscreet group to get a plate, I had no choice but to continue my consideration of the canapés.

"Apparently they're both going—Jüliger doesn't trust Horchheimer. I mean, fair play, if I were the old man I wouldn't trust Horchheimer after what he did! Bit of a coup, taking over that source in the Zone!" the younger one guffawed and lit a cigarette. "Mind you, he's clever, the Baron, always finding new ways to put pressure on Jüliger."

"So they're going to Strasbourg?" interrupted another. The waitress they'd been leering at had passed to the far side of the ballroom, and the men found a new object for their gaze. As one, their heads turned in the direction of a waitress reaching over a table to pick up empty glasses, causing her white blouse to gape, revealing a hint of lace-enclosed breast.

"There could be fireworks—things still haven't calmed down after the Baron announced he was bringing in the pet Stasi. Could be a good show"

Another pitched in with an anecdote about further friction between Horchheimer and Jüliger, all the time staring at the waitress.

"Let's see how they are when they get back, I for one would enjoy it if those two started arguing in public again—that'd brighten up my day no end."

"A plate, sir?"

The question came from behind me. At the sound of the waiter's voice, the posse of gossips turned to stare at me. As one, they moved off, suddenly having lost interest in the young woman whose breasts they'd been gawping at.

56
WIESBADEN

I left shortly after being caught eavesdropping. The mistrustful looks I was harvesting throughout the ballroom was tiring.

The doorman offered to order a cab, but I waved him away, preferring to walk down the hill to the main station while I digested the new information and adjusted my plans.

Weber had been right to insist I come to the party—I was more than satisfied with the nuggets I'd panned from the small talk and chit-chat. If it was true that Horchheimer and Jüliger were locked in a dynastic struggle, and importantly, that the younger man had taken over the star source in the East, then I'd been wasting my time targetting Jüliger's office. I needed to refocus my activities, and with both BKA officials planning to attend the TREVI meeting, all I had to do was find out when that was if I wanted a free run at Horchheimer's office.

It was while changing trains in Mainz, waiting for the stopping service to Bingen, that I noticed the shady character. He was shady inasmuch as he preferred the shadows between the columns that supported the platform canopy. He knew enough to avoid the pools of light cast by the lamps, and he kept his face obscured between the turned-up collar of a heavy herringbone overcoat and the narrow visor of his US Army-style jeep cap.

I ignored him, pacing instead to the end of the platform and lighting a nail as I waited. Only when the lights of the locomotive loomed out of the cutting did I walk back up the platform, just far enough to board the last carriage. I only looked directly at where the man had been standing once I'd pulled open the doors of the *Silberling* coach and was hauling myself up the steps. The niche that Mr Jeep Cap had occupied was empty.

Once aboard, I sat myself down where I could keep an eye on the interior door that led to the rest of the train, but my caution went unrewarded: I spent the journey alone, no other passengers were in the carriage, nobody used the connecting door. And when I alighted at Bingerbrück, the station nearest the safe house, the platforms were deserted. I climbed the steps up to the bridge, keeping my head bowed against the cold as I crossed the tracks and went down the other side, over the main road and on my way home, same as any other citizen.

On foot, the direct route to the house winds up the hill, alternating between residential streets and footpaths that cut between the hairpin turns the road takes. At the start, the route is wide and well-lit, but the further up the side of the valley I climbed, the narrower and more windy the path grew, until finally, the last section was a muddy, unlit track through the woods. I paused to light a cigarette, turning out of the slight breeze and giving myself a chance to look back down the hill. Had that been a shadow slipping to the side, or was it just my fantasy, fired by all the Rhenish *Sekt* I'd enjoyed at the party?

Once I had the cigarette glowing nicely, I turned back to the track. If the man in the jeep cap was following me then he was probably harmless, sent by the BKA to keep an eye on me. And even if he wasn't, I now knew he was there, and as the old ladies like to tell each other: *Gefahr erkannt, Gefahr gebannt*—danger detected, danger averted.

I reached the top of the footpath and crossed the road to enter the garden of the safe house. Once completely among the trees and bushes, I pinched out my nail and glissaded neatly into the shadows.

Whoever was following me, if he was still there, was clever enough to stay back far enough that I couldn't hear him, and it took me more than a minute to locate him. He was waiting on the other side of the wrought iron gate, not making any move to follow me into the garden. Instead, he was looking down the road, as if expecting company.

He wandered up and down like a sentry, out of my sight at the far ends of his chosen round, but now I knew where he was, I could almost catch the sounds of his boots grating and scuffing on the tarmac.

As the parallel lights of a vehicle strobed the woods, I eased myself lower to remain in the shadows as the car rounded the final switchback on the road below. It stopped by Mr Jeep Cap, who opened the passenger door and got in, exchanging a few low words with the driver as he did so.

The clumsy five-point turn that followed, with the car shunting the bushes to the right and the left, gave me enough time to recognise the shape of the headlights and the size of the body. Round lamps, like a Trabant's but spaced more widely, on a hatchback-style car: I was looking at a VW Polo.

I waited and watched as they headed back down the hill, leaving me to my shadows.

57
BINGEN

Weber left the safe house early on a dull, drizzly Monday morning. From my bedroom window, I watched her carry her single suitcase to the lime-green Polo that had come to collect her.

I was at the wrong angle to see the driver behind the windscreen, I couldn't tell you whether he was wearing a jeep cap or a dark woollen coat, but the fact that a VW Polo had turned up was a pretty big coincidence, if you choose to believe in such things.

Shortly after my babysitter had left, I walked down the hill to Bingerbrück station and caught the train to work where I was obliged to endure the usual shakedown at the gates. As the previous work day, and the one before that, they checked my pockets and patted down my legs and arms.

Finally permitted to proceed, I found my desk at the back of the hangar-like open office and began sketching out a report based on the notes I'd made the previous week.

I didn't possess enough actual facts to provide anything convincing, so had to use my imagination a little. As I sketched out my fantasy of made up facts, I reflected how Ewald and Schur should have foreseen this situation, This was a wasted opportunity to inject disinformation into the heart of West German intelligence operations, potentially wrapping them in confusion for years to come.

But without prepared material or a strategy, I could do little more than fabricate a range of plausible lies—everything from statistics on light industrial output to stock maintenance at the supermarket in the Berlin Centre compound.

Once I had written a fair draft, I went to see the head secretary, a thin, elderly woman with permed and dyed hair who favoured washed-out knit dresses. She sat at a high desk from which she could comfortably superintend the entire office.

When she noticed me heading in her direction, she closed the leather-bound notebook she had been writing in and crossed her hands over it, waiting patiently for me to arrive and tell her what I wanted.

"I need a typewriter."

Her lips pursed and one index finger began drumming on the notebook. "Have you written up what you want typing? I hope it's legible?"

"I'm to type it myself," I replied, in what I hoped was an authoritative air.

The finger stopped drumming, the lips narrowed further but eventually she must have decided to indulge me, nodding towards an ownerless electric typewriter a couple of aisles away.

Flattening my sheaf of notes, I started the report, the keys chattering busily with each peck of my index fingers. I didn't need to turn around to imagine the chief secretary pouting and rolling her eyes at my technique, but it had always worked fine for me.

After I'd rolled out the last page, I squared the small stack of paper against the top of the desk. The chief secretary called me over.

I gave the papers an extra couple of taps for good luck, then strolled across to her desk.

"Please sign for this," she said, handing me a ballpoint pen and sliding a form in my direction. Once I'd taken the pen, she picked up a long white envelope.

I signed on the dotted line and took the envelope, lifting the flap to see what was inside: four green 20 DM notes and a couple of grey tenners.

"One hundred Marks. Initial allowance for the procurement of items pertaining to the establishment of your household, to be set off against future income obtained through your engagement by the agency."

I was used to bureaucratic language, but the West Germans speak their own version, and I didn't quite catch her drift until I saw the pre-printed form she had taken from a drawer: *Temporary Assignment of Living Accommodation.*

Below the dense prose quoting relevant laws, ordinances and regulations, a section had been filled in with a typewriter:

```
Unmarried accommodation,
Sertoriusring, 6500 Mainz-Finthen
```

"Please sign there." She tapped a pulpy finger at the bottom of the form and I obliged.

Another receipt, then a pair of keys on a ring. I read the house and flat numbers typed on a piece of paper inserted into the plastic tag.

"I'm to move?" I asked.

"Your new accommodation is available from tomorrow afternoon. Have you finished typing your report? I'll put it in the tray for Herr *Kriminaloberrat* von Horchheimer."

I kept the report under my arm and took a step back. "Is Herr *Kriminaloberrat* not present today?"

"Meetings until 1530," she said, a little too quickly. She held her hand out for the report I'd just typed up.

"I shall give it to Herr *Kriminaloberrat* myself," I replied, pocketing the keys and money.

Back at my desk, I waited until the chief secretary had vacated her perch for a moment before I asked the fellow one row over where to find Horchheimer's office.

Having listened to his directions, I picked up my report and marched out of my building and across to the more upscale block where the brass hung out. Horchheimer's office was a floor below Jüliger's and in a different wing, but the dark brown carpets on his corridor were equally deep, although the artwork on the walls was more modern watercolour than heavy oils.

Finding Horchheimer's office next door but one to the Gents toilets, I gave his door a good rap. When no answer came, I waited a little longer before trying the handle.

The man himself was barely visible behind a rampart of stacked files. Looking over the amassed paperwork, he took off a pair of wire-framed aviator-style spectacles and made use of his eloquent eyebrows to let me know my intrusion was both unexpected and unwelcome.

"Herr *Kriminaloberrat*, my report." I took a few steps forward, far enough to place my pieces of paper on one of the piles near the edge of his desk.

He slid his reading glasses further up his nose and picked up my report, flicking through it.

"You type this yourself? Well, don't. Let Frau Pfaff take care of it next time." He placed the sheets on a side table, then returned to whatever he'd been reading before.

Now his attention was no longer on me, I looked around the office. Smaller and with average-sized windows instead of the floor to ceiling glazing that Jüliger enjoyed, but with exponentially more evidence of actual work being done. A row of mismatched filing cabinets—the last three of the same make and model as in Jüliger's office—paraded along two walls and a computer, this one a standard IBM-clone, stood on its own desk next to the windows.

"Anything else?" Horchheimer clearly hadn't thawed to my presence.

I gave him a salute and backed out of the office, my eyes taking in as much as they could as I slowly closed his door.

The last thing I checked before treading soundlessly back along the plush corridor was the lock. It was the same kind as Jüliger's, which meant it would be just as easy to open with the pick gun. But Weber would need to source some lock picks if I were to have any chance of getting into those filing cabinets.

The next day Horchheimer came to find me at my desk.

"Interesting report, Herr Reim."

I sat back in my chair and watched his mobile eyebrows, trying to work out whether he was mocking me.

"How much more of this kind of thing can you give me?" He looked at the pages of notes spread over my table, picked one up and tried to read it but gave up and put it back down. It had taken me years to develop a shorthand so arcane that only I could decipher it, and even I sometimes struggled.

"A good report—I want more. But first ... here, could you ...." he fished around in the inside pocket of his jacket and pulled out a piece of paper. I recognised it as being a page from the report I'd given him the previous day. "This bit here —do me an authentic looking report based on this."

I read the paragraph he was pointing at, it was something I'd made up about increasing the production of 64kb RAM modules. I knew they had something to do with electronics, but had no idea what these modules were, what they did or where they were used. I'd need some help if I was going to fatten it up for even the shortest report.

"Authentic looking?"

"What we need is something that looks like a copy of an internal document on production schedules for these RAM modules," Horchheimer said. He was stooping over my table, the cigarette in his hand shaking a little.

"An MfS internal report? Or one from the Robotron production sites?"

"Your lot, the Stasi." He sipped at his cigarette for a moment or two, looking at the smoke, then, tapping his temple to show he'd just had a brainwave: "Can you make it look like it's been through Counter Intelligence's hands? Yes, that'd be good—can you do that?"

He wanted me to make it look like this fabricated report had been leaked from Lieutenant Colonel Schur's department.

"Not a problem, I'll make that look like it's come from HA II. But then it'll need a distribution list and a name or code for the author."

"Don't worry about all that—we'll do it in such a way that it looks like the circulation directions have been cropped off the top—just make sure there's something in the text that clearly links it to HA II. Start on that right away, any other tasks can wait."

"It'll be ready by tomorrow midday, Herr *Kriminaloberrat*."

"Actually, no. No need—Thursday sometime will be fine. Yes, hand it to Frau Pfaff on Thursday morning and she'll have it typed up for my return."

I watched Horchheimer disappear down the aisle between the desks, stopping every so often to lean over one pretty female assistant or another.

It sounded like my man would be going to the TREVI meeting tomorrow.

58
WIESBADEN

I left the office soon after Horchheimer's visit. Had anyone bothered to ask, I would have told them I was off to find supplies for my new flat, but other than the burly guards at the gate, nobody was interested in my movements.

It's a forty-minute walk from the BKA Headquarters to the station, along leafy streets lined with oversized houses, then through the pedestrianised city centre. I stopped at the first bookshop I saw and broke the hundred Marks I'd been given on a street map of the twin cities of Mainz and Wiesbaden, a small notepad and a soft pencil. With my purchases stowed in a sports bag given to me by Weber along with the rest of my belongings, I continued towards the station.

A little further on I came to the Church of St. Bonifatius, a squat red sandstone building with spindly towers that reached for the grey sky. As a rule, I've no time for churches, but that afternoon I pushed open the heavy wooden door and entered the cheerless scent of dust and frankincense. Tapping and shuffling noises drew my attention to the choir gallery above the main entrance, a couple of men in overalls were dismantling an organ pipe in the glare of a portable spotlight. Scaffolding had been erected for the renovations, and I had to thread between the steel legs to enter the body of the church.

I sat myself in a pew in the right aisle, prepared to think pious thoughts and observe the rhythms of the church. But my thoughts were neither pious nor pressing—the operation was progressing nicely, even if Weber had proved to be less of an asset than hoped—so with nothing much else to occupy my mind, I concentrated on the observation side of things.

It was gloomy in the nave, the hanging lamps did little to pierce the thin darkness, but I could still see the priest bobbing around the chancel clearly enough. He wandered around, seemingly without reason, kneeling and crossing himself every time he passed the altar. When he finally disappeared from view, the discreet clatter of a door told me he had left.

Above me, the workmen were still scraping and hammering, occupied with their own tasks.

I tore a page out of my new notepad and, resting it on the back of the pew in front, wrote a short note.

On my way back out of the church, I slid the note into the open mouth of a horizontal scaffolding brace and, on the next but one standard along, I turned my hand slightly so that the piece of chalk held between my fingers could scrape across the metal, leaving a yellow mark.

It took me much longer than could be reasonably expected to reach the estate I was to call home—but catching trams in the wrong direction tends to slow down travel plans. It also helps to show up idle tails who think they know where you're going.

I alighted at the wrong end of Mainz, indulged in a cursory dry-clean and then went hunting for a phone box.

Once in the yellow cabin, I slotted thirty Pfennigs home and dialled a number in Munich.

"Bierberg und Wieps, *grüss Gott.*"

"I have a case I'd like Herr Wieps to take a look at—is he still practising? He was my father's lawyer."

"Shall I put you through to his office?"

"No thank you, I'll call again in a couple of weeks."

That was it, a message would now begin its circuitous and covert journey to Berlin, telling them their operative was in position and had begun work.

★

Back at the main station, I changed to the tram for Finthen, alighting again just off a few stops later when I saw an Aldi store. The shop assistants were as unfriendly as those at any HO or Konsum back home, but here the shelves were stacked with cardboard boxes, the fronts ripped open to allow customers to take whatever they wanted. Having done the rounds, reminding myself of the sheer, glistening abundance available here in the West, I waited in a long queue, finally being permitted to pay for my bread and sausage, putting them in a plastic bag along with a bottle of cheap schnapps and a couple of beers.

Waiting for the next tram, I shivered in the chill air; the year was ebbing away and I needed a warm coat. But I also needed to keep as much of my initial cash allowance as I could —if I had to make a run for it then a bundle of readies in the pocket could mean the difference between escape and starvation.

59
MAINZ FINTHEN

The tram tracks looped under an elevated stretch of motorway and through a stained new-build district which almost gave me another spike of homesickness.

It seemed every block of flats in the housing project—over 300 of them, going by the house number I was looking at—had an address on Sertoriusring, and I couldn't work out what logic, if any, there was to the numbering system.

The day had already given up the struggle in this abandoned corner of Mainz, and the underpowered street lighting wasn't up to the job of helping me navigate between spindly saplings and expanses of deep mud, broken glass and general rubbish.

Aggravated by the general gloom and struggling to find my block, I didn't notice the gang until I'd practically walked into them.

They were kids, really. Lads who hadn't yet had the pleasure of legally ordering a schnapps at the bar, but that didn't make the situation any less alarming. Five of them were arrayed across the path in front of me, and a reserve hung back in the shadows beyond a knocked-out lamp.

I straightened a little to appear taller, threw my shoulders back to widen my silhouette and aimed for the largest gap. The nearest two, both sporting permed mullets, thin sweatshirts and stone-washed jeans moved together to block my way.

"Alright, lads?"

"Where's he from? Anyone understand him?" demanded a

short but wide kid to my left. He sounded adenoidal.

The others moved close enough for me to admire their pimply coupons, a few began to mimic my Berlin accent, also giving the general impression of suffering from congested sinuses. Perhaps it was just the local dialect.

Seeing the ring tighten around me, I let go of my Aldi carrier bag, swivelled on my heel, dropped a shoulder and, without hesitation, rammed the biggest lad. He staggered backwards, folding over to try to get some air back in his lungs, and while he was busy with that, I hooked my foot around his calf and tipped him in the mud. He went down with a squelch, and only then did his mates think to react. The next one in line made a grab for my jacket, another pulled at the sports bag still slung over my shoulder, but ignoring them, I put my shoe on the throat of the boy I'd just dropped. I pressed on his Adam's apple a little, enough to show I meant business, but not enough to cause any lasting harm, then once I was satisfied he'd understood, I lifted my foot a millimetre or two so he could get the air he needed to start whining.

"Any of yous make a move and he's history." I didn't need to raise my voice, I just used my foot to regulate the volume of the whimpering coming from ground level. I played him like an organ until the others backed off a little, their faces inscrutable in the darkness, then I bent down and pulled the lad out of the mud by his wrist, quickly twisting the arm behind and up his back before he got any clever ideas. He realised he couldn't move, but that didn't stop him moaning about it. I shoved his arm further up his back until he shut up, his knees weakening.

I moved backwards, pulling him with me until I was up against a junction box that stood in the middle of the mud like a gravestone. Feeling less exposed, I took my time assessing the group that still surrounded me.

"You can drop that right now," I told a tall, thin kid in a grimy nylon jacket. I stared at him until a sliver of light fell to the concrete walkway.

"Kick it over to me," I ordered, and he gingerly tapped the knife with his foot so that it skittered over the edge of the cement pathway and onto the clogged grass. I dragged it towards myself with the heel of a shoe, then stamped it into the mud.

"Anyone else got anything they don't need any more?" A couple of hands moved towards pockets, the others remained where they were, hanging sullenly by shivering torsos. "OK, listen. I live here, and I'm glad I came across you lads, because now I know you and you know me. I know where you live. Any hassle off any of yous"—I looked around the faces and momentarily tightened my grip on the big lad's arm so he gave a dramatic whine—"I won't be running to the bulls. No, I'll be coming for every single one of you—and if I can't find you, I'll find your families and your mates. Got that?"

I waited until each of them had either nodded or murmured something that could be interpreted as reluctant agreement, then let go of the kid, giving him a quick push to tell him to join his crew. "A bit of respect, and we'll have no problems."

I reached into the mud below my feet and freed the knife, a short hunting number with a serrated blade and gutter for the blood. Not the kind of thing children should be playing with.

Another look around, one or two of my antagonists had backed off, others were staring at their feet, avoiding both my gaze and that of their humiliated friend who was trying to work out whether to rub his arm or his throat. Keeping the knife ready in my hand, I picked up my sports bag and shopping and continued the search for my accommodation.

60
MAINZ FINTHEN

I found my flat near the northern end of the housing project, at the top of one of the grey blocks. The light in the stairwell had blown, so it took me a while to get the door open, but when I did, I found a pokey one-roomer with grand views of brittle trees, mud and other flats.

I dumped my bags next to the bed. There were no bedclothes, the kitchen was empty and where you'd expect the light fittings, wires poked from a ragged hole in the concrete ceiling.

"Welcome to the degenerate excesses of consumerism in the capitalist West," I said to myself, standing in the scraps of moonlight that managed to penetrate the uncleaned windows. Hardly the hero's apartment a defector dreamed of, but at least the size of the place and the absence of a second bed told me I would no longer be expected to put up with a babysitter.

The light above the mirror in the bathroom worked, so I used it to check my watch. Nearly seven o'clock—shops would be shut by now, I couldn't even go and buy some basics like a light bulb or a bar of soap, never mind bedsheets and blankets. The hundred Marks I'd been given looked less generous now I knew it would have to stretch to everything from coffee to pillows.

I pulled a kitchen chair across the room and sat down to examine my new street map by the light that fell through the open door of the bathroom.

★

The next morning I left my flat in the greyness of morning and hiked across the mudfields towards the tram stop. As I reached the junction box that marked the site of the previous night's altercation, I paused. Had I overreacted? No, the hunting knife I'd confiscated proved I hadn't overestimated the threat.

Reminded of the knife, still in my jacket pocket, I realised I had to get rid of it before arriving at the BKA—wouldn't want the goons at the gate to get the wrong idea about me.

About to continue on my way, I saw a movement beside the low enclosure that held a clutch of waste bins. I watched the corners and vague shadows until I was sure: it was the big lad, the one I'd tripped into the mud.

"Hey! Get over here!" The shadows resolved themselves into a more solid shape which began to shuffle towards me.

As he made his slow way, I lit up a nail, keeping pack and lighter in hand. Once within attacking distance he stopped and looked down at his white trainers, still smeared with dry mud.

I held out a cigarette. He looked up, surprised, then took it. I let him borrow the lighter.

"Wasn't counting on seeing you this morning, shouldn't you be in school?"

His grey face was studded with acne and he was shivering beneath his cheap, grey sweatshirt. He puffed on the cigarette as if convinced it would warm him.

"What's your name?"

"Jens," he managed, after a pause to think. He probably didn't want to tell me, but without his mates here to back him up, he calculated he couldn't afford to give me any cheek.

"Right Jens, remember this?" I held up the hunting knife and he took a step back. "Give it back to the lad I took it off, yeah?"

He nodded, holding out a shaking hand.

"I'm not here to cause trouble, but if it comes my way I can deal with it. Know what I'm saying?"

Another nod. This time he raised his face far enough to meet my eyes for a whole second or two.

"You get around a bit, don't you? Well, I need you to do me a favour—it'll be worth your while." I pulled out a few of the twenties that were still weighing down my suit pocket and showed them to him. "See these? Here's twenty Marks now, call it an upfront payment. You in?"

He nodded again and reached for the money, but I pulled my hand back.

"I haven't told you what I want yet. Now listen—if anyone comes snooping around here, I want to know about it. You know where my flat is don't you?"

Another nod, a little more confident this time.

"How?"

"F-Followed you last night."

"Good lad," I let him have the money. "You see anyone hanging around, anyone who doesn't belong, tell me. Got that?"

"Do I get more dough if I see someone?"

"Yeah, all of you do—but you've got to be on the lookout— all of yous, all the time. Got it?"

The kid had found his confidence again, the humiliation of the previous night forgotten. He nodded with enthusiasm as he pushed the money into his jeans pocket. The knife had long since disappeared, though I'd not noticed where he'd stowed it —looked like this kid could teach me a trick or two.

"Here." I passed him a piece of yellow chalk. "You see anyone who doesn't belong, put a mark on the shelter by the tram stop, about so high. One for each person—two men come, put two little lines there. And when they go, cross them out. That bit's important—cross it out, don't rub it out. I want to see whether you're doing your job. You don't do that, you don't get paid."

"Not even half?"

I grabbed him by the front of his sweatshirt and jerked him towards me, keeping an eye on his hands in case the knife decided to make a reappearance. "Nothing. Either you do the job properly or I get someone else to do it. *Capito?*"

He nodded again, so I let him go.

61
WIESBADEN

I took a detour through a park on the way to the BKA offices, hoping to see a chalk stroke on the memorial dedicated to a long-dead worthy, but when I pushed through the dripping bushes to check the back of the stonework, it was marked only with moss, lichen and droplets of condensed water vapour. And no sign in yellow chalk meant no response from Weber after my note the previous night.

I was being a little unreasonable, hoping for a reply so soon —we'd agreed to check the central dead drops every few days —but that didn't stop me feeling a little resentful about the fact that Weber hadn't checked the dead drops in the last twelve hours.

Nevertheless, time was pressing. Unless she came through with a set of lock picks by the very next day, I'd lose this opportunity to search the filing cabinets while Jüliger and Horchheimer were at the TREVI meeting in Strasbourg.

Resigned to the possibility I might have to wait for a long time before another opportunity to raid Horchheimer's office came along, I trudged further up the hill towards the BKA, along quiet roads of villas and parks. Even up here, a hundred vertical metres above the Rhine, trails of mist floated past, sometimes twisting into transient fog before fading into wisps of haze.

The inevitable pat down at the entrance to the BKA Headquarters was just their way of welcoming me to another eight hours of creating valueless *Katzendreck* for my temporary masters. I'd been here for a matter of days, yet already I could see what life would be like if I remained in the West—days spent spinning up worthless material—perhaps later graduating to assessment and report writing, punctuated by barely tolerable lunches in the canteen and cigarettes at my desk.

Yet the Westmarks they'd already given me provided a faint gleam of comfort that morning. With money in my pocket I'd been able to decide which brand of nails I wanted to smoke, the first time I'd been able to choose since I'd come over here.

Trouble was, it had been a difficult choice—so many brands on offer: Lucky Strike, Marlboro, Eve, Kim, Benson & Hedges, Stuyvesant, Ernte 23, West, Gitanes, John Player Special ... I stood by the kiosk at the main station this morning, eyes flicking from one colourful packet on the shelves to the next, trying to guess which might taste the most of home.

I recognised a few of the decks—I'd had a couple of *Polizeirat* Portz's Gauloises in the days we'd been thrown together in Berlin and Rostock, I'd smelled the flat tang of Marlboro around the upper corridors of Berlin Centre, had tried Weber's HBs and during my interrogation, the clones and the interrogators had always given me Camels or Lucky Strikes.

Unsure which to go for, and unsettled by the kiosk owner's palpable impatience, I'd plumped for a red soft-pack, attracted by the old-fashioned line drawing of a hand on the front. I added them to the tourist map of the Rhine-Main area that I'd already selected.

But when I lit up my first filterless Roth-Händle I realised I'd chosen the hard-core option—even stronger than Merkur's filterless Gauloises, more like the sharp papirosas KGB Major Pozdniakov sometimes offered me. When I inhaled, the smoke tore at my lungs, causing me to cough and pat my chest as I turned away from the appalled gaze of commuters hurrying out of the station.

Now, in the early afternoon, I was on my ninth Roth-Händle and had grown used to the dark tobacco. Mind you, I still had to be careful not to inhale too deeply—the prim Western drones in the office wouldn't appreciate Roth-Händle-induced fits of expectoration.

When I alighted from the tram at Finthen that evening, my eyes went first to the concrete shelter on the other side of the tracks. A couple of passengers were waiting, so for the moment, I did nothing but peer surreptitiously into the dimness of the shelter—was that a yellow mark above that old gent's shoulder? Unsure, I walked a hundred metres south, away from the housing project, and lit another of my new brand of nails, waiting until the audience had departed.

The tram screeched around its turning circle and rattled up to the stop, pausing to take on the new passengers before beginning the long trek back to the centre of Mainz. Only once it had ground round a bend in the road did I finish my cigarette and walk back to check whether what I had seen was indeed a chalk mark.

And there it was—a long yellow stroke, bisected by a hasty vertical. My young scout had spotted a stranger.

It didn't necessarily mean much, but it was more than enough reason to show some caution as I approached my flat.

I saw Jens, lurking around the bins again, and I stopped beneath the broken street lamp, lighting another cigarette and waiting for him to come over. When he did, he was trailing a couple of his pals a few metres behind. They gave me sidelong glances, like cats unwilling to meet a potential adversary's gaze.

"Y'alright," he said in his congested accent.

"You've been keeping your eyes open, I see." I offered him a Roth-Händle, noting how he clocked the red pack and put the cigarette behind his ear to smoke later, possibly when no one else was around to sneer as he spat up his lungs.

"Yeah, you know—me and the lads are always on the lookout. Got to look after our patch, know what I'm saying?" He was playing up for his pals, squaring up to me a little, talking like an actor on a badly scripted American television show. The two adjutants, emboldened by his attitude, came closer. One of them was the straggly kid who'd pulled the hunting knife on me the previous night.

"OK, who did you see?" I pulled out a ten Mark note, holding it folded between my fingers.

"Some bloke. Never seen him before. Blue overalls and blue jacket—went into your block."

"When?"

"Dunno. About three—what do you reckon lads? Three o'clock?"

"Yeah, about then."

"Carrying anything? Any tools? A bag?"

"Yeah. He had, like a box it was. Looked heavy. Took it up to Frau Weyer."

The two teenagers at the back laughed, one of them slapping Jens on the back. He grinned. "Bo-Frost man, it was the Bo-Frost man!"

I didn't know the Bo-Frost man, and Jens was sharp enough to pick up on my ignorance.

"Don't know the Bo-Frost man, innit!" he said, turning to the others to share his incredulity.

"Has he been here before?" I asked, keeping my voice level.

"Nah, always a different one, but they always look the same in their sad-case uniform. Always Tuesday when the freezer delivery van comes." He smoothed the air in front of him. "Bo-Frost, it says on the side of the van."

"OK, keep it up—there's more in it for you if you spot anyone interesting." Jens snatched the ten Mark note from my hand and the three kids ran off, yelling something unintelligible in their asthmatic dialect.

A false alarm—home deliveries of frozen goods seemed to

be a regular occurrence here, as alien as the idea seemed to me
—but I still carefully checked the paint-smeared stairwell and
hallway before letting myself into my flat.

Cursing myself for forgetting to buy or steal a lightbulb, I
switched on the lamp above the sink in the bathroom and
scanned my accommodation in the meagre light. Nobody here,
no subtractions to my few belongings, and certainly no
additions. Not even a pack of frozen peas or cream spinach
from the Bo-Frost man.

62
WIESBADEN

The weather the next morning somehow contrived to be even more dismal. I stared through the train window, hardly able to see any further than the steel latticework of the bridge over the Rhine. Freighters pushed through grey water, lonely foghorns vibrating the woollen mist.

When I left the station, I found the centre of Wiesbaden barely more tangible than the Rhine had been—the soft edges of high buildings appeared and disappeared in the sporadic beams of car headlamps, and the visible stench of exhaust fumes added to the fog.

Instead of clearing as I climbed higher towards the BKA Headquarters, the mist seemed to emerge from the forest above, rolling down the hillside and through the streets to the river valley. But up here, the moisture-laden air was odourless. I sniffed again, missing the homely spice of brown coal smoke and the sharpness of two-stroke exhaust that would be hanging over Berlin on a foggy day.

Once I entered the little Dambachtal Park, the whiteness tightened its chilly grip and the rufous leaves of the oaks and horse-chestnuts segued into a blank backdrop. Visibility was no more than fifteen metres, and the dampened sound of cars and pedestrians dopplered in from all directions and none. I paused by the industrialist's monument, listening for a moment before stepping closer to examine the chalk marks at the back: two circles.

Weber had actioned my request.

★

The guards at the BKA gatehouse were a little disconcerted by my enthusiasm that morning. They'd become used to surly acquiescence, so my change of mood was enough of a reason to search me more thoroughly than ever. Instead of the usual dip into my pockets, the contents were placed on a table before me and investigated in the manner of our own customs officers at border crossings into the GDR.

For the first time, the younger of the two guards spoke to me. He'd opened the brand-new packet of Roth-Händle cigarettes, tearing the foil off the top to look inside, then, as he returned the deck to me: "Acquired a new taste in cigarettes?"

"Want one?" I stepped forward and held the packet out to him, my other hand reaching for my lighter, waiting on the table next to the broken sticks of yellow chalk.

He hesitated, glancing at his colleague who was distracted with prising the inner-sole out of my left shoe, then shook his head. Interesting dynamics, I thought. And interesting also that he was observant enough to note the recent change in my brand of cigarettes.

My Roth-Händle were enjoyed outside that day, an excuse ready on my lips, but no one was interested in hearing how I feared further complaints if I smoked the dark tobacco at my desk.

Standing by the door of my own block, I contributed to the general haze lying over Wiesbaden, keeping an eye on the building where the brass had their offices.

The general traffic in and out seemed to be at usual levels: the occasional secretary with an armful of files, a dark Mercedes pulling up at the door and disgorging senior officers and identically besuited minions. But thankfully, no sign of Horchheimer, who I knew enjoyed a wander around his fiefdom, nor of Jüliger, whose movements were, if anything, even more arbitrary than the young pretender's.

★

I left for lunch late, waiting until my colleagues began to drift back, brushing droplets of moisture from their shoulders and sleeves as they entered the office. Noting the absence of the chief secretary, I rolled up my latest typed report and put it in an inside pocket, then went to the canteen.

I chose and ate a meal without knowing what I was tasting, waiting it out until the place was empty of any face I even vaguely recognised. Once the time was right, I took myself off to a storage cupboard on a little-used corridor on the second floor.

Using the steel shelves as a stepladder, I pushed at a tile in the corner of the ceiling and stuck my hand into the cobwebbed darkness, groping around until I had hold of a plastic bag. Catching the weight as it slipped through the gap, I opened it up: a pair of cotton gloves, the pick gun and a decent set of lock picks in a leather wallet.

Slipping them into my pocket, I left the building to cross the courtyard to the block where Jüliger and Horchheimer had their offices. I entered just as a group of suits exited; I didn't look at them, and they didn't bother to look at me.

Taking the stairs to the fourth floor, I paused long enough to peer through the glass fire doors while I checked the air was clear. Seeing no passing bigwigs or secretaries, I marched across the open space of the floor lobby and into the corridor that led to the south wing.

The framed modern art hanging in the hallway outside Horchheimer's office was as sparkling and clear of dust as the last time I'd been here, the carpet immaculately vacuumed and the recessed strip lighting buzz- and flicker-free. The only sounds in the hushed wing were the crackle of my heart and the rap of my knuckles on Horchheimer's door.

Hearing neither an answer to my knock, nor the shuffle or scrape of human movement, I pulled on the cotton gloves and inserted the pick gun and torsion key into the keyhole. A final look up and down the corridor, then I pulled the trigger and twisted the lock.

I pressed on the handle and pushed the door open far enough to slip inside, then stood for a moment, taking in the whole of the room. Piled files still cluttered the desk and the row of pregnant filing cabinets were still waiting to give up their secrets.

Mindful of my narrow escape in Jüliger's office a few days before, my first move was to the window, looking down to check on any activity in the courtyard below, but the fog had closed in again, turning the world outside grey.

With a nimbleness borne of years of handling files, I sorted through the folders on Horchheimer's desk, reading each title for mentions of the source I'd been sent to identify, or anything else relating to the GDR. Practically the whole stack was of criminal cases—Chancellor Kohl's visit to the People's Republic of China being the only exception—so I left the desk and positioned myself by the filing cabinets, looking out of the window again as I passed.

The drawers were labelled alphabetically, so I put my picks to use on the cabinet containing the Ds. It was a difficult lock, and I had to try out a couple of the hooks before I found the one that fit. Concentrating on my task, I turned the plug fractionally with each pin that I managed to push up, until, when lifting the fifth pin, the whole lock turned smoothly, pulled around by the torsion key I'd kept under pressure the whole time.

I pulled open the bottom drawer, marked *Do-Fa* and let my fingers march through the hanging folders until they reached several that were fattened to bursting point.

I pulled out the first and flicked open the cover to reveal the title page, rocking back on my heels with self-satisfaction: *Agent Dresden (1984)*. The next few files bore similar titles: *A. Dresden (1983/i)* and *A. Dresden (1983/ii)*, then *Agent Dresden (DDR) (1981-82)*.

I took the first file for 1983 to the desk, automatically

glancing out of the window as I passed—the fog had cleared a little, I could guess at the outlines of the block where I worked —and I spread the file open ready for the miniature camera and wound on the film.

The first hundred or so pages of file 1983/i looked familiar— the material tallied more or less with the reports I'd spent a couple of weeks analysing in the half-built signals base back in June. I took a picture of the schedule that showed the material had been passed on by Agent Dresden, then leafed through the pages rapidly, my eyes catching odd snippets of new material. But I didn't stop to read. My priority was to find anything that might help us identify Source Dresden—only once I'd found that could I afford to find out what other secrets he'd betrayed.

The pages I flicked past were smooth, slightly shiny, as if each had been ironed—photocopies. But just over halfway through, the quality of the paper changed, and I lifted about a centimetre of paperwork out of the way to get to that part.

And there was Agent Dresden, staring back at me from a photograph: sitting at a table on a terrace, a glass of wine in front of him, the grey shoulders of men in suits cropped out of the shot. Autumn-bright vines curled up the iron stanchions and over the wooden handrail of a balustrade, and behind the table, further vines climbed the rendered walls of a two-storey residential building. The plaster around the windows was picked out in a darker colour.

The roofs and half-timbered gables of neighbouring houses queued up beyond the terrace, and over their shoulders peered a high, naked cliff. I leaned in to identify a couple of blotches of colour near the top of the rock: flags.

Letters and numbers were typed below the picture—a classification mark—followed by a short description:

```
09.09.83 Agent Dresden's
house-warming in 6532 Urbar
```

I slumped into Horchheimer's chair and stared at Agent Dresden, the source I'd been searching for.

It was a clear enough photograph, there was no doubt who I had in front of me. His white-blonde hair and light eyes showed clearly on the black and white print. One side of his mouth tugged down in a sneer, even at his own party.

This was the man who had killed friends of mine, both old and new, and had nearly done for me. This was the man I'd come to the West in the hope of finding.

This was *Oberleutnant* Gerhard Sachse.

63
WIESBADEN

I took a photograph of the page with the picture of Sachse and his West German house, along with the following pages of accounts showing payments made to him since the beginning of that year. Turning over again, I found a property contract, signed by Horchheimer and Sachse (using the alias Dresden) and notarised, but no address to link the contract to the house in the picture. The first clause referred only to the *Property subject to the Contract signed by the below parties on the 9th of September this year.*

This was good material, but I still lacked a trail of evidence so wide and clear that even the brass back in Berlin could follow it. I needed something in writing to definitively identify Source Dresden as Sachse, and to show how he was profiting from selling out his country. Without that, Sachse and the HV A could still deny he was Dresden, find some clever way to cover up that fact he was committing treason.

Leaving the thick folder open on the desk, I crossed back to the filing cabinets and pulled out the earliest file, marked 1981-82. If this were an asset's file in Berlin Centre, I'd expect to find a handwritten statement of commitment signed by the subject himself—but did the West Germans also insist that an asset incriminate himself in that way?

Carrying the papers back to Horchheimer's desk, crossing in front of the window, I took another look at the grey world outside. The fog was thicker than ever, there was nothing to be seen beyond the glass.

But as I turned back to the desk, about to put the folder

down, the grey blankness outside lifted for a moment, the gaps between the tatters of cloud giving a clear view of much of the yard. I stepped towards the window, looking down at a couple of figures four storeys below. Dark woollen coats buttoned up to their necks, both of them tall, one wearing a felt hat, the other with blonde hair bared to the damp day.

The mist dropped again, leaving only ghosts where a moment before two men had stood. I glanced at the desk, at the file in my hands, and back out of the window. The blonde man reminded me of Sachse—could he really be here in the BKA compound?

Unsure, I stepped closer to the window to get a better angle on the area directly in front of the building. I hoped for another breeze to whisper out of the nothingness and blow a hole in the mist, but at the same time aware of the need to find and capture evidence of Sachse's treachery in the file I held in my hands.

I remained where I stood, scanning the blank canvas before me, my eyes continuously darting between where I'd last seen the two men and the front doors—and there it was, the movement of air I'd been waiting for, twisting and thinning the mist until I could see them again. They'd reached the doors of the building, I could see the shape of them—both tall and thin, the one in the hat almost Prussian in appearance with his straight back and arrogant tilt to his head: Horchheimer. The blonde man with him raised his face to look up at the steel and glass facade, and before I stepped back, I took in his height, his build, the thin line of his off-kilter mouth. I hadn't been imagining it—Sachse was here.

Another moment wasted, staring uselessly at the cover of the file in my hands, anticipation and satisfaction swirling through my chest and mingled with—could it really be?—yes, fear. Or apprehension. Call it apprehension, I told myself, as I took the files back to the cabinet, slotted them into place and slid the door shut. No time to lock it again with the picks, so back to the desk to pocket the camera. Hand into the other pocket to check I hadn't left the pick gun lying around, then over to the door.

I eased it open and listened. Not hearing anyone, I widened the gap and slipped out of Horchheimer's office. Another pause to listen before using the pick gun—voices, the swish of the glass door just around the corner. Horchheimer and Sachse were already on their way.

Giving up on the lock, I padded back into Horchheimer's office, looking desperately for a hiding place I knew wasn't there: no corners, no other doors, not even a pair of long curtains. So I did the only thing I could do: I plumped myself down in the visitor's chair in front of Horchheimer's desk.

I leaned back and crossed my legs.

64
WIESBADEN

Horchheimer stepped into his office, already pulling off his coat and swivelling to hang it on the hatstand to the side. Behind him, I heard another door swing shut further down the corridor.

Horchheimer unwound a plaid woollen scarf and draped it over a hook. That's when I decided a discreet cough was in order.

He wheeled about, eyes wide, still holding the end of the scarf.

I proffered the report I'd brought with me, eyebrows raised in query and apology. "The door was open—I understood you were expecting me."

Horchheimer's scarf still trailed from his hand, his eyes were narrow and his brow creased in indignation.

"Get out of my office. Now!"

"But the report-" I broke off and stood up, fascinated by the worried Horchheimer threw at the open door.

"My apologies, Herr *Kriminaloberrat*. A misunderstanding." I clicked my heels and saluted, knowing he didn't like it—I couldn't help myself, I was enjoying his discomfort. But since it was also in my interests to get out of the office, I didn't hang about to watch him froth.

I didn't go too far, just to the corner of the corridor where I positioned myself, out of sight but within earshot of Horchheimer's office. It wasn't long before I heard the shuffle of a heavy door being pulled open, followed by a drawn-out wheeze as it was pulled shut again by a mechanical closer. I poked my head around the corner.

As the toilet door juddered home, a man walked away from me. I could see the long back and the white-blonde hair of Sachse as he headed for Horchheimer's wide open door.

As soon as I heard Horchheimer's door shut, I took myself out of that building. Hesitating halfway across the fog-shrouded yard, I changed direction and walked towards the gatehouse.

"Leaving early?" It was the young guard I'd spoken to this morning. Recalling my earlier good mood, I pasted a smile on my face.

"Still a few Roth-Händle in the pack if you've got time for a gasp?" I put my hand in my pocket for the deck, but instead of the soft, paper packet, my fingers encountered the hard plastic grip of the pick gun.

Sweat prickled in my armpits and at the back of my neck as realisation stole up on me—I'd forgotten to stash the tools. Concentrating on keeping my breathing steady, I pulled my hand back out of the pocket and, with my other hand, tried the other side.

"I've lost my lighter ..." I stated casually, as the fingers of my left hand probed beyond the lock picks and the soft gloves, reaching for the cigarettes beyond. I grasped the smooth paper packet, teasing it past the leather pouch of picks and out of my pocket. I took a nail for myself then offered one to the guard.

I watched his eyes—they were fixed on the red packet in my hand, greedy for nicotine. He looked away, over his shoulder to the unoccupied desk by the window where his colleague usually sat.

"Lighter?" I prompted.

He picked up a box of matches from the desk, and I jerked my head in query—*smoke outside?* He nodded, and I held the door open while he stepped through.

He lit me up first and I inhaled. I ignored the dribble of cold sweat carving its way down my back and watched the young guard bite back a cough. I took small puffs, concentrating on keeping my breathing even.

"I'm Reim," I told him, holding out my hand, even though he already knew my name—it was printed on the BKA pass he examined every morning.

"Engert." He took my hand and we nodded companionably.

"You're from the East?" he asked, then shook his head slightly. "Sorry, shouldn't ask that kind of thing ... security."

"No, no. No problem. Yes, I'm from the East. Helping out with a couple of things—you know how it is." Engert clearly didn't know how it was, but he nodded anyway, keen to appear knowledgeable.

"What about you? Been here long?"

"Since six this morning."

I smiled to show I got the joke.

"Just since last year, starting at the bottom, working my way up—right?" And he was young. Now I looked more closely, I could tell he was barely out of his teens. Could I soften him up enough that he would forget, or be too embarrassed, to search me? Or did his inexperience make him more likely to stick to the book? I had to make a move before his older colleague returned, once he was back to oversee matters, my young friend would have no choice but to at least pat me down.

The adrenaline kick from being discovered in Horchheimer's office was seeping away, my pulse was slowing, allowing room for rational thought—I should make up some excuse about having forgotten something, return to my desk. Backing out was the only sensible course of action right now.

Remembering the report still rolled up in my pocket, the one Horchheimer hadn't let me present, I decided to use that as an excuse to head back into the complex. Waiting for the right moment while pretending to listen to Engert tell me about his career plans, I ran the words through my head: *Damn, forgot to hand in this report—back in a couple of minutes ...*

But just as the guard's monologue slowed, two things happened: a dark Mercedes S-Class purred up to the gates and a woman in a tight business suit with wide shoulders tippy-toed up to us on her patent high-heels. In her arms, she cradled several centimetres of paperwork.

Engert looked at the big car, then the secretary. Deciding the car had priority, he ran up to the driver's window to check identification documents. Satisfied, he doubled back to the gatehouse to press a button for the electric gate. Meanwhile, the woman had homed in on him as he stood by the desk, she was already talking to him even though he was concentrating on the car as it edged closer to the tall steel gates as they swung open.

Seeing my chance, I waved to Engert as I walked alongside the car leaving the BKA complex. I didn't look back to see how he reacted, but I could feel my shoulders stiffen as I went, expecting alarms and shouts. It wasn't the kind of trick I'd dare to pull back home, not unless I wanted my legs shot from under me, but this wasn't the right moment to second-guess my own actions—I kept up the pace, chucking the spent cigarette as I crossed the line and turned right along the tall wall bordering the site.

The Mercedes pulled past me and took the corner. Knowing I was out of the direct line of sight of the gatehouse, I broke into a run, not stopping until the thick mist had not only swallowed me, but was threatening to overwhelm my tarred lungs.

65
WIESBADEN

I stopped, out of breath, opposite a park, it was one of the standard posh green spaces Wiesbaden goes in for, and feeling the need to get off the streets, I crossed the road and went through the gates.

Bent over, hands on thighs, gulping damp air into my lungs, I felt alone for the first time since I'd crossed the border. Grey trunks and sparse leaves surrounded me, showing up only slightly darker than the dishwater greyness of the mist.

My chest was burning, my blood was screaming for nicotine, but for the time being I kept my hands away from the deck of cigarettes. I leaned against a tree and listened to the soft dripping of damp branches, breathing ever more easily as my lungs slowly unclenched. I could see my breath in the air, thicker bubbles of mist that hung around my head. My gasping slowed and quietened, leaving me in a murky cell of calm.

No scrunching of footsteps through leaves, no susurration of small animals disturbing the dying undergrowth, no alarm calls from startled birds. There were no eyes on me, no microphones pointed at me.

Alone.

I dropped to my haunches, the serrated bark of a tree catching at the cheap material of my suit jacket. I put my head in my hands and breathed deeply a few more times. This mission was taking more out of me than I cared to admit—a month of prison for intense preparation, a further week or so of interrogations followed by the full-time role I was playing for the BKA—enough to dent even the hardest operative.

I gave in and lit a nail.

If I was honest, it wasn't just the last couple of months that had been hard. Things hadn't been the same for over a year, ever since Major Fröhlich had sent me into the sandy wastelands around Berlin to tidy up after one of his affairs. Since then, whenever work seemed to be settling back into comfortable routine, some superior officer—whether in my own service or the KGB—had taken it into his head to send me off on one unofficial mission after another.

And if I succeeded this time—if I brought back watertight evidence that Sachse was the source we'd been looking for, if I found them iron-clad proof that he'd leaked state secrets and endangered the security of the Socialist Fatherland—even then, there'd be no flowers or medals for me. Not for an operational process like this, carried out completely under the radar.

No promotion, either.

I'd be back on the treadmill, waiting for Schur or Kühn or Pozdniakov or any of the other brass to decide I was the right operative—the one with the necessary qualities of being both able and expendable—to deal with whatever pile of shit they currently needed clearing away.

I felt heat on my fingers and dropped the cigarette—I'd let it burn down without taking more than a single hit. That didn't happen often.

I toed the butt into the wet grass at my feet and eased another out of the deck.

And what if I stayed here? The BKA would never really trust me, but they would probably give me a steady job—no operational duties, assigned only boring but comfortable desk work. Not the most exciting future, commuting between a concrete workers' silo in a sink estate and the offices in leafy Wiesbaden, but it wasn't without appeal. What did I have to go back to the East for anyway? The bureaucrats at Berlin

Centre were right to question my West Confirmation—I had little to hold me in Berlin: no family—wife had long since left me, parents both died peacefully in their beds nearly a decade ago—and no friends. The only person I had really called a friend was dead, as good as killed by Sachse.

Which brought me neatly back to now. Here, in Wiesbaden, in West Germany—within a few hundred metres of this damp park, Sachse was having a cosy chat with a senior officer of the West German Federal Crime Agency.

And if I had one motivation to continue this operation, it was revenge. Not only for my dead friend Holger, but also for my drowned colleague Sanderling, pushed under the ice by Sachse because he suspected she might know too much.

I finished the cigarette, allowing my thoughts to slow. I'd overreacted back at the BKA. I should have stashed the picks and the camera, gone back to my desk, continued doing the job of producing *Katzendreck* for Horchheimer, acted as if nothing was amiss.

But now I thought back on it, Horchheimer's reaction to my sudden appearance in his office had been a little off. Sure, his indignation had been both predictable and justifiable, yet he had wanted me out of his office not because he was concerned about security and angry at the intrusion, but because Sachse was in the Gents, just a moment away from walking into the office.

Why didn't he want me and Sachse meeting? What did he think would happen?

Personally, I had plenty of reasons to avoid a face-to-face with Sachse, and I'd been glad of the excuse to leave before he turned up. But did Sachse know the BKA had a 'tame Stasi' working for them? And did he know that I was that tame Stasi?

As interesting as this was, I could see no tactical advantage in speculating any further—it was time for me to act: either stash my hardware and go back to work at the BKA, or stash it and go home.

The thought of walking back up that hill and through the gates of the BKA made me droop further against the tree trunk.

I lit another cigarette.

66
WIESBADEN

Making use of the privacy provided by the mist and the trees in the park, I wound the film back into the canister and took it out of the camera.

Finding a stationer on a back road, I made a few purchases, then, outside the shop—considering the quiet byway was as discreet a place as I'd find in the centre of town—I wrapped my burglary tools in tissue paper and placed them in a cardboard box.

I addressed the package to *Frau A. Weber, Poste Restante* the post office at Frankfurt am Main central station, then went in search of a post office.

Having passed the parcel to the care of the postal service, my final stop before the railway station was the chilly interior of the Church of St. Bonifatius. I sat quietly in a pew for a while, shivering and observing. A few old ladies dressed completely in black sat or kneeled near the front, and a handful of tourists were glotzing at one of the side chapels. There was no sight or sound of the organ renovators that day.

Once the tourists had grown bored of the unspectacular ecclesiastical architecture, I followed them out, and as I passed the scaffolding brace I'd used last time, I inserted the film canister into the end, plugging it with a piece of screwed up tissue paper.

★

Free of incriminating objects, I stepped more lightly on the short walk to the station. I bought a bottle of vodka at the kiosk and continued on my way to my flat.

It was late afternoon when I arrived at the concrete estate I currently called home. There were no chalk marks at the tram stop and no sign of Jens or his gang. In fact, the place felt even emptier and more spectral than usual, but it was probably just the dusk gathering early at the edge of the mist, causing the grey blocks of flats to bleed into the colourless air.

Switching on the striplight over the sink, I settled in the chair near the open bathroom door with a glass of vodka, feeling the stones in my stomach dissolving with each sip. That was good. Another nip, let it do its work, undo the choking knots of worry. Then, reaching for the tourist map of the region, I unfolded it and began to gen up on the local geography.

But my head still hadn't settled after the events of the afternoon, it was too difficult to concentrate on the map. Running away from the BKA had been the right reaction, although now I was wondering how clever it had been to return to the flat. Sachse's arrival posed a threat to me and my mission. How much danger I was in depended on how long Sachse was here for, and how much Horchheimer told him.

I put my glass on the floor by my feet and turned back to the map—if I had to duck out quickly, then knowing where to run to would be essential. I needed an overview of the terrain: not just the topography, but the location of nearby towns, the transport infrastructure, how to get out of town fast. I traced the roads and train lines to the closest destinations, and made a mental note to check the timetables for the tourist boats that headed downstream for Koblenz and Cologne.

Topping up my glass, my thoughts returned once again to Sachse, trying to get inside his head. If he knew I was here, that I was the BKA's tame Stasi, would he come to my desk to gloat over me, the MfS operative brought low, working as a plumber for the BKA, piecing together bits of information into something that might be useful to his new masters?

Or would he see me as a personal threat, as he had done when our paths last crossed, back in February?

My concentration was broken by a faint scratching at the door. Turning to look into the poky hallway, I rose silently from the chair, picking up the vodka bottle by its neck as I did so. It wasn't much of a weapon, but it beat a folded tourist map by a long way.

Looking through the spyhole, I couldn't make out anything but shadows—the bulb in the stairwell was still out. I waited, eye at the lens, until the shadows shifted and I made out the torso of a man—tall and broad. He came closer to knock gently at the door again and I recognised the outline of his mullet hairstyle.

"Alright Jens?" I said quietly as I opened up, bottle still held tightly in hand.

He looked back down the stairwell as if expecting an eavesdropper to be there, took a short step forward and whispered, "Some blonde's been hanging around, outside your block," he gestured needlessly to the front door at the bottom of the stairs. "Couldn't get past her to warn you."

"Where is she now?"

"At the caff, the one next door to Schlecker." He shrugged. "Mebbe she needed to warm up a bit."

I reached into my pocket and pulled out twenty Marks—that was over half my float already gone—and handed it over.

"Cheers Jens, you're sound."

He clattered off down the concrete steps, all sense of discretion forgotten, and I waited until I heard the outside door scrape across the uneven cement before I put the bottle down and pulled the flat door shut behind me as I left.

★

I stood in the lee of a building opposite the little café, trying to see past the condensation that dribbled down the inside of the wide windows. The place was pretty much empty, a figure moved from table to table, wiping them down and placing chairs on top, ready to mop the floor. Another woman was hunched over a cup by the window. Other than that, there wasn't much to see.

Stooping to comb the grass with my fingers, hoping I wouldn't encounter anything too nasty down there, I scooped up a couple of small stones.

I pitched the first pebble sidearm, not too fast, aiming for the café window. It hit home with a click that made the two occupants start. The person who had been tidying went back to work, and the other woman left her drink, saying something over her shoulder as she walked towards the door.

She came out, peered into the shadows for a moment, then crossed the path and headed straight for the patch of darkness in which I was lurking. I waited for her.

It was Anna Weber.

"What are you doing here?" I knew she wasn't here on official business, nor was it a personal call, a friend popping by. If it had been either of those, she would have knocked on my door like any normal visitor.

"I didn't come up," she answered, reading my thoughts, "someone was watching. When I realised it was just a kid, I thought perhaps you'd recruited him, so I cleared off to let him make contact with you."

"What are you doing here?" I repeated. The question came out sounding a little shorter than I'd intended, she was my only ally in this country and I knew I should try harder to be nice.

"Our friend Sachse, he's in town-"

"I know."

That stopped her for a moment, but she recovered and

continued: "I went to Wiesbaden today, wanted to speak to Ingo again about getting my old position back, but I didn't get to talk to him—he and that man Sachse were at your desk, looking through the drawers."

"Anyone else with them? Jüliger? Maybe someone from the BND or *Verfassungsschutz*?"

She shook her head and we stood like that, close together in the shadows, shivering in the dank night.

It took me less than thirty seconds to make up my mind.

I didn't even bother going back to my flat—the most important item there was the half bottle of vodka I'd left in the hallway, and I didn't expect any problems with replacing it.

67
MAINZ

It was early the next morning when Weber drove up to the gates of the allotment colony in a familiar-looking VW Polo.

"Flask on the back seat," she said as I climbed in.

I held the plastic cup with both hands, glad of the chance to warm myself after the damp night in a garden shed. Weber reached down to turn up the heater while I poured myself another coffee, holding and sipping it, enjoying the warmth from inside and out.

Behind us, the sun lipped the horizon, a white haze in the fog of the Rhine valley.

We pulled in at a service station for a break, taking a spot far from the restaurant and filling station.

"Try this for size," said Weber, who was at the back of the vehicle, poking through some boxes. She pulled out a heavy dark green coat with moss green collar and lapels and horn buttons down the front. I slipped into it, enjoying an anticipatory pleasure as the bulky coat settled on my shoulders. Wearing this, I'd soon feel warm.

When I turned around, Weber had another gift for me, a felted hat of the kind I associated with beer-drinking Bavarians. I tried it on, pulling the brim low over my eyes to shade out the sun that was still struggling to free itself from the hills behind us.

"And these, roll them up over your trousers." She held out a pair of thick woollen socks in forest green and stood by while I perched on the back of the car to pull off my shoes.

The socks covered my trousers as far as the skirts of the coat, and with the coat buttoned up, my suit was no longer visible.

"They'll think I'm a Bavarian," I said. Not exactly my thing, but I wasn't complaining.

"Don't worry, it's the local style. Nobody will mistake you for a Bavarian. Still, shame about the shoes."

We looked down at my black, smooth-soled office shoes.

"Who looks at shoes?" I protested.

"Spies do."

"Hans wears this stuff when he goes hunting, I'm sure he won't mind you borrowing it," Weber said as we got back into the car.

"Was that Hans who picked you up at the safe house on Sunday?" I asked as I turned down the heating, I was warming up nicely.

"He's an old colleague of my husband."

Husband? She'd never mentioned a man in her life before, and something that big usually is usually dropped into the conversation early on in any relationship, whether it's professional or personal. I get nervous when assets hold back something that's important to them—not that Weber was an asset, and not that this was the right time to delve into her private life, but at some point I'd have a few questions for her.

But right now, I was more concerned about the car we were sitting in, and whether it was the same one that had picked up my shadow after Saturday night's soirée.

"So Hans is happy to lend you his car for a secret mission involving a member of an enemy agency?"

She didn't answer—she didn't even smile—as she manoeuvred us down the slip road and back onto the motorway. It was a pretty effective way to close down the conversation.

★

The blue sign told us that Koblenz was twenty kilometres away, and I took that as my cue to ask Weber again about the layout of the contact site.

"*Deutsches Eck*. Bit of a landmark. Originally a monument built in honour of the Kaiser when he unified the German states in 1871, now it's dedicated to the reunification of East and West Germany."

I managed not to snort too loudly. I had no idea whether and when Weber thought re-unification might happen, but any fool could see the two Germanys were worlds apart, that the idea our two states would somehow come together again was nothing more than revanchist fantasy.

"Built at the confluence of the rivers Rhine and Moselle—the Moselle joins the Rhine from the south-west—there's a headland that juts quite far out into the stream, and the monument stands between the access paths that run along the banks of either river.

"It's really just the plinth for a bronze of the first Kaiser, but it's big—think of a plinth on top of a plinth—about twenty metres high. Then there's a high stone pergola which blocks direct access, so if you want to get to the monument you have to go along one of the two river paths."

I'd never seen it, but I had it in my mind now—a wedge of land between the two rivers, the only way in or out being along the promenades fronting the two rivers. Simple enough.

"And you're sure you have a red scarf with you?" I asked.

"Stop fretting."

68
KOBLENZ

Weber let me out of the car a few blocks from the main station in Koblenz old town and I continued north on foot. There were few people around at this time of the morning—a handful of shop workers opening up, a few pensioners queueing outside bakeries for bread rolls fresh out of the oven, but otherwise the streets were quiet.

It wasn't hard to do my usual dry cleaning routine under these conditions, and when I finally neared the *Deutsches Eck* twenty minutes later, I was pretty sure I was clear of unwanted company.

I took a right, down to the Rhine promenade that I'd avoided thus far on the premise that the streets offered more cover than an open vista along a river bank, and, standing at the corner of the last building before the Kaiser's plinth, I observed the dog walkers and the few tramps that had unwisely bedded down in a park, exposing themselves to the endless mists that wheezed down the Rhine.

In contrast to the narrow streets I'd just left, visibility here was poor: the joggers and walkers lost definition at just fifty or sixty metres, mere shadow puppets in the grey morning.

Lighting a cigarette, I checked my watch—I had only five minutes until the rendezvous, but I was in sight of the end of the stone pergola. So far, I'd seen nothing that worried me, all was running according to the schedule I'd been given in the emergency phone call to the solicitor's office in Munich last night: *Check your tail and wait on the headland at precisely 0735 hours.* And here I was, tail-free and perfectly positioned to be in the right place at the right time.

Another look around before I lost the cigarette and turned towards the *Deutsches Eck*.

As I came abreast of the steps that led up to the heavy stone pedestal, empty now of the bronze Kaiser on his horse, I spotted Weber. She was taking a lot of interest in the elaborate frieze, a *Mischmasch* of imperial symbols and, bizarrely enough, snakes. Her scarf was tucked into a pocket, a mere tail of red peeking out: all clear.

Reassured, I strode along the railing above the Rhine until I reached the point where it met the Moselle and turned around to take in the full extent of the monument. Weber hadn't been kidding when she'd said the thing was big. Steps led up to the base where my partner admired the stonemasons' craft; further steps climbed to the stone pergola at the rear of the ensemble.

I turned my head to look across the waters of the Moselle— as grey and featureless as the Rhine and the mist that blanketed the whole valley.

I lit another cigarette and leaned against the railing, the lack of visibility was a problem—from my position on the headland I couldn't make out who was approaching until they were abreast of the monument. A squad of cops could be charging towards me and I'd be cornered before I knew it was happening.

But there was no reason for cops to turn up mob-handed, the only people who knew I was here were Weber and whoever the lawyers in Munich had passed my message to.

A dog walker edged along the bottom of the steps, his head not even level with Weber's feet—she'd moved on, was now at the side of the plinth, running her fingers over the carvings on the side of the stone curtain at the back. I watched him being pulled onwards by a dog the size of a large rat, its short legs pumping so fast they blurred in the thick air.

A tenor note from behind distracted me—a long hoot from a

ship as it emerged from the fog that hung over the Moselle. I watched as it steadily took form, a high windscreen and short roof for the pilot, benches for passengers running the length of the open deck.

Keeping one eye on the promenade along the Rhine, I watched the boat's outline grow in confidence as it first neared the headland, then swung against the current to make for what must be a landing stage hidden below the lip of the high embankment.

Back on land, a man appeared around the monument, approaching along the Rhine. He walked with purpose in my direction.

This was my contact. He was bringing me my ticket home.

69
KOBLENZ

I leaned against the railing as the man closed the gap between us—he was one of our men here in West Germany, and he'd come to tell me how I was to be exfiltrated from the Operational Area.

For a moment I allowed my thoughts to stray back to Berlin, I saw myself on Alexanderplatz, sitting at an outside table in front of Café Polar. *Schwedeneisbecher* sundaes aren't really my thing, but I'd be due some leave once I'd been debriefed, and after being away from home for so long, I intended to spend every moment I could in the noise and stink of my home city.

Over the man's shoulder—he was still some thirty metres distant—I saw Weber flicker into view from around the back of the monument. I couldn't see her features clearly in the mist, but I could tell she glanced my way, and I noticed the scarf still hanging from her pocket. She slipped back around the side of the pergola, better to keep an eye on the approaches.

As my contact drew closer, our eyes locked for a moment and we nodded in greeting. It was nobody I knew, but I was familiar with the type: a nondescript grey face under fine grey hair, the kind of person who'd blend into any scenery. The perfect bagman for agents in hostile territories.

"Looks like summer's over," he observed, his hand outstretched for me to shake. "The wife tells me we should go to Hawaii, she says the sun always shines there."

Hawaii? Who thought up these ridiculous challenges? But I was a good boy, I wanted out of here as soon as possible, so I played along and kept to the script I'd received down the phone last night: "There's always the skiing to look forward to. I like the Tyrol myself."

The grey man nodded and reached into the inside pocket of his coat, pulling out a deck of Marlboros. He offered me one and lit me up, and we both stood around, letting out little clouds of smoke.

I wanted him to tell me what my next move would be, I was impatient to put some distance between me and the BKA and Sachse in Wiesbaden, but he made me wait while he smoked his cigarette.

"My team should be here by now—they're very good, experienced lads. Can't think why they've been delayed ...."

He was suddenly talking too much, blethering on about how his team was never normally late. And all the talk about a team didn't suit me either—surely Mr Grey was here to give me instructions, at the most to take me to a safe house?

I flicked the cigarette into the river and started stamping my feet as if suffering from the cold, but using the movement to disguise the fact I was taking a good look around. My companion didn't react. He was nervous, his eyes flicking between me and the broad walk along the Rhine, as if expecting his team to come from that direction.

But having started to listen to the doubting voices in my head, I couldn't stop assessing him, trying to predict his intentions. Even when he looked at me, he no longer met my eyes. In fact, he hadn't looked directly at me since passing me a cigarette. As far as I was concerned, that was another mark against our Mr Grey.

I carried on stamping and shuffling, every step taking me a little further away from the man, and as I danced out of his reach, I divided my attention between the man, the Rhine promenade and the monument, but saw neither the advertised team of experienced lads nor Weber, who was supposed to be playing sentry for me.

I didn't like the situation, but this contact was my best way home. And since Weber hadn't raised the alarm I decided it was in my interests to stick around a little longer.

"Here they are," said the man, his voice pitched high in relief. He took a step forwards, closing the gap between us, his back suddenly straighter, his eyes no longer flickering—the overall effect was more reassuring. So when he set off to meet the two men gradually emerging from the mist, I stayed at his side.

Weber was still out of sight, the tiny rat-dog was sniffing the edge of the steps over by the Moselle, its owner still hanging onto the lead. On this side of the triangle of headland it was just Mr Grey, myself and the two tall young men we were going to meet. They moved easily through the thick mist, I could see them more clearly now, recognised them as operatives: they were in good physical condition, aware of their surroundings and looking very proficient.

The experienced lads who were here to take me home.

At a distance of ten metres—we were now level with the bottom of the steps to the monument—I could see their eyes, the way they stared at me, observing every move I made. Unease whipped its way up my chest, like a bad case of heartburn.

I stared back at them, but a movement, a flash of colour in the monochrome world pulled my eyes to the top of the steps where Weber was waving her scarf. A red flag signalling danger.

70
KOBLENZ

The two operatives didn't see Weber waving her red scarf on the steps behind them, but Mr Grey did, and the goons picked up pretty fast when he turned his head to get a better look.

By the time the goons had reacted, I'd bolted.

I darted across the dimpled concrete surface, splashing through puddles. I didn't bother wasting time with looking over my shoulder, I knew they were after me. Young and full of beans, they were in much better condition than I was, they'd soon catch up. So when I heard the heavy splash and a hard footstep behind me, I sheered to the right, my loden coat dragging on my shoulder as the kid made a grab for me, his fingers clawing at the heavy green felt without quite catching it.

I ran on, along the front of the monument, heading for the embankment above the Moselle, but a shade of movement in the corner of my eye warned me to swerve again. A few steps to my right, then back on course, parallel to the stone steps.

But the goon was already overhauling me, his arms out, he crabbed along, trying to shepherd me into the wedge of land between the two rivers so he and his pal could corral me.

I sprinted for a metre or two, surprising myself and my pursuer with the sudden burst of energy, then, just as he skipped to the side, arms wide to prevent me from passing him, I used my forward momentum to plant a heavy fist in the centre of his wide chest.

He was too fit and too well wrapped in warm clothing for my punch to even wind him, but it knocked him half a step backwards, and he dropped, tripped by the lapdog's lead.

I didn't wait to see how that particular scene played out, but as I sprinted the last few metres to the railing above the Moselle, I heard shouts, yapping and growling. Bouncing off the railing, I launched myself onto a new trajectory, this time along the Moselle and away from the headland. The little ferry I'd seen a few minutes before was still at the landing stage at the bottom of a flight of steps cut into the embankment—the pilot had a mooring line in his hand, was unwrapping it from a ring.

Another spurt and I reached the top of the steps just as the pilot cast off. The stone treads were slick with moisture, but I didn't let that slow me—taking them two at a time, jumping onto the jetty just as the pilot pulled on the throttle. I didn't stop, but crossed the boards, leaping over the widening gap to the boat—as my left leg scissored out to bridge the distance, the smooth sole of my right shoe slipped on the damp planks. Throwing my arms forward, trying to give myself enough momentum, I managed to grab the gunwale as I flew over the top. I made it halfway into the cockpit, my ribs crunching across a metal cleat, my legs jackknifing over the side of the hull, one foot caught up in a fender, the other trailing in the freezing grey water of the Moselle.

The pilot turned, his hand instinctively pushing the throttle to neutral

"Keep going!" I screamed at him, the pain in my chest giving my voice urgency, scaring the two passengers who had hold of my coat and were trying to pull me in.

The pilot looked over my head at the embankment behind, and as I was dragged aboard, I twisted to see the two goons on the landing stage. One was reaching inside his coat pocket, the other looked up at Mr Grey, who was standing at the railing five metres above.

"*Polizei!* Get this boat moving!" I shouted again.

The magic P-word did the trick, the captain flicked the

control lever forward and span the wheel to starboard as the ship slowly picked up speed.

I moved forward, pushing past the knees of anxious passengers.

"Zig-zag as much as you can! And give her some welly," I ordered, pulling out my BKA gate pass and giving him a quick look while I checked what was happening on the shore. There was a pistol on the landing stage, aimed directly at us. I reached over and pushed the ship's wheel hard, surprising the pilot—as soon as I felt the stern kick about, I pulled the wheel the other way, but other than making the boat wiggle, it didn't have much effect—we were moving too slowly to provide a difficult target.

But when I looked back at the goons on the shore, they were both looking up to Mr Grey on the embankment. The last thing I saw as the mist closed around us was the pistol disappearing back into an inside pocket.

71
KOBLENZ LÜTZEL

I stayed at the captain's side until we reached the far side of the Moselle then, in the hope of forestalling any pursuit, told him not to cross back to the other side for at least half an hour.

But as soon as I started up the slope to reach the road, I was forced to slow down again—my lungs were fighting to draw enough air, but when I breathed deeply, pain sliced beneath my chest. Gasping for breath, I probed gently beneath my coat. I'd broken a rib, maybe two. Probably not dangerous, but more than enough to slow me down.

There was a wide slipway to my left, a camping ground to my right, and when I finally reached the top of the incline and read the board, I found out that the block of offices fringing the slip belonged to the Waterways and Shipping Office.

A white Volkswagen Transporter flatbed was coming through the gates outside the offices, and I did my best to speed up, trying to reach it before it turned onto the road. I grimaced as I scuttled along, a hand pressed to my chest to hold back the pain.

"Which way are you heading?" I asked the driver as I flicked my BKA pass at him.

He looked at me, he looked in his mirrors, then picked up a clipboard from the dash and had a look at that.

"Shipyard in Brohl-"

"That'll do." I had no idea where Brohl was, but anywhere would do so long as I got out of Koblenz. I walked around the front of the van and climbed in beside him.

He looked at me, then in his mirrors again, then put the clipboard back on the dashboard. "Who did you say you were?"

I gave him another flash of my pass, it was impressive enough—the same thick green, watermarked paper they use for passports and identification documents, with my photograph held in place with rivets. A West German eagle proudly sat at the top with *Bundeskriminalamt* written in capital letters alongside—but if anyone got a proper look, they'd soon notice the words printed at the bottom edge: *Temporary Pass—this is not an identification document.*

But people rarely ask for a second look at official ID, and when they do, they can usually be discouraged by a few robust questions of my own.

We soon hit the dual carriageway along the Rhine, the signs all pointing north to Bonn and Cologne. The driver tried to make conversation, but after I'd shut him down a few times he got the message and stuck to smoking cigarettes and humming along to the hits that leaked from the radio.

Free to think my own thoughts, I allowed my mind to flit backwards through the previous quarter of an hour, alighting first on the operative on the jetty who levelled a pistol at me. He wouldn't have pulled the trigger, I told myself. Whoever he was, whoever he worked for, firing on a passenger boat with innocent parties aboard would draw too much attention.

Spooling back a little further, I took the mental image of the grey man and held it up to the light, angling it this way and that, trying to get a handle on him.

Who did he represent?

At the time, I'd assumed he was an IM, a non-professional MfS asset, sent as a messenger to guide in the exfiltration team. But the two operatives had accorded him a measure of respect back there, they'd looked to him for orders. That, to my mind, decisively shifted his status from non-professional to professional.

But one of us, or one of them?

And what about Weber? She'd waved her scarf to warn me —but how had she recognised the danger?

Had she been spooked by the sight of the two operatives marching my way? Or had she seen something else? More troops waiting in the wings? Perhaps a *grüne Minna* police wagon? Whatever it was, she'd definitely seemed very certain when she'd waved that scarf.

And where was she now? Had she been taken by Mr Grey and his squad?

I had no answers, and I couldn't think how to get any, not without risking my own freedom. I couldn't even work with probabilities—I'd have given even odds on those men being West Germans or from Sachse's department at the MfS.

72
BROHL

The little town of Brohl arrived sooner than expected. The driver dabbed at the indicators and slowed to rattle over a level crossing by the side of a narrow river harbour. A few metres away, a train of open wagons hitched to an undersized diesel locomotive edged along tracks under a crane.

"This is us," he said unnecessarily and gave me an expectant look.

I took the hint and climbed out, ignoring the squelching coming from my left shoe. I murmured a word of thanks as I left.

The mist had burned off, or had perhaps never made it this far up the Rhine valley, and I had a clear view of the few houses on the other side of the road, tidy and square in the West German fashion, a restaurant nestled between them, not open for breakfast.

Having seen a railway station near the highway, I crossed the busy road and walked back the way we'd come.

Intending to buy a ticket for anywhere east of here, I joined the queue at the station. The far wall of the ticket hall was covered with a hand-painted map of the Middle Rhine, showing the sights, ferries and railway stations along the way. Beside me, framed posters in glorious technicolour boasted of castles, white wine and young women dressed in traditional costume sitting beneath, in and on the castles while somehow simultaneously smiling and drinking wine.

One poster was mostly devoted to a picture of a high bluff

that rose from the waters of the Rhine, dwarfing its wooded flanks. An inset photograph in the corner showed a sparsely clad blonde playing what could have been a tiny harp.

"Where's this?" I asked the man at the counter when I got to the front of the queue.

He looked at the picture I was pointing to, then at me, wondering whether he was dealing with an idiot. Clearly deciding my Berlin accent was explanation enough for any amount of ignorance, he told me it was the Loreley.

"The Loreley? The one with all the songs about it?" I asked, but he didn't bother to answer. "Any other rocks like that?" I asked, risking further contempt.

"It's the Loreley," he repeated, as if that were all the answer I needed.

"Second class to the Loreley." I proffered the rest of my cash, examining the poster again while he set the machine to print the ticket. On the poster, I could just about make out two flagpoles at the top of the cliff, one flying a black-red-gold West German flag, the other a smudge of black and red.

Sankt Goar, when the train finally pulled alongside the low platforms, proved to be little bigger than Brohl, and despite the ranks of hotels and manufactured tourist shops, was twice as pretty.

When I hurried down to the bank of the river and looked over to the other side, there was no sign of the Loreley cliff. All I could see was a strip settlement along the road at the foot of a heavily wooded slope. And when I turned around to look at my side of the river, I had practically the same view.

"The Loreley?" I asked a shopkeeper who was opening up a kiosk of kitsch and souvenirs.

He jabbed a thumb upriver, not bothering to look around as he hung up racks of postcards and strip maps of the Rhine.

So I walked in the direction the thumb had pointed, taking it easy to spare my rib, and half an hour later I stood on a narrow bend of the river, taking in the crag on the far bank. Although the perspective was different, I had no doubt this was the same slate cliff I'd seen filling the background of the photograph in Sachse's file.

Not only was the perspective from which I was looking at the Loreley wrong, but there was no cluster of slate-roofed houses obscuring the view. Right rock, wrong place.

I looked up the valley on my side of the river—a retaining wall beyond the main road held up the corniche along which the railway lines ran, and beyond that, bushes and trees marched upwards, shelving out of sight.

I decided the houses had to be somewhere up on the plateau beyond the top of the valley.

A few minutes search revealed a path that tunnelled first beneath the railway lines then dog-legged up the steep side of the valley. The sun appeared, hanging over a short stretch of the winding river as I climbed higher, pausing frequently to catch my breath. I breasted the top of the slope and stopped to admire the small village on the edge of the plateau.

Putting my felt hat back on and pulling the brim low to shade my eyes from sun and human scrutiny, I walked the last few hundred metres across mown meadows to the nearest houses. From here I had a view that skimmed the tops of the trees and out over the river gorge. Less than a kilometre away, on the other side of the Rhine, the rock named Loreley caught the sun, the twin flags at the top stirring in the slight breeze.

Looking out at that cliff, then at the slate-roofed houses behind me, I knew I'd found the place Sachse had his luxury accommodation in the West.

73
URBAR

It was midday before I found Sachse's house, and as soon as I was sure, I left the village. I couldn't make a move during daylight, and in any case, I needed to source a couple of tools. In the meantime, I had to find somewhere inconspicuous to wait out the afternoon. The tourist town of Sankt Goar on the Rhine was likely to meet my requirements, so I stumbled back down the hill to the river.

I long ago learned the art of making a coffee or a beer stretch, and I spent the rest of the day in the corners of twee, wood-panelled establishments, counting out my last Pfennigs and pushing away thoughts of the risks I was about to take. My cover as a defector had been blown for nearly twenty-four hours and if the police got hold of me, I wouldn't see daylight for a long time to come.

Nursing my drink, I wasted time watching American tourists. I'd seen enough of them in uniform over on our side of Berlin, buying up half the Centrum department store on the Alex, and I knew how capable they are of taking up more space than you'd think a human body merited. But the species on display here in the Rhineland was different—perhaps they felt safer in West Germany, they certainly seemed less aware of their surroundings than the GIs who came over to East Berlin.

The tourists around me were tucking into oversized meals of sauerkraut with pork knuckles and dumplings with liver, demanding more beer and dishes of fries on the side. They forked up chunks of meat, cabbage and potato and entertained the other guests with wild gesticulations and loud stories.

Fascinating as their eating habits were, I was more interested in how they treated their valuables. Most seemed to keep their cash in capacious money belts wrapped around generous bellies, either under or over their clothing. But despite this healthy respect for the safety of their dollars and Marks, they seemed less interested in looking after other possessions. Fine jackets and expensive cameras hung over the backs of chairs, even left on the coat hooks near the entrance.

With this in mind, I returned to a restaurant which had been particularly popular with Americans during the lunch hour and sat myself at the back, nursing a beer and observing.

Once I'd made my target—a large American with a bright red sweater that matched his florid complexion—I waited until his main course had arrived before I signalled for my bill. Formalities out of the way—the last thing I needed was a waiter chasing me down the street and demanding payment—I headed for the door, taking a slight detour to pass behind my mark.

He didn't even notice when I walked out with his camera bag hidden beneath my loden coat. As quickly as my broken rib would allow, I headed for the pedestrian tunnel beneath the railway tracks and the path up the hill to the village of Urbar.

It was already dusk when I reached the viewing point halfway up the side of the valley. I opened the bag and examined my bounty: a Canon A-1 SLR camera, spare films and a couple of lenses. I swapped out the film and attached a lens suitable for close work.

As the light of day receded beyond the horizon, the moon rose over the Loreley's shoulder—a full moon that laid down a flat, glinting path up the last incline to the meadows surrounding the village.

★

In the village, blue light flickered through some curtains, steady yellow light behind others, but Sachse's windows were dark. I took a look at the letterbox by his garden gate—the neatly printed card behind the little plastic window didn't spell out Sachse, but it was close enough: Sacher.

Reassured, I tried the gate, pushing it open just far enough to slip through, and made my way down a weed-free path. Slipping off to the side shortly before the front door, I used what shadows were available to creep around the edge of the house. With the exception of the patio doors on the terrace, the roller shutters on every ground-floor window were down, and by cautiously lifting the wooden slats, I could see the place was in darkness.

Climbing over the creeper-overrun balustrade, I observed the nearby houses. They were all further down the hill, so Sachse's ground floor was level with their upper storeys or roofs—only in a couple of cases could I even see the lit windows of their kitchens, dining rooms and living rooms.

Taking off my heavy coat, I draped it over the back of a metal garden chair, then picked the whole thing up and swung it at the terrace window.

The first strike bounced off the glass with a resonant thud. The second strike went through with a sharp crack followed by a cascade of shards, tinkling and ringing as they hit the tiled terrace.

Stepping into the shadows beside the window, I watched and waited, alert for any sounds or movement from the house or its neighbours.

A minute passed, then two. Only when I was sure there had been no reaction did I put my hand through the broken glass and release the catch.

74
URBAR

I remained outside for another moment, then, heart drumming against fragile ribs, I parted the heavy curtains and stepped into the room, patting the curtains back into place as I did so. I edged past furniture recognisable only as black silhouettes in the darkness, finally reaching the doorway—another deeper patch of shadow recognisable only by its shape—and looked out into the hallway.

A tiled floor shimmered in what little moonlight came through high windows flanking the front door, and, treading softly, I moved to each doorway in turn, waiting on the threshold of each, watching and listening for signs of another presence.

Satisfied that I was alone, at least down here on the ground floor, I moved gently up the stairs, testing each step before I trusted the wooden treads. Once upstairs, my job was made easier by the low moon that shone directly through uncurtained windows, allowing me to make out the basic features of the furniture.

I looked into the bathroom and touched the soap by the sink. Dry, but not so dry it had cracked—either a fresh bar, or it saw regular use, just not in the last couple of hours.

Returning downstairs, I put the light on in the hall and glanced into each room again, paying more attention to the kitchen. It was a modern affair, cabinets and surfaces fitted around an oven that hadn't yet lost its virgin lustre. A fridge big enough to hide in hadn't even been plugged in, but the cupboards yielded up coffee, sugar, powdered milk and a good selection of tins.

I crossed the hall to the room I'd first entered and checked the curtains wouldn't leak light around the edges, then flicked the switch. The furniture was an assortment of expensive but unmatched antique furniture. An old-fashioned roll-top writing desk took up a decent proportion of the space available, but my attention was drawn to the large black and white photograph hanging above a 1930s wooden armchair.

I stood in front of the simple frame, taking in the picture of Sachse smiling and shaking hands with a middle-aged man with a round face, full grey hair swept back from a side parting and a pointed, but not prominent nose. I didn't know who it was, but I'd seen his portrait in the canteen—he was some big fish in the BKA.

I raised the American's camera to my eye and twisted the lens to focus on the picture, pressing the shutter and winding the film on to expose a second frame, just in case.

Putting the camera down, I turned my attention to the desk. It was solid and old, made of good hard oak, and the locks on the drawers were simple, but also well made. If I wanted to get in there, I'd need something to attack the soft brass escutcheon surrounding the keyhole.

Not seeing a hefty letter opener or any other handy implement, I decided to check the cellar, hoping to find a bag of tools down there.

Back in the hallway, I opened a small doorway under the stairs and followed the narrow, concrete steps down to a full workshop. The workbench, vice and tool racks had never been used and were covered in dust, a few steel edges were already succumbing to rusty eczema.

Selecting a narrow cold chisel, I turned to climb the cellar steps and stopped. Hadn't I left the door at the top open? It was shut now, perhaps it had swung to in the draught coming through the broken patio windows?

I mounted the stairs, chisel held low in my hand like a

knife, and twisted the handle.

It turned easily and the door swung open. I pushed it until it bounced off the wall—nobody was hiding behind.

From my position at the top of the cellar steps, I could see most of the hall—the bright bulb lit every corner, no opportunities to lurk in the shadows here. Easing around the door frame, taking in the rest of the hall and the stairs as they came into view, I breathed out. Nobody here, it seemed the door had blown shut.

Marching across to the study, still gripping the chisel, I paused—the door here had also swung shut. I reached down and twisted the knob. But as I nudged the door open, I could see the room in darkness. A familiar kick of adrenaline sparked its way through my body.

A breeze might blow a door shut, but it takes a person to turn a light off. Someone else was in the house.

75
URBAR

Keeping my back to the wall, I reached over and flicked the hall light off. But waiting and listening by the door to the study wouldn't help if whoever else was in the house was keeping still.

Was the person even in the study—or had they moved to another room? Perhaps they were watching from the top of the stairs? And was that person alone, or would I have to deal with a whole troop of adversaries?

It's hard to retreat, particularly when you know a little more effort and a pinch more luck is all you need to fulfil the operational objectives. Nevertheless, life still had some meaning for me, and now I was aware I wasn't alone in this house, I knew I was at a distinct disadvantage. I took another step to the side, away from the study and towards the front door. Then another, treading as softly as I could over the tiled floor. Reaching out, I depressed the handle on the front door, it went down, but when I pulled on it, I got little more than a click as the bolt hit the edge of the mortise. The front door was locked.

If I wanted to get out, I'd have to find another way. Moonlight peered through windows high up either side of the door, mocking me. But even if I hadn't been nursing a broken rib, I wouldn't have fitted through those narrow openings.

There were no other possible exits in the hall, my next move would have to be through another of these darkened rooms, and even then, the windows, particularly on the ground floor, were most likely locked. Smashing double-glazing makes noise and takes time—a poor tactic when you're looking for a discreet retreat.

I didn't like it, but going back out the way I'd come in—through the study and the patio doors—was my best option.

Extending my arm, I nudged the study door further open and stepped back out of the doorway to make less of a target of myself. I felt rather than heard the soft sigh of the door as it swung open, but the dull bump as it hit the wall was unmistakable in the hush.

I paused at the edge of the door frame, tensing the muscles in my legs, ready to move. Bringing the chisel back into position, I sprang into the study and dropped, rolling to the side.

I heard a grunt of pain. It surprised me—I hadn't bumped into any bodies, and I couldn't even locate the direction it had come from. Up onto my knees to spin away and the smothering pain pulling at my chest made me realise the moan had been my own.

On my feet again, my back to the wall, I surveyed the darkness, recognising nothing but the outlines of the closest pieces of furniture.

Then a chuckle, coming from the hall. A shift in the shadows, a plastic click and the room crashed into brightness. My pupils narrowed in the sudden light, struggling to focus on the pale, pitiless eyes of Sachse.

He was standing in the doorway, alone. But don't start thinking that this would be a fair fight. Sure, we'd been building up to this for months—he'd taken out my friends and colleagues one by one, injuring and humiliating me in the process—and it was time for retribution, with or without the broken ribs.

But he had a gun.

★

I stared into the blued-metal mouth of the muzzle. I wasn't particularly surprised that Sachse would be carrying, but I was a little taken aback by the gun itself: he had hold of an old stalwart of the armed organs in the Socialist bloc, a Makarov pistol.

"Showing off again, Sachse? Just like you to bring your service weapon over here. You use it to impress the girls behind the bike sheds?"

"Drop the metal!" Sachse had never been one for small talk.

I looked at the chisel and decided to keep hold of it for a little longer.

"Don't piss me around, Reim. Apart from you, nobody's going to get upset if I shoot you in the knee. And let's be honest, I'd enjoy doing it."

I dropped the chisel, hoping the point would gouge his polished parquet flooring. Sachse didn't react.

"What else you got?" He gestured at my right hand, the one clutching my ribs. It felt like somebody was poking a stick in my lungs—with every breath the stick jabbed a little harder and a little deeper, but Sachse obviously thought I was holding my own piece.

"I'm unarmed," I said simply, trying to shrug but giving up halfway through.

"Take it out and put it on the floor."

"I'm unarmed," I insisted. I held my coat open and took a step forward. "See for yourself."

He switched the pistol to his left hand and moved towards me, I met him halfway, still holding my coat open.

"You move those hands, I'll shoot you in the thigh and let you bleed to death," he warned, slowly moving a hand forward to pat down my suit pockets.

I did what I was told, I didn't move my hands, and I didn't make any clever comments about how he needed to make his mind up about where exactly he was going to shoot me. But I did kick him—and I scored a bullseye. Right in the eggs.

While he was bent over in pain, I dived to the side, lashing at his knee as I went down. Another direct hit, he crumpled and I scrambled to my feet. I was managing the moves, was concentrating on taking only short, shallow breaths, but I was too slow. By the time I was in position for the next strike, I was out of breath. I slumped over, trying to maximise the air I could take in, and that was how I missed my chance to get hold of the Makarov.

Never interested in giving opponents a sporting chance, Sachse seized his pistol by the barrel and closed the gap between us. Swinging his arm up, he brought the Makarov grip down hard on the back of my skull.

76
URBAR

When I came to, I found myself on a kitchen chair, hands bound behind me. With my arms twisted around the back of the chair, every breath I took felt like being jabbed in the chest with a sharp broom handle.

Keeping my eyes closed for the moment, I tried to scope out my situation. Light glowed beyond my eyelids, the buttery hue of a lightbulb. A shifting chill tickled my right cheek. And the only thing I could hear was the rasping of my own lungs as they struggled for air.

Needing more information, I opened my eyes and saw Sachse in the wooden armchair in front of me. He was leaning back, legs crossed, his customary sneer dominated his coupon and his Makarov was balanced on the armrest.

"Back with us, Reim?"

I looked around the room—an occasional table and a stained-glass *jugendstil* lamp had fallen victim to our little struggle. The curtains rippled in the breeze drawn through the smashed patio door. But most interesting to me was the ormolu clock above the door: ten o'clock. I'd only been out for a few hours—the night was still young.

I turned back to Sachse, the movement causing pain to swill past my eyes. When I was able, I focussed on him. I'd examined his photograph often enough, had met him a couple of times in real life, but until now never felt the need to take a good look at the man, to see him properly.

Predictably enough, he looked like all the photographs I'd seen of him. His pupils were so light they were almost translucent, his hair was blonde to the point of whiteness. All that was familiar. But when my scrutiny moved onto the lower half of his face, I realised that the constant sneer was less the physiognomic symptom of the inevitable internal changes brought about by his counter-revolutionary activities, and more to do with simple scar tissue. Aware of my stare, Sachse swallowed, and the evidence became more visible: the tracks of long-pulled stitches sharpened and deepened the natural fold at the corner of his mouth.

"What happens now?" I asked, looking away from his scarred face. "You going to finish me off like you did Bruno and several of our colleagues? That's what you do, isn't it? Whoever gets in the way, you-"

"Shut your trap!"

"Am I bothering you? Sorry, did you plan to use this time together to tell me how clever you are? Did you want to lay out your cunning scheme to a captive audience? Because I can't wait to admire your organisational skills." Sachse moved his hand to the pistol. "Is this what you did to the others? Don't tell me—Holger Fritsch didn't kill himself because you were blackmailing him—he did it because he couldn't face yet another of your arrogant, overweening lectures-"

"Trap. Shut!" Sachse was on his feet now, holding the Makarov by the grip. He whipped the muzzle across my face, once for each word. I felt the skin on my cheek split, warm blood dripped down my chin, drying quickly in the cold air that fanned past the curtains. Painful, but it woke me up. And it took my mind off the rib that was still jabbing at my lungs.

He remained standing over me, pistol raised in warning like a club. *Keep him talking*, I told myself, staring into those disturbingly colourless eyes of his. The ropes binding my wrists had enough give for me to move my hands up and down a few centimetres and with a little more time I might still work those knots loose. Sting him with enough words, he might start talking and allow me a few more minutes of life.

"What the hell are you doing here?" he demanded, returning to his seat.

"That's funny, I wanted to ask you the very same—okay, okay!" At the sight of his raised gun I switched to a gentler tone. "I was looking for you. They sent me here to find you."

"Who?"

"Main Department II."

"I asked *who*?"

"Lieutenant Colonel Schur. If you ask me, I'd say you went a wee bit too far—don't know if that was your fault or the bosses at HV A. They showed the Minister some of that material you've been selling—dropped Schur and his department right in it, made him look incompetent. You can imagine how the Minister heated up hell for Schur, so now he has no choice but to retaliate."

"The brass in Berlin, they're like swine, shoving their snouts in the trough. They've got themselves in position and they're making the most of it. No privileges in Socialism, except for the Party *Bonzen* and the Firm's brass—they're living a different version of Socialism than the rest of us; they're helping themselves to the property of anyone who tries to emigrate, looting mail from the West—do you know how the old men in the Politbüro steal their medicines from their own citizens? Department M have a list of people whose relatives in the West regularly send medicine. If Honecker needs more beta-blockers, Department M checks their lists and keeps an eye out for any pills coming through the post." He picked up his Makarov and pulled the slide back to drop the magazine, fingering the bullets in the rack before slotting it home again. "Those are the people we work for. That's the Socialism they believe in."

He walked to a Biedermeier drinks cabinet and poured himself a reasonably sized glass of brandy. I watched him lift it to his mouth, my own lips and tongue anticipating the burn of the alcohol, but anticipation was as far as it went—I knew he wouldn't offer me any.

Downing the brandy and filling up again, he returned to the chair and settled back, more comfortable.

Looking anywhere but at his drink, I tried to think of something to say, anything to keep him talking while I sawed away at the rope with my wrists.

"So you thought you'd like a bit of what they have—you thought you'd sell our secrets to the West and you'd be rewarded. You've done alright, too, your gamble almost paid off. But not quite, because when HV A hear about your plans to move over here full time, they won't be happy. You know what happens to your sort."

I thought he'd rise to the bait, demand to know what I meant by his sort. But he smiled to himself, or maybe he didn't. I didn't trust myself to guess right any more.

"I'm just the first," I told him. "If I fail, the colleagues back in Berlin will make sure HV A are told what you're up to ... they still think you're the blue-eyed spy, bringing back all that lovely material from the class enemy. But one report and all that will change."

"You know nothing!" Sachse snapped.

"So tell me." Had those ropes loosened a little? Or was it wishful thinking? I jiggled my hands around to try to get the circulation going.

Sachse was silent, he was staring at his hand-laid parquet.

"And what about Pozdniakov? Oh, I imagine he won't be happy either," I decided to add a little more pressure. To me, the KGB major was scarier than General Mielke himself, but that was probably because I'd never come face to face with the minister in charge of the MfS, whereas Pozdniakov seemed to know everything about me and had already used his knowledge to press-gang me into several illicit operations.

Sachse went to pour himself another drink.

"The KGB will protect me, I'm useful to them." He wasn't slurring his words or anything, but he was speaking more slowly, more carefully. I didn't want Sachse drunk, he was unpredictable enough when he was sober.

"You know that Pozdniakov gave me the green light? I told him I was hunting you and he washed his hands-"

"I told you to keep your trap shut!" His face was pale, it was like looking at one of the inmates of Hotel Magdalena. Had I pushed him too hard? Far from buying myself time, had I only succeeded in bringing forward my own death? I ignored the whining inside my own head, dug my fingernails into the rope, desperate to loosen a loop in the knot my fingers had already teased out.

"Enough!" Sachse shouted, even though I hadn't spoken again. He put down his glass and picked up the Makarov.

I found myself staring into the darkness of the muzzle, a black hole about to suck me into oblivion.

"Wait! Before you shoot—tell me ... why did you kill Holger Fritsch?"

"I didn't—the wimp killed himself. They told me you were there when he did the deed." He snorted. "How did you feel, watching him die?"

The gun's unwinking eye stared at me, and I couldn't help but stare back. "You made him kill himself. Why?"

"Same as the other one, Sanderling. Got in the way, knew too much. They both talked to Bruno, and Bruno was in the same department as my contact. Couldn't risk it, they had to go. And now—you do too."

"So you admit to poisoning Bruno? It was you who drove Holger to suicide, and you pushed Sanderling under the ice?"

"Don't worry—your death will be quicker than theirs." He chambered a round, the clacking of the slide echoed across the wooden floor and around the room. The last thing I saw before I closed my eyes was his thumb flicking the safety off. The whimpering in my head sharpened and grew until it was screeching deep in my skull, deafening—so loud I didn't hear the gun when Sachse pulled the trigger.

77
URBAR

I opened my eyes. I was washed out, nerveless. But alive. Alive enough to want to know what, why, how ... I took in the scene before me: Sachse crumpled on his beautiful wooden floor, clotted blood seeping from his blown head.

My sight blurred, another image muscled its way into my consciousness—a past image, my old friend Holger, moments after he'd shot himself.

"You alright?"

My vision steadied again and I looked in the direction I thought the voice had come from. But it wasn't Sachse, he was still lying on the floor. But over there, by the windows, Weber was there, next to curtains that swelled and swung in the draught.

She was shivering. Her right hand hung by her side, clutching a Walther PPK.

"He killed Arno," she said, her voice surprisingly steady.

I was hurting, seeing things, pushing away the voices inside. Then it clicked. Arno, her colleague Arno, my Source Bruno. This wasn't the time to get soppy over fallen friends and enemies—who knew how many neighbours in this tidy little village had heard the gunshot and were right now dialling 110 to tell the cops that the Russians had invaded.

"My hands are tied, Anna."

That did the job. Weber slipped the safety on her pistol, pushed it into a pocket and crossed the room to undo the rope that bound my wrists.

78
URBAR

"Where to?" asked Weber when we reached the green Polo, parked a couple of hundred metres from Sachse's house. She looked dazed, but the cold night air had woken her enough for me to trust her behind the wheel. More than myself, at least—a sharp buzzing behind the eyes and a sore head were enough to make me take my concussion seriously.

"Nearest motorway—let's put a bit of distance between us and this ...." I didn't finish the sentence, bewildered by the various options: *traitor* would be a good start, *murderer* fit the bill, too. But the words *mess* and *crime scene* were perhaps the most relevant at that moment. I needed to be out of sight when the West German *Kripo* began their investigation.

I looked at the paperwork I'd taken from Sachse's house, still clutched in my hands. After Weber had untied me, I'd delayed our departure only long enough to slip the bottle of brandy into my pocket and use the cold chisel to make a mess of the desk. It was a shame to damage the marquetry around the lock on the drawer, but more than worth it—the search unearthed a sheaf of pay slips going back a couple of years. On top of this house, the BKA had been providing Sachse with a salary of 3000 DM for the material he was passing on to them.

I rolled the papers and slipped them into an inside pocket, feeling calmer than I had done at any time since a West German police officer named Arno Seiffert walked into a local MfS office nearly a year ago.

But I hadn't finished yet. I still had one or two niggles.

"How did you find me?" I asked once we'd joined the light traffic on the motorway.

"When you escaped from those men in Koblenz this morning, I didn't know where you'd go, how to contact you. So I went back to Mainz, checked the dead drops and found the film canister. Took it to the chemists shop for the same day service, and when the prints came back I saw the photograph of Sachse on his terrace, the name of the village conveniently typed below ..."

Weber was good, I was glad I had her looking out for me. But was she really on my side? I needed to check.

"Pull in here," I told Weber as we approached a motorway service station.

"I thought you wanted to get away?"

I didn't answer, I was occupied with rooting around in the glove box. The car slowed to take the turn just as I put my hands on what I was looking for. Testing the torch I'd found, I waited until Weber had parked up at the end of the car park, far from the restaurant and filling station.

I got out and, leaning through the car door, pushed my seat back. Turning to lie on the floor with my head in the footwell, I directed the torch beam under the dashboard. I poked around until I found a couple of wires tucked into the plastic edging and tugged, following them up to the central console where they disappeared into the plastic moulding. Back in my seat, I pulled the ashtray right out and shone the torch into the gap. There it was.

"Your hands are smaller—can you get at that?"

Weber shoved her hand into the slot, her fingers scrabbling to gain purchase, then she pulled out a small plastic box trailing a couple more wires. I took the case off her and forced a broken fingernail into a join, levering it open to slide the microcassette out.

"Whose car did you say this was?"

"Belongs to a colleague, Hans-"

"And did you take it back to Hans last night, after you dropped me off at the allotment gardens?" I waited for her to nod. "We discussed my instructions last night on the way to the shed, and then you took the tape of our conversation directly to them. They knew all about Koblenz, they knew exactly when and where I was to make contact this morning."

Weber looked away, hand rubbing the back of her neck. "How did you know?"

"I was followed home the night of the party. The person tailing me was picked up by a Polo, might have been a coincidence, but then again ..."

"Sorry." Weber still couldn't meet my eyes.

"Don't break your head over it—it's easy to overlook danger when it's so near to home."

I closed the door and Weber started the engine. Her remorse seemed genuine to me, I didn't believe she knew the car had been wired. And my belief in Weber had to be good enough for the next few hours, because like so much in this game, I wasn't going to get proof either way.

"Where to?"

I'd already thought about this. I wanted to get home, but it wasn't as easy as driving up to the nearest border crossing. The West German BGS and customs kept an eye on who was going through, and by now I'd be on their watch list.

Jumping over the border fence wasn't an option either—I'd just avoided being shot that night and was in no hurry to try my luck with trigger-nervous border guards.

But there could still be a way. Maybe it would work, maybe it wouldn't. But I was hopeful.

"Well?" demanded Weber as we picked up speed and moved into the middle lane.

"Let's head north." I uncorked the bottle of brandy I'd taken from Sachse's study and took a swig. It was smooth, very smooth. The same round and complex taste as on that first night in Wiesbaden, before the interrogations began.

79
LÜBECK

It took half the bottle of cognac and most of the night to reach Lübeck, a small city in the far north, where the inner-German border runs into the Baltic Sea. I'd dozed for much of the way, letting Weber do the driving after my knock on the head.

"How are you going to do this?" she asked once we entered the quiet Lübeck suburb of Eichholz a couple of hours before sunrise.

"I know some of the crew at the border crossing in Herrnburg." I was exaggerating—I'd been to the border crossing earlier in the year when I'd been tasked with expelling *Polizeirat* Portz from the country. I'd had some interaction with the Pass and Control Unit there, and if I was lucky, they'd remember me. "I need to check which shift is on duty before we cross."

Weber frowned. "Herrnburg is a rail crossing—how can you get on the train? The BGS will be checking passengers at the last station in the West."

I had a plan. Not the best plan, but a workable one. The first station in the GDR is just a few hundred metres over the line that divides East and West. The trains reduce speed when they cross that line, slow enough to jump aboard. Even if the border guards spotted us, they wouldn't be able to stop the train before it got to the station anyway. Once there, I'd have to persuade PKE on the platform to let me put a phone call through to Lieutenant Colonel Schur in Berlin, ask him to send a clean-up squad to Sachse's house and arrange my transport back to Berlin.

I told Weber all of this, but her frown didn't lift.

"You can't stay here," I told her. "They know you helped me. Horchheimer suspected it from the first—why else wouldn't he let you return to work?"

Weber didn't answer. She lit a cigarette and stared at the smoke drifting across the inside of the car.

"You and I are linked now, and once they notice Sachse is missing, they'll follow the trail straight to you. If you stay here, you'll end up in prison ..." I paused. I'd been so used to seeing her as a Western agent, competent and self-contained, that I hadn't thought of her as having another life, one outside her work at the BKA. But then I thought of the conversation we'd had on the way to Koblenz, just twenty-four hours before: "I forgot—your husband, you don't want to leave him."

"There's no husband, not any more. He's dead."

"So come with me—a hero's welcome awaits." It was a little grandiose, but I was nervous about getting across the border and back to Berlin, and I liked the idea of bringing her with me—it wouldn't harm my career, bringing a defector like Weber.

And I liked her.

I remembered the first couple of times we'd met, in a smokey bar in Warnemünde. Her flirtatiousness at that time had been part of the role she was playing, but it hadn't made her any the less attractive to me.

I respected her. And there's not many people I can say that about. Sachse may have taken away the only person I really thought of as a friend, but he'd brought us two together.

"Let's go," she said, opening the car door.

We lay on the hard slopes of the railway embankment, hidden in the brittle undergrowth.

Six hundred metres up the arrow-straight track, I could see the Pass and Control Unit moving around on the floodlit platform of Herrnburg train station—I didn't have binoculars, but I did have the American's camera. Adjusting the telephoto lens, I focussed on the figures.

I couldn't read the shoulder boards from this distance, but I could make out the Head of PKE's office at the far end of the platform. Two men stood smoking—the short, thin one looked like the NCO I'd dealt with back in February, and the broader man next to him, the one with slow, lazy gestures, reminded me of the major in charge that day.

Was I sure? No. But without decent binoculars I wasn't ever going to be any surer. So now it was time to wait for a goods train to pass, and hope it arrived before the next West German patrol discovered us.

I heard the train long before the triple headlamps swung into sight a kilometre to the west. The grumbling diesel and the rattling wagons told us to get ready.

As the locomotive neared, I unslung the camera—too bulky and unwieldy to keep hold of—and checked my pockets. Negatives from the pictures I'd taken in Horchheimer's office, film cartridge from the American's camera and Sachse's pay slips, all safely stowed.

"Ready?" I asked Weber as I raised myself into a crouch. The locomotive had already overtaken us, closed goods wagons were now clattering past. I had my eye on an empty flatbed with steps and a grab rail at each end—that should be easy enough to catch hold of and swing ourselves up onto.

But Weber hadn't moved.

"You can't stay here." If I couldn't persuade her, I was thinking about using force to get her on that wagon. But she had the only gun, and I had the broken rib.

"My husband ...." I had to lean down to hear her over the clanking and squealing of the wagons and wheels, less than a metre away. "He was over there, on your side of the Wall. He died because the Stasi ... he was killed by Sachse-"

The flatbed was the next wagon along, I watched it

approach, the front edge with its steps and rail swayed past, but I looked back at Weber. She was saying my Firm had killed her man.

The back end of the flatbed was upon me, all I had to do was jog a few steps to get up to speed and grab the rail to pull myself up. I looked at Weber, but she didn't look back.

My Firm had killed her husband, and she'd only collaborated with me because she knew I could help her find some sort of justice.

"Anna—what's your real name? Who was your husband?"

She looked up and I saw it in her face. I didn't need to hear her speak the name, I knew the answer already. But I waited anyway, I owed her that much. I gave her enough time to find the strength to say it aloud.

"Seiffert. My name is Anna Seiffert—my husband was the man you called Bruno."

I jogged after the train, reaching out for the rail and jumping up. I lifted my foot to reach the next step and turned to lean against the railing, gasping from the pain in my chest.

It was time to go home.

LIST OF MAIN CHARACTERS

MfS staff

Eberhard **Dupski**, captain, Reim's immediate superior.

Bernd **Ewald**, captain, HA II, answers to Lt Col Schur.

Holger **Fritsch**, Reim's friend in HA XX.

Heinrich 'Heinz' **Kühn**, major, head of section II in ZAIG.

Horst **Lütten**, second lieutenant at BV Rostock, Abt XV.

Erich **Mielke**, general. Minister for State Security.

Georg **Prager**, corporal, BV Rostock, Abt XV.

Hans-Peter **Reim**, second lieutenant, ZAIG/II at Berlin Centre.

Gerhard **Sachse**, first lieutenant, foreign intelligence, BV Rostock.

Sanderling, code name for **Ruth Gericke**, lieutenant, HA II.

Walter **Schur**, lieutenant colonel, head of HA II/2

Matthias 'Matse' **Stoyan**, second lieutenant, HA VI.

Other characters

Source **Bruno**, codename for Arnold Seiffert.

Agent **Dresden**, a Western asset sourcing material in the GDR.

Herbert **Heller**, Agent Dresden's courier,

Ella, Freiin **von Horchheimer**, wife of Ingo von Horchheimer.

Ingo, Freiherr (Baron) **von Horchheimer**, Kriminaloberrat, BKA.

Hermann **Jüliger**, Polizeidirektor in the BKA.

Codename **Merkur**, codename for Andreas **Portz**

Frau **Pfaff**, secretary at BKA central HQ.

Andreas **Portz**, Polizeirat, BKA. Arnold Seiffert's superior.

Dmitri Alexandrovich **Pozdniakov**, major. KGB.

Renate Vera **Reim**, née Kubzyk, Reim's wife.

Arnold 'Arno' **Seiffert**, officer of the BKA, defected to the GDR.

Anna **Weber**, Kriminaloberkommissarin (senior inspector), BKA.

GLOSSARY

MfS units

Abteilung – Department. The **Hauptabteilungen** (**HA**—main departments) were based in Berlin (most, but not all at Berlin Centre in Lichtenberg), responsible for national co-ordination and strategy in their areas of responsibility.

The *Abteilungen* were sub-departments of the HAs, either based in Berlin, (e.g. Abt. M, Abt. 26) or the equivalent departments in the *District Administrations*. Most local departments kept the number of the Main Department they belonged to (e.g. Abt. II represented HA II), the main exception being Abt. XV, the local level of the HV A.

Main Departments were further divided into Sections.

Abteilung XIV – security and administration of the MfS remand prisons (**UHA**) in Hohenschönhausen (UHA I), Lichtenberg (UHA II) and each of the 15 District Administrations.

Abteilung XV – District and local level departments reporting to the **HV A**.

Bezirksverwaltung des MfS, BV – District Administration. Each of the 15 administrative districts in the GDR had a MfS District Administration, which co-ordinated operations in that area. The next administrative level down, the counties (*Kreise*), had offices in each county town (**Kreisdienststelle, KD**).

Department see *Abteilung*.

District Administration see *BV, Bezirksverwaltung*.

HA, Hauptabteilung – see *Abteilung*, or the specific Main Departments below.

HA II – Main Department II, counter-intelligence.

HA III – Main Department III, signals intelligence, monitoring of electronic (radio) and telephone networks.

HA VI – Main Department VI, passport control, tourism, transit traffic, where Reim was posted until autumn 1983.

HV A, Hauptverwaltung A – Main Administration A, foreign intelligence. Represented at district and county levels by Department XV.

Main Department see *Abteilung.*

Kreisdienststelle, KD – see *Bezirksverwaltung.*

PKE, Paß- und Kontrolleinheit – Pass and Control Unit at border crossings, part of *HA VI* .

ZAIG, Zentrale Auswertungs- und Informationsgruppe – Central Evaluation and Information Group, general staff unit with wide-ranging responsibilities, notably archiving, general reporting and, in Reim's section (ZAIG/II), control and measurement of professional standards.

Ranks (DVP, MfS, NVA etc)

Hauptmann – captain.

Kriminaloberkommissar(in) – West German rank, equivalent to first lieutenant.

Kriminaloberrat – West German rank, chief superintendent in criminal investigation. Equivalent to lieutenant colonel.

Leutnant – lieutenant.

Major – major.

Oberleutnant – first lieutenant.

Oberstleutnant – lieutenant colonel

Polizeidirektor - West German police rank, equivalent to colonel.

Polizeirat – West German police rank, equivalent to major.

Soldat – soldier, private.

Unteroffizier, Uffzi – the lowest rank of the non-commissioned officers, also generally used to cover all NCO ranks.

Unterleutnant – second lieutenant.

GDR/German/other terms

Ausweis – identity card. **Personalausweis** was the civilian identity card, **Dienstausweis**, service identity card (eg for work or in the armed organs, including the military **Wehrdienstausweis**). These *Ausweise* were little booklets, most with a cardboard and/or plasticised cover.

Bautzen – town in Dresden District, best known for its mustard and its prison, STVE Bautzen I.

Berlin Centre – MfS headquarters in Lichtenberg, Berlin. Also known as *Stasi Zentrale, Ruschestraße* and *Normannenstraße*.

Bezirk, district – the GDR was administratively divided into 15 *Bezirke* (districts), each of which was further divided into *Kreise*, which I've translated as counties (NB some authors and historians translate *Bezirk* as county and *Kreis* as district).

BGS, Bundesgrenzschutz – West German border patrol.

BKA, Bundeskriminalamt, Federal Crime Agency – West German investigative police agency, answering to the Federal Ministry of the Interior.

BKK, KoKo, Bereich Kommerzielle Koordinierung, Commercial Co-ordination Division – responsible for procuring hard currency. Activities included weapons exports, import of hazardous waste, running holding firms and shell companies in the West as well as **Intershops** and **Interhotels** in the GDR, negotiating the sale of political prisoners.

BND, Bundesnachrichtendienst – West German foreign intelligence service.

Bonze – bigwig, (mil.) brass, party leaders.

Catterpillar carriers, Raupenträger – senior officers (major and above), on account of the braided shoulder boards.

Centrum – department stores run by the *HO*.

Cheka – originally the Bolshevik secret police agency set up by Felix Dzerzhinski in 1917 in the Soviet Union. The secret police agencies in socialist states, and particularly the Stasi, drew on the traditions of the Cheka, seeing themselves as *Chekists*.

Chekist – member of the Cheka.

Clapperboard – Reim's term for the MfS ID document, commonly called *Klappfix*.

Comrade, Genosse – member of the Socialist Unity Party (Communist party of the GDR); member of the army and other armed organs of the GDR.

Deutsches Eck – lit. German Corner, headland at the confluence of the rivers Rhine and Moselle in Koblenz, West Germany.

District see *Bezirk*.

Doppelkorn – grain spirit, schnapps.

Federal Republic of Germany; FRG, Bundesrepublik Deutschland, BRD – West Germany

Fischkopf, Fischkopp – fish-head, derogative term for a resident of the coast.

Freiherr – baron.

GDR, German Democratic Republic; Deutsche Demokratische Republik, DDR – East Germany.

Grenade, Granat – (mil) jargon for 0,7l bottle of spirits.

Groschen – ten Pfennigs.

Gründerzeit – in architectural terms, the period between 1871 and the First World War.

Grüne Minna – police wagon for transporting prisoners.

GÜST, Grenzübergangsstelle – border crossing point.

HO, Handelsorganisation – one of the two main retail organisations. State-run.

Hohenschönhausen – borough in Berlin, location of MfS central remand and interrogation prison *UHA I*.

Hopse – Berlin name for hopscotch.

IM, Inoffizieller Mitarbeiter – unofficial collaborator of the MfS.

Interhotel – chain of international standard hotels in the GDR.

Intershop – hard currency store selling Western products.

Jugendstil – German equivalent of Art Nouveau.

K1 – Department 1 of the *Kripo*, which although it was not directed by the MfS, had close connections to it.

Karl-Marx-Stadt – name for the town of Chemnitz, 1953-1990.

Katzendreck – lit. feline excrement, Reim uses *Katzendreck* to refer to low-value intelligence material.

KKW, Kernkraftwerk – nuclear power station.

Kombinat – vertically and horizontally integrated industrial group.

Komplexannahmestelle – shop accepting consumer goods for servicing. Repaired everything from tights to televisions, accepted bed linen for ironing, filled gas bottles and much more.

Konspirative Wohnung, KW – safe house/flat.

Konsum – one of the two main retail organisations, a consumer co-operative.

Kontakt Person, KP – Contact Person, an informant, particularly in the *Operational Area*, not usually registered as a regular *IM* informant.

Kripo, Kriminalpolizei, 'K' – Criminal Police, the criminal investigation agency for police forces in German-speaking countries. The abbreviation *K* was unique to the GDR.

Magdalena, see *UHA*

Ministerium für Staatssicherheit, MfS, Stasi – Ministry for State Security, secret police and intelligence agency.

Mitropa ran sleeper cars, station buffets and kiosks as well as motorway service stations.

MZ - VEB Motorradwerk Zschopau, popular motorbike.

Neue Wache – the Memorial for Victims of Fascism and Militarism on Unter Den Linden in Berlin.

Neues Deutschland – national newspaper in the GDR, central organ of the *SED*.

Nordhäuser Doppelkorn – brand of schnapps.

Operational Area, Operationsgebiet - field of operations, usually referring to West Berlin or West Germany.

NVA, Nationale Volksarmme – National People's Army, the GDR armed forces.

Operationsgebiet, OG, Operational Area – field of operations, usually referring to West Berlin or West Germany.

Perspektivagent – sleeper agent, long-term prospect embedded in a target organisation.

Petschaft – aluminium seal with unique numbers and coding, provided to persons with security clearance for sealing doors to offices and safes, using wax and thread.

Pfeffi – square sweets, originally peppermints, but in later years other flavours were available.

Platt – north German dialect, particularly from coastal areas.

Politbüro – the Politbureau of the Central Committee of the *SED*, executive council of the GDR communist party.

RD, Rückwärtige Dienste – rear services in the **NVA**, responsible for supplies, provisions and accommodation.

Red Army Faction, Rote Armee Fraktion, RAF – West German terrorist group, originally formed around Andreas Baader, Ulrike Meinhof and others. At times, the GDR provided some logistical support and training.

Republikflucht – fleeing the republic, illegally crossing the state border of the GDR.

Reichsbahn, Deutsche Reichsbahn, DR – GDR railways.

Robotron – producer of electronics and office equipment.

Roth-Händle – West German brand of filterless cigarettes, renowned for their strength.

Rotkäppchen – domestically produced sparkling wine.

SB, Służba Bezpieczeństwa – Polish secret police.

Schwalbe – moped made by Simson, who also produced inter alia, the S50 and S51 light motorbikes.

Schwedeneisbecher – popular variety of ice cream sundae.

Silberling – carriages used by West German railways on stopping services, named after the brushed steel exterior.

Softeis – soft whip ice cream, soft serve ice cream.

Station der jungen Naturforscher und Techniker – Centre for Young Naturalists and Engineers, after-school centres encouraging interest in the sciences.

Strandkorb – wicker or wood covered seat, used on beaches.

Stullen – sandwiches.

Tacheles – straight talk. From the Yiddish.

Trabant – most widespread car in the GDR.

Transportpolizei, Trapo – East German transport police.

TREVI – Intergovernmental Security Forum in Western Europe founded in 1975. Commonly held to be the precursor to Europol.

UHA, Untersuchungshaftanstalt – remand prison. UHA I was the Hohenschönhausen complex; UHA II, the smaller prison on Magdalenenstraße (known as *Magdalena*) next to Berlin Centre.

Verfassungsschutz – West German domestic intelligence.

Volkspolizei, Deutsche Volkspolizei, DVP – GDR police force.

VVS, vertrauliche Verschlußsache, Top Secret – one of the highest level classifications for secret documents.

West confirmed, westbestätigt – entry in personnel files indicating that an individual could, in principle, be allowed to travel to the West. Other than political reliability, an important factor was usually an established family (spouse and children) who would remain in the GDR during any Western travels.

White mouse, weiße Maus – traffic cop, so called because of their white uniform jacket and cap.

Zone – pejorative term for the GDR, derived from *Soviet Occupation Zone.*

Made in United States
Orlando, FL
05 March 2022

15424960R00159